# COMMENDABLE DISCRETION

## A DETECTIVE NOVEL OF THE OLD WEST

BY

J. HOOLIHAN CLAYTON

*WITH ILLUSTRATIONS AND ENGRAVINGS*
*FROM HARPERS WEEKLY*

DOG SOLDIER PRESS

TAOS

Published in January 2021 by
Dog Soldier Press, PO Box 1782,
Ranchos de Taos, NM 87557
dogsoldierpress.com

Graphic Design: book interior and cover
Ananda M. Sundari, Alchemy Arts
AlchemyArtsllc.com



Library of Congress Control Number: 2021930337
Printing: Ingram Sparks
Print ISBN: 978-1-7362743-0-9
eBook ISBN: 978-1-7362743-1-6

*"I have seen the day of wrong through the little hole
of discretion, and I will right myself like a soldier."*

*Love's Labour's Lost, Act V, Scene 2,*
- William Shakespeare -

*"Major Reno is very confident that there were a
number of white men fighting with the Indians."*

- General Alfred H. Terry in his official report
to the War Department of June 28, 1876,
entitled "Camp on the Little Big Horn." -

*History of Montana 1739 -1885*
D. J. Stewart, Chicago:
Warner, Beers, 1885.

# Prologue

His eyes smarted from the glare and sweat. The screaming was endless and he could no longer differentiate between the wounded horses and men or the horde of devils, slaughtering and slaughtering any living being on the field of battle. He realized he was crying and the shredded flesh of his right arm was streaming a steady rivulet of blood into the powdered dust upon which he sat and that rose up to fill the air with a fine, opaque curtain. His arm did not even hurt. He had no idea what had happened to his army-issue Springfield and his ears buzzed with the sound of angry bees. A long time ago, back in Ohio, he had taken honey from a wild hive and the noise seemed vaguely reminiscent. A man fell nearby and lay twitching savagely. Then the soldier looked straight at him, appeared to want to speak and died, his upper back a forest of arrow shafts. A shadow fell across him and when death came, he saw it was delivered by a blue-eyed man in war paint with auburn braids. The incongruity dismayed him. Then he thought he heard his mother's voice calling to him from the distance and the screaming abruptly ceased.

# 1

Dust motes filtered through a beam of sun, slanting past the President's left shoulder. There was a smell of cigar smoke, leather bound books, and furniture polish in the room and a slight odor of stale alcohol emanating from the President. His eyes were rheumy with hangover and the bags under his eyes were prodigious. C.W. Collins liked this man and hated to see him do anything to further the rumors circulating about him. The redoubtable general sat silently behind his desk making a tent with his fingers in a pose that he must have thought made him look authoritatively pensive. C.W. waited in the settled way he had learned to assume at rest. It was not unpleasant sitting in an oak and book filled room awaiting the pleasure of a great man.

Finally, President Grant took the cigar out of his mouth and spoke. "I have always attempted to be acutely aware of the *reality* of what is taking place in this country." He coughed and seemed to be choosing his words very carefully. "I say reality, as opposed to the decorated and embellished landscapes painted by newspapers, Congress and the *Harper's Weekly*. There is always a schism." He sighed deeply and C.W. could see that Grant's weariness was decidedly more encompassing than mere alcohol withdrawal.

"As you no doubt are aware, I felt no love for George Armstrong Custer. Despite the tragedy of the loss of his men, I am not unduly sorrowful that he has been removed from the political and military stage. What Phil Sheridan saw in that swaggering fool, I shall never know. He talked me into granting Custer's request to accompany the 7th." Grant leaned back and looked at the ceiling. His chair squeaked.

"The nation, however, is overcome by mourning; a result of the dramatic literary lamentations of the *Bismarck Tribune* taken up by newspapers all over the country. So be it. The public would mourn any mountebank if led to it. My concern..." Grant leaned forward suddenly and set his eyes on C.W. in a grand gesture, "is that my friend Marcus Reno's credibility and the rationality of my Indian policy are being called into question by the machinations of Libby Custer." The President paused, still holding Collins's gaze, as if gauging his reaction. C.W. returned the president's scrutiny with aplomb. Although some people quailed before Grant's steady gaze, C.W. was fully aware that his own piercing blue eyes tended to unsettle both women and men.

"Some information has come to my attention that could fuel the controversy she is fomenting. There was an official military report given by General Terry that was, let us say, ill advised." General Alfred Terry had been the commanding officer of the Dakota Column in the Powder River Campaign and C.W. knew he was solely responsible for sending Custer out on reconnaissance. Terry had known that Custer would never limit himself to simple reconnaissance and C.W. figured the general was presently afraid of the ramifications of Custer's demise.

Grant seemed to be waiting for something. Collins finally spoke. His voice possessed a muted Irish brogue that he could restrain or unleash as the occasion warranted. "What was the nature of the report, Mr. President?"

The President scratched behind his left ear, stirring

the dust floating in the sunlight. "Damn the man! It would have been better for him to have been killed, you mark my words!" Grant visibly steadied himself. "Reno reported to Terry that there had been white men fighting with the Indians. Not just a few, but a *number* of white men."

C.W. raised his eyebrows in response. This was surprising news, made all the more so by Terry choosing to report it formally. What *had* the man been thinking, given that General Terry had been privy to military bureaucracy and its concomitant perversity for many years?

"The Adjutant General mentioned it to Taft, who quickly got his hands on it and sent it directly to me," the President told him. "Except for a very few, you and I are the only ones who know about his communiqué. This information *must* remain a secret. It could not only hurt Terry and Reno's reputation as officers, but absolutely rout the credibility of my Peace Policy toward the Indians. As it is, the public is clamoring for retribution and Miles has taken over the chase. He has been ordered to set up a headquarters on the Tongue River. Imagine word getting out that white men were on the side of the Indians...the potential of generating inquiries into our policies toward them. The Democrats have control of Congress and are seeking ammunition against the Republicans. This is an election year, as well as the nation's centennial, and we must appear to be completely justified in all our dealings with the Indians. The Quaker missionaries and the Unitarians, who have been so beneficial on the reservations, could be held accountable. There are many who do not approve of their beliefs or their sympathies with the Indians."

Grant reached into a drawer and pulled out two stout glasses and a half-filled bottle of whiskey. He poured and handed a glass to Collins, who placed it untouched on the desk and watched as Grant knocked back a tremendous gulp. The physical relief was apparent on the President's face as the whiskey spread into his blood. C.W. knew the sensation well.

"There are those who have drawn a bead on my head," Grant said, cocking an eyebrow and significantly not smiling. "But the government cannot withstand a storm of criticism at this time, what with the economic depression, elections coming and now Custer's unfortunate martyrdom... not to mention that debacle with the Whiskey Ring. Of course, I know the situation with the Indians is criminal, but the settlers and miners keep moving into Indian lands and demanding we protect them. Red Cloud wiped out Fetterman and burned our forts. The Powder River Campaign was our first attempt to punish the Sioux, almost ten years later."

"They have a treaty. We violated it." C.W. said quietly.

"Yes, yes I know." Grant rubbed his face briskly. He looked at C.W.'s untouched glass of whiskey on his desk. "You quit drinking?"

C.W. nodded, offering no explanation. The President looked him over then obviously decided to leave it alone. He examined his cigar and struck a match to relight it.

"Look, it does not matter that we have a treaty. What matters is that this country is spreading west and no one can stop it...not the president, the U.S. Army or even God himself. Gold has been found in the Black Hills. Predictably, hostilities there have grown out of the avarice of the white man. The first immigrants to the area were removed by troops, but the rich discoveries have increased their numbers. Any further efforts to remove the miners will result in the wholesale desertion of the troops sent to remove them. We must be practical."

Collins shook his head. "Are the Sioux to have no protection from the abuses of treaty stipulations? Are they to be wiped out entirely?"

Grant twisted his face in mock pain. "God's teeth,

you can convolute the point. There is gold out there. That is the only real salient point. Gold that is free for the taking. When did social conscience *ever* come before gold?" Grant reached for C.W.'s untasted whiskey and drank it. "How many people balked when Chivington displayed Arapahoe and Cheyenne scalps in Denver? Who really cares how many people the Masons hang in Montana Territory?"

The rhetorical question hung in the air. Collins looked out a window at the rusty leaves of a maple tree. They fluttered lightly, making shadows dance on the corner of Grant's desk. Grant was studying him again, but there was nothing to say. He could see that all the scandals, self-doubt, and alcohol had virtually thrashed this honorable man to a pulp.

"I gave Sherman the authority to assume military control of Sioux reservations. The Indians are now to be treated as prisoners of war," the President said without sentiment. "Congress will no doubt approve a bill ceding the Black Hills and approaches to settlement by citizens. This will be the punishment for going to war with the United States Army."

"Custer attacked them."

Grant waved his hand impatiently, as if shooing a fly. "A commission has been sent to secure signatures transferring the Black Hills to us."

Truly unsettled by this new information, C.W. decided to wrest the topic back to Reno's report. "What do you think it means to have white men allied with Indians?"

"I am afraid of what it could mean. They could be renegades, remnants of Quantrell's men for example, leavings from the galvanized Yankees, Mormons, escaped criminals...overly zealous missionaries...anything."

"How about men who do not espouse the philosophy of Manifest Destiny?"

Grant gave him a sour look. "Few men are willing to

die for the cause of another race."

"I do not think that all Americans buy the myth that the U.S. is ever on the side of might and right. I think that there are at least a few immigrants who are not entirely enthralled with their new land."

Grant grinned. "Bitter?"

C.W. let the question pass without comment. He was past being baited by anyone. Grant appeared to regret his sarcasm and changed his tack. "I have a job for you to do."

C.W. had expected as much, having been summoned from an assignment with the Pinkerton Agency in San Francisco all the way to Washington D.C. "I am always at your service," he said. C.W. had previously performed covert duties for Grant, beginning during the war and always requiring extreme tact and secrecy.

"Whether it is expedient or just, you and I both know the country is moving west at an alarming rate. Railroaders, prospectors, miners, farmers... even flocks of scarlet women... are migrating toward the setting sun. I need to know exactly what the situation is with Reno's information. If there are armies of renegades supplying the Indians with rifles and swelling their numbers with able bodied men, I need to know about it." Grant rubbed his face with both hands, exacerbating the flush that the whiskey had brought to his cheeks. "Understand me, Collins...there cannot be a whisper about what you are looking for."

Collins nodded. His discretion was legendary. "What exactly is Elizabeth Custer doing to get under your hide?"

"What is she doing?" Grant asked with counterfeit incredulity. "She and some writer named Whittaker are working on a book that is to be imminently published. According to one of my sources, this will be a grandiose work of fiction posing as an extended eulogy of the Custer that never was. It is my understanding that Terry, Benteen, and especially Reno are to be vilified, not to mention my humane treatment of the Sioux. It will cause a stir, Collins. It will be...vituperative." Grant paused. "Have you met the lady?" he asked.

"Only once. I found her...overbearing."

Grant was visibly pleased. "Reasonably attractive until she opens her mouth to speak."

Collins found this rather amusing, as Grant's wife was excessively homely. He changed the subject, asking, "Why does she feel the need to hound poor Marcus?"

"I assume to remove attention from Custer's follies. Someone must be blamed for the massacre and she will not wish to be the widow of a pariah. She is causing all sorts of mischief with newspapermen, friends in the military, widows of the fallen soldiers... Reno has already gotten into a drunken brawl over malicious gossip." Grant poured himself another short drink. "Did you know I received a petition two weeks after the massacre with 236 names affixed, requesting a promotion for Reno?"

Collins shook his head.

"The non-commissioned officers of the 7th Cavalry wished to have Reno promoted to lieutenant colonel... and now...." Grant shrugged disgustedly. "He is at Fort Abraham Lincoln. Go there first and see him. You may confide in him to a point, but remember the man drinks and a drinking man talks." With this, Grant drank his whiskey and smiled at the corner of his mouth. "I want you to get every detail out of him about the white renegades; their clothing, their weaponry, even their hats."

"Their hats?"

"Confederate braid, kepis, captured uniforms, that sort of detail."

C.W. felt dimwitted to not have understood. "What shall I tell Marcus?"

"That you are looking into Terry's report. To keep his

mouth shut.”

“Has he been spreading the story?”

“Good god, I hope not.  I think he has more pressing matters to deal with at the moment.”

“Do I leave immediately?”

“Immediately.   Usual arrangements and communicate by telegram directly to me. Encoded, of course. Speak to Babcock, my secretary.”

“Anything else, sir?”

“Yes.  Take it easy on Marcus.  He was an outstanding soldier in the war and of great service in the Freedmen’s Bureau.  He is a good man and it pains me that instead of being lauded as a hero for saving his men, he is being viciously maligned by Libby Custer and her minions.  I fear he is headed for a fall.”

“I know him and respect him.”

“Good.”  Grant shifted in his chair and C.W. could see him donning an official air.  The meeting was over.

C.W. rose to his feet and retrieved his hat from the expansive desk.  “I will take the train today and will have a report for you soon.”  Grant was already chewing vigorously on his cigar and looking through some papers. He gave him a dismissive salute.  C.W. was long used to Grant’s peculiarities and left the room without a backward glance.

# 2

C.W. Collins watched the landscape slide by as he headed northwest through Minnesota toward Dakota Territory and Fort Abraham Lincoln. He had always been pleasantly lulled by trains and tended toward deep thought.  He perused the farm country, the fields, the barns, and livestock, but was carefully reviewing the totality of his knowledge of Indian conflicts in the western territories.  The most significant event of which, alluded to by President Grant, had been the Fetterman Massacre; the absolute destruction of eighty-one souls, including two civilian scouts.  Fort Phil Kearny had been built on a spur of the Bozeman Trail called the Montana Road. This road led directly to Virginia City, a mining town in Montana Territory that was purported to have some of the richest gold strikes in the west, prior to the discoveries in Last Chance Gulch and the Black Hills.  The road, however, cut through land claimed by the Sioux and guaranteed them by treaty.  After ongoing attacks, settlers and miners demanded protection from the U.S. Army.  After the fort had been built, outraged Indians harried wood cutting crews and hunting details until Colonel Carrington, the post commander, and his contingent were barely eking out an existence.  In defense of a wood cutting crew, he had sent out Lt. Colonel Fetterman with eighty-one men, one civilian riding his daughter's pony, with express orders to not pursue the Indians once the crew had been rescued.  Predictably, Fetterman's ego had gotten the better of his sense and he had led his men into an ambush. Fort Phil Kearny had been subsequently abandoned.

Stretching his legs, C.W. smiled at a pinch-faced old woman sitting caddy corner to him, just to see if she would smile back. She averted her eyes. His smile broadened as he contemplated the smallness of human nature. He would have bet a twenty dollar gold piece that she was a devout churchgoer. A herd of milk cows grazed bucolically alongside the train window and smoothly slipped from sight. C.W. actually loathed farm country and farmers, considering them to be the most dull and mortally ignorant louts. He came from fishing folk on the coast of Ireland, although his father had been a blacksmith. Farmers had always seemed to him to be as limited as their round of toil and especially prone to accepting British injustice and atrocities. He pondered the similarities between the history of Irish oppression by the English and what was happening to the Indians at the behest of the U.S. Government. The purposeful starvation, broken agreements, self-justification, and outright massacres were all recognizable themes to the Irish. Oh well, he thought philosophically, he had fought for the emancipation of slaves and sent a few racist "crackers" to perdition, so perhaps he could be forgiven for being in the employ of an aggressive government, especially under someone like Grant.

Even at the speed of twenty miles an hour, his destination of Bismarck was still days away. The town would be a beehive of activity due to the recent and crushing military defeat, as well as the heightened prospecting and mining in the Black Hills. Not surprisingly, Custer's perfidy had had much to do with the current rush on the Black Hills. C.W. had difficulty assigning the man any respect of a military rank, let alone the brevet rank of general bestowed upon him. He had always referred to and thought of him as Custer.  He was not alone in this.  Until the man's death, all sorts of unflattering nicknames for Custer were common around the barracks of the west, not the least of which was "Iron Butt" or "Ringlets" due to his ridiculous hair. After Custer had abandoned some of his men at the Battle of Washita, he had earned the enmity of Captain Benteen and several other officers.  His tendency for meting out brutal punishment for minor infractions made him generally unpopular among the soldiers under his command.  C.W. found it disturbing that general amnesia had taken over and now his heroism was being praised to the skies even amongst those who had known him well.  He felt terribly sorry for the soldiers who had been haplessly led to their deaths by this self-aggrandizing ass, many of whom had never seen combat, let alone an Indian in full battle regalia.  He had spent time on the Great Plains in summer and could imagine the grueling heat, the choking dust, and the abject, gut-wrenching terror of young recruits as they first heard, then saw, the grimly painted warriors bearing down on them.  All in the name of one man's personal glory.

Custer's foray into the Black Hills, violating treaty rights with the Sioux and Cheyenne, and his subsequent dissemination of the news of gold, had led to frenzied prospecting and a good many deaths.  C.W. suspected that Custer had had some financial interests in mining speculation and more than a passing motive in helping to force the government to move against the Sioux Nation.  Ironically, Custer had ultimately eluded any punishment for his actions and, due to Libby Custer's efforts, would probably be remembered as a true American hero.  His fate would, no doubt, mirror that of Andrew Jackson, Collins mused, a monumental impresario of self-veneration who was nearly deified in the collective American memory.  C.W. held a profound disdain for the need of heroes, especially because their lives and deeds were either entirely fabricated or thoroughly cleansed posthumously. Incongruously, he was named after a great Irish hero, Wolfe Tone, but Charles Wolfe Collins had been so christened by an Irish mother with revolutionary sympathies and because of this, he was proud to bear the name. Theobald Wolfe Tone, in point of fact, had not finally achieved a united Ireland, but his legend still inflamed Irish revolutionaries.

Thoughts of Ireland brought to mind his friend Myles Keogh, once a member of the Vatican Guard and a veteran of the War Between the States. Keogh had been killed with Custer and much was being made about his horse as the sole survivor of the battle. C.W. could imagine that Myles had fought like a demon, in fine Irish mettle when all hope was lost. Another good man sacrificed on the altar of Custer's ambition. Perhaps he could do something to save Marcus Reno from being scapegoated by Custer's overweening widow. He recollected the night he had met her. There had been a dress ball in Washington D.C. to celebrate Christmas. Her manner had been somewhere between reptilian insinuation and the enthusiasm of a puppy.

As the train gently rocked its way toward his destination, Collins observed his fellow passengers and found them to be as uninteresting as he found most people. He possessed no great admiration for the human race. This caused him little concern and gave him the talent of dispassionate, somewhat scientific, powers of observation. Such a talent had been invaluable during the war, when he had been working as an operative for the Union cause. Now, he used his abilities to perform all types of duties in the civilian realm, freelancing as a detective for Alan Pinkerton, wealthy citizens and, on occasion, President Grant. Collins had definite parameters for the work he was willing to do, however, and refused domestic spying, employment from foreign governments, political blackmail, union busting, and any other jobs that lacked integrity or challenged his sense of honor. Over the years, he had frequently irritated Alan Pinkerton by what Pinkerton called his "damnable Irish delicacy." C.W. refused most work offered to him by the Pinkerton Agency, either due to the nature of the work or a conflict of interest involving a case. Sometimes, he refused merely because C.W. had never really liked the opinionated Scotsman, who had fought for Scottish independence in his youth, but had become increasingly involved in cases that protected big business against the working man. Pinkerton's recent sabotage of the Molly Maguires had truly affronted Collins' sense of justice. A case involving bank fraud in San Francisco and dwindling personal finances had lured him back to the agency, but Collins had been relieved when the summons had arrived from the White House.

14
LIBERTY
MUS HALL
B PRINTING
TIMES
POST
OFFICE
R D THAL
EXCH
SAL
PHANT

BOOM TOWN

# 3

Bismarck had grown up swiftly with the arrival of the Northern Pacific Railroad.  Although spread out in the haphazard fashion of most western towns, houses were abundant, as were various businesses, saloons, brothels, hotels, and freighting offices.  The wide main street was bustling with buckboards, freight wagons, horses and pedestrians.  Collins strode along the thoroughfare, dodging piles of manure, children and dogs, making his way to the riverfront.  He hoped to catch a ferry or steamboat down the Missouri to Fort Abraham Lincoln without too much bother or time lost.  It was plainly obvious that the new wealth of the Black Hills mining concerns was already pouring into Bismarck.  It was also evident that heightened prejudice toward Indians was infecting the town, what with the tortured effigies of feathered demons hanging about and a couple of actual rotting and battered heads of Indians displayed with pride outside prominent saloons.  Collins had no stomach for such atrocities and wondered, if given the chance, whether he would not fight alongside the Indian factions against migrating droves of ignorant white settlers.

Down at the riverfront he had little difficulty securing passage to the fort on a small barge carrying goods to the military personnel stationed there.  He sat on a crate and watched the water skim by, smoking his pipe and contemplating the general meanness of the human spirit.  He had read much of the Enlightenment thinkers and, despite his admiration for John Locke, just could not agree with the notion that humans were motivated by good intentions if left to their own devices. In the American frontier, people were left greatly to their own devices and the results could patently prove to Locke that his theories were faulty.

He wondered whether it was human nature to hate others of disparate origins. Most societies presumed their own superiority. The British Empire and its citizens expressed their certitude as they plundered and oppressed cultures around the world. In Rome, there had been absolute conviction that Roman society surpassed all else. Herodotus had been intrigued by, yet ever disdainful of, foreign cultures. The United States exhibited the profound belief that all lands bounded by the Atlantic and Pacific should surely belong to the intrepid white pioneer and frontiersman, but most definitely not to the red heathen. There was one incontrovertible fact, he thought sadly. The Indians would not stand a fighting chance against the onslaught of Manifest Destiny.

The barge bumped up against a primitive gravel quay and Collins helped secure it to a couple of stout posts. He left the barge, waved farewell to the pilot, and followed a wagon road along the river, then up onto its broad, grassy bank. He walked leisurely toward the clustered buildings of the fort, passing a wagon headed, no doubt, to pick up the supplies brought in on the barge. The driver nodded and slapped the lines to pick up the pace of the team. The air was warm and humid, full of buzzing insects and the cries of water birds. As he neared the fort, he heard the shouting of commands and other sounds of military life. He spotted a young private sitting on the porch of a long barracks, polishing a pile of boots. Collins walked over to him.

"Good day to you," he said pleasantly.

The private looked at him sullenly. "Yeah"

"Looks as if you have earned a bit of work," Collins observed.

"No bloody fear."

"Looking for Major Reno."

The boy sneered. "What the hell for?"

C.W. drilled him with an eloquent look. "No reason you need be privy to," he said after a pregnant moment.

The young man seemed to believe him. "Major Reno is probably down at the stables."

"Thank you."

The private gave him directions and Collins realized he must have walked right past the buildings near the river landing. He found the stables and went around the back where he could hear some activity. Several soldiers were leaning against corral railings watching a man working with what appeared to be an extremely unbroken horse. He examined the group and picked out a face that seemed familiar. He walked over.

"Major Reno?"

"Yes?" The face was aged beyond its years and much more haggard than the last time he had seen it.

"I am Charles Collins. We were associated together in the Freedmen's Bureau after the war."

Recognition came into his eyes. "Of course." He took in Collins' civilian clothing. "What in the hell are you doing here?"

Just then there was a burst of cheering from the men as the young soldier in the corral vaulted onto the back of the horse, which stood quivering in fear.

"Can we go somewhere to talk? It is quite important."

Reno seemed interested. "Come with me."

Although they had not been close in the days in Atlanta, the two men had respected each other. They walked in companionable silence to the porch outside the officer's quarters. They sat down on high backed wooden chairs in the shade.

"Well?" Reno asked unceremoniously. Collins had always liked the man's directness.

"I have come here at the behest of President Grant."

"You, sir, are joking." Reno said, without a trace of mirth.

"No, sir, I am not. If you recall, my work in the latter part of the war, and later in Atlanta, was more of a non-specific nature."

"You mean spying."

"If you care to put it that way. Let us just say I specialized in gathering sensitive information."

"And you are doing it again for Grant."

"Occasionally."

"Fucking great." Reno was notoriously profane. "I suppose I am to be burnt upon the altar of national politics."

"Nothing of the kind. The President is concerned for your future. He is distressed by the attacks of Elizabeth Custer and others."

Reno seemed to soften. "God, I worship that man. I am heartened that he has not forgotten me."

"Not at all. I must tell you, however, that he is also concerned about certain information you provided to General Terry that was considerably unwise."

"Oh shit. I knew that would bite me on the ass." Reno rubbed his jaw. "It seemed important at the time. I had no idea Terry would pass it on."

"He did. Now it is up to me to glean through your recollections in order to ascertain the ramifications of what you observed."

"I understand." Reno got up and, taking a dipper from a hook, scooped some water from a bucket hanging on the wall of the building. He drank deeply, then offered another dipperful to Collins. When they were finished, Reno returned to his seat. "It was mighty odd, if you ask me," he said, looking at his boots.

"What was odd?"

"Well, firstly, the number of them. And it was not as if they were attempting to disguise the fact that they were white."

"The President was quite interested in their garb."

Reno appeared to be trying to remember. He frowned for a while, then said, "Really not very noteworthy. Some Indian duds mixed with white clothing."

"Hats?"

"Civilian. Nothing military, until later."

"Later?"

"Yeah, when the fuckers had killed some of my men trying to get to water. We were all dying of thirst."

"Of course. So they joined the Indians in stripping the dead?"

"Sure as hell did." Reno started shaking. "I do not want to talk about this. I cannot sleep as it is."

"I must ask you to recall everything."

Reno shot him an angry look. "There is nothing. Some were blonde, some darker. They were yelling in Sioux and in English. The Indians obviously trusted them, since they brought them to kill other whites. I cannot tell you whether some were in on killing Custer. I assume so, since most of them showed up after Custer must have been dead." Reno got up and began pacing. "I will tell you, Collins...I despised the bastard. I simply will not stop just because he is dead. I have more reason now than ever."

A group of mounted infantry rode into the parade grounds and dismounted. Reno leaned against the porch railing and watched them. A stray horse with four white stockings wandered over to the group.

"That's Keogh's horse."

"What?"

"Keogh's horse, Comanche. He was one of the few creatures left alive in that field of putrefaction. He was too badly wounded for the Indians to take him, although one of the stories going around was that Keogh still had hold of the reins.  I never saw that myself. ”

Collins thought about Keogh's last moments.  He took a deep breath and said, “I want you to tell me everything that happened from the beginning... from the moment Terry decided to send Custer on reconnaissance.”

Reno turned and there was real anguish in his face. “You want me to go through that entire hell all over again,” he said, flatly.

“Yes.  I am sorry, but I need to understand.”

“Grant's orders?”

“Near enough to.”

“I will need whiskey.”

“That,” Collins said, “can be arranged.”

# 4

They found a quiet stretch on the Missouri River beneath a large old cottonwood tree. The golden leaves filtered autumnal amber on the drying grass beneath. Both men took off their coats and Collins pulled out the pint bottle of whiskey that had been stowed away in his pocket. Knowing Reno's penchant for alcohol, C.W. had made sure to bring enough to loosen him up, but not enough to make him drunk. Reno broke the seal and yanked out the cork. After a long swallow, he handed it to C.W., who shook his head.

"All yours," he told him.

Reno shrugged and took another drink. He recorked the bottle and leaned it against an exposed root. He gazed out over the river and Collins read all manner of pain in the lines of his face. Suddenly he was filled with a profound compassion for the man and an equally profound gratitude he had not been with him on the Little Big Horn. C.W. felt certain Reno's story would only increase the sensation.

Reno began talking abruptly, as if diving into cold water. "I had been the one originally sent out on reconnaissance. In the valley of the Rosebud, my men and I discovered a trail...well not really a trail...more like a thoroughfare of churned earth, tracks, horse manure and litter." He looked at Collins. "I swear to you, it was at minimum a mile wide. A mile wide, for god's sake." He turned his gaze back to the river. "I returned to the

*Far West,* the riverboat being used as command head-quarters, and gave my report to Terry and Gibbon. I told them what I had seen and my belief that there were thousands of Indians on the march toward the Little Big Horn Valley. Mitch Bouyer, one of the scouts, had told me that it was likely that the Sioux, Cheyenne and their allies would be headed for their summer rendezvous, in spite of the War Department's demands they surrender themselves to the agencies. In fact, as it turned out, many of them had *left* the reservations. I reported this as well. They scoffed at me. I think General Terry believed me, from the look of anxiety on his face, but you knew Custer. He kept working the men up, claiming I was exaggerating in order to avoid confronting the Indians."

"The man was insufferable," Collins concurred.

Reno nodded. He reached for the whiskey and took a drink, carefully replacing it against the tree root. "Never, in my entire military career, have I given anyone cause to doubt my bravery. But the staff was willing to be bullied by Custer as everyone was keyed up for a fight and anxious to not be left out." He sighed. "At any rate, my report was summarily dismissed and that is when plans were made for us to follow the trail to where the Indians were no doubt encamped."

"I understand the estimated number of Indians camped on the Little Big Horn was somewhere around fifteen thousand?" Collins asked.

"Including women and children. I know the camp was about three miles long, maybe more. It was like riding into a hornet's nest." He picked a dry grass stem and twisted it around a finger pensively. "Terry told Custer to report back after we found the camp. None of us believed he would obey Terry. I tried to urge the bastard to take the Gatling guns the general offered him, but he would have none of it. We followed the trail to the Little Big Horn Valley and camped. Then he had us pull up stakes after dark to push further along.  Later, he left us behind and went to look around.  While he was gone, some hostile scouts found us and we exchanged fire.  When Custer heard about it on his return, he got all stirred up again, saying he had found the camp and now the Indians had found us and we must attack immediately.  That damnable newspaperman, Kellogg, was spurring him on and all his family members got excited."  Reno snorted mildly and shook his head. "Christ what an entourage. You should have seen them, happy as school children on a Sunday picnic. The rest of us felt uneasy. I remember looking at Benteen, who was of much the same mind as myself, and we knew each other's thoughts.  Nothing would be spared in the name of furthering Custer's career.  I think my greatest discomfort came from the greenness of the soldiers.  Some of them were still having difficulty handling their horses." Reno paused.  "There was a boy from New York.  The kid looked to be around twelve years old, but I know he had to be older.  Anyway, every time we mounted up, he went all white around the gills and commenced shaking.  He was that scared of his horse."

Collins found himself being drawn into Reno's account and sadly considered that the boy had probably not survived. "Go on," he said.

Reno uncrossed his ankles and sat up, as if preparing himself.  "We followed the crest of some low hills.  Then we stopped again and he divided up the regiment, placing me and Benteen at the command of three companies apiece and keeping five for himself.  Captain MacDougal and the other troop were to escort the pack train in the rear.  That is when he sent Benteen on his wild goose chase to the south.  We progressed again and a couple of miles from the Little Big Horn, he informed me that I was to head west across the river and into the south end of the Indian camp.  He planned to parallel the river and the Indian camp and attack precipitously on the north-ern end.  I protested that I would have probably engaged the enemy before him, but he smiled that damn conde-scending smile of his and told me that if he heard gunfire prior to his own attack, he would certainly return to my aid."  Reno turned to Collins.  "That is the god's truth. He told me he was to come to *my* aid.  At no time did he ask that I come to *his*.  His exact orders, as clearly as I recollect them, were that I was to move forward at a rapid gait, charge afterwards, and that the whole outfit would support me....support *me*."

Collins knew that one of the most insidious stories circulating about Reno's supposed shortcomings in the battle was that Reno had failed to come to Custer's aid in his hour of need.  Having known Custer better that he had ever desired, Collins was fully aware that Custer would never have asked for help under any conditions.

"I believe you," he told Reno.

"From our position on the ridge, we could already see the smoke rising from the cooking fires in the camp.  Je-sus, it was daunting.  And the Crow and Arikara scouts had been posturing and making faces and entreating Custer to rethink his plans.  I had the sense that we would not survive the day.  But that fucker was as sure of himself as always and there we parted company, the sun baking down and a great plume of dust making his approach as visible as a Fourth of July parade.  Myles Keogh and Colonel Cooke stayed with us a bit longer. That damned Keogh was smiling his big mick smile and boasting he would be in at the finish before we even ar-rived. I spoke to my men, bolstering their courage, and we headed down hill toward the river.  It was the last I ever saw of either of them."  Reno reached again for the whiskey. "I believe you knew them both well," he said, wiping his mouth.

Collins nodded.  He knew the rest of the story would

come harder. "That is when you rode into the camp?"

"Not yet. First we had to ride down that fucking steep embankment on the east side of the river. A couple of the new recruits fell off their horses and it took us a while to cross the river, but it was the best spot we could find to cross." He took a swig of whiskey and held onto the bottle. "I remember wondering why we had not been attacked yet, given our proximity to the village, but perhaps they were busy watching Custer's cloud of dust. We assembled on the west side and rode hard through the brush and cottonwoods toward the village. I was out in front with the other officers and the closer we came to the camp, the more it became plainly apparent that there were vastly more Indians and tepees in front of us than we had been able to see from above. Remember what Grant used to say about his first charge into Harris' camp at the beginning of the war? How his heart kept getting higher and higher until it was in his throat?"

Collins nodded.

"I felt that for the first time on the Little Big Horn and it was odd, because I had never experienced it in the war. I cannot imagine what the boys behind me were feeling...something far worse, I suppose. And then the Indians came boiling out of everywhere. In truth, there are no words for the unspeakable sight of those devils and the piercing cries emanating as if from the depths of hell. We looked to see if Custer had come to our rescue as promised, but had no sign of him. I ordered the men to stop and dismount, so that we could take defensive action. We laid flat on the ground and fired repeatedly until we checked them a bit. We retreated into a thicket of brush and trees, but we were crowded and it looked as if we would soon be overwhelmed. It was then I ordered the soldiers to remount and make for the river. I heard someone say something behind me and turned to find Bloody Knife. I could not make out what he was trying to tell me and a moment later his head exploded, spattering my face with what must have been his blood and brains. I was shaken, I admit, but the safety of my men was foremost in my mind and I herded them helter skelter to the river." Reno rubbed his face with both hands, as if remembering the sticky sensation of Bloody Knife's detritus.

"I tell you, the worst part of that initial skirmish was the sight of one young boy who lost control of his horse. The animal bolted right into the heart of the enemy with him screaming all the way. I was later told by one of my men that his head was found rammed onto a stump in the southern end of the abandoned village." Reno had tears in his eyes. "It haunts me, Charles. It haunts me."

Collins watched as he drank down a large measure of the remaining whiskey. Then Reno seemed to get a hold of himself again.

"The men were in full panicky flight. The horses were tired and soon the Indians were among us, stabbing, clubbing and shooting guns and arrows. About a third of my men were wounded or killed in that desperate race to the Little Big Horn. The worst part came when we reached the river. We had to jump from a fucking six-foot bank. Many of the troopers fell from their horses into the water. On the other side, the wet horses and men turned the embankment to greasy clay, with the horses slipping or falling backward and the Indians picking us off from the opposite bank. I yelled myself hoarse and pushed them and at last we made it to the top of the hills in front of us where we stood for our last defense, or so we thought. We were astonished to find that very few Indians had followed us and became more astonished when those few went tearing ass down the valley to the north. I guess that was when word reached them that Custer had been engaged."

They sat in silence for a few moments, Collins imagining the terror of men and horses. Reno was obviously bracing himself to continue his grim tale. He fingered the bottle, but decided not to drink.

Reno sighed and went on. "We formed a perimeter on the crests of the hills, the men sheltering themselves as best they could behind saddles, dead horses, sagebrush, anything. I ordered a call of the roll. Three officers and more than forty men were missing; either killed, wounded or hiding, which proved successful for some of them. Most of our scouts were missing and I noted that Isaiah, our colored interpreter, was gone. Not long after, we noticed a great amount of dust to the southeast. We watched it grow nearer with trepidation until we were able to make out our own troops. Benteen rejoined us and not long afterward, Captain MacDougal showed up with his cavalry troop and the train of pack mules. There was a momentary jubilation, then the horses and pack animals were herded into a depression behind the crest of hills and the packs were used to fortify our position. Our conferences naturally revolved around where Custer was and what we were to do next. Some of the officers came close to quarreling and some felt strongly about moving north to find Custer. As the highest-ranking officer there, I made the decision to remain fortified and to care for the wounded. That damned Burkman, Custer's orderly, made quite a little fuss. I thought he was about to commence weeping."

Reno finally decided to take another drink of whiskey. "Earlier, just after our arrival on the hills, there had been a lot of dust and smoke north of us. We heard some shots fired, but as it turns out, Custer was over three miles away and sometimes we thought we heard something and sometimes not. Then there was what could have been a couple of volleys, but I cannot be sure. All I know is that about five p.m. the Indians came on us in thousands. We fought desperately until dark. About nine p.m. the Indians withdrew and we feverishly began to further fortify our positions.  Benteen took up a defensive position on a hill to the south and I placed him in command there.  We dug rifle pits with knives, plates, whatever came to hand, with one soldier even using a side of bacon as part of his shelter.  There was a damned sharpshooter up on a high hill overlooking our position.  Every time he shot, an animal or a man went down.  He was there on the 25th and the 26th and the demoralizing effect on the men was terrible.  Finally, Sergeant Ryan brought him down.  He had a big bore Sharps with a telescope. It was a great relief.  But I will tell you, Charles... I swear he was white."

Collins was confused. "Ryan?"

"No," Reno shot him an impatient look. "The sharpshooter."

"Surely there are Indians who can shoot that well," Collins suggested.

"Perhaps...but this fellow took his hat off a couple of times.  One of those times I happened to be glassing his hill."

C.W. frowned.  He had no reason to doubt Reno's word. "Go on," he said.

"Our thirst was terrible, especially that of the wounded.  Many of the men talked of Custer and every little noise made them think his men were sneaking back to join us.  Many of the soldiers were cursing him roundly. The ones who knew about Elliott at the Washita were the most vehement, claiming he had abandoned us as he had abandoned Elliott.  I will admit the thought had crossed my mind as well.  Anyway, we were left undisturbed until half past two in the morning of the 26th when two rifle cracks opened one of the heaviest fires I have ever witnessed.  We defended ourselves rigorously, but our most desperate need was water.  We sent volunteers crawling for the river in the dark.  Most of these brave fellows were killed. I had reserved all the canned fruit for the wounded, figuring the juice would give them some relief. It was that night I discovered those fucking civilian packers eating several cans and I admonished them roundly. God, how I wanted to shoot them. Later, we discovered they had also stolen personal items from several of the officers. Around about eight in the morning the Indians made a concentrated charge on Benteen's position. He told me later that one of them came close enough to tap a dead soldier with his coup stick. He will never touch another, that is for damn sure."

"And the whites?" Collins asked.

Reno looked over at him as if coming out of a deep reverie. "They were ubiquitous. In every charge, in every attack on our water parties. I heard them yelling to each other in English. But it seemed that some of them spoke Indian as well, as they were obviously communicating with their red brethren."

"What happened next?"

"The heavy firing continued until half past nine a.m., or thereabouts, when the fury of the attack subsided. The question of obtaining water was then becoming vital for the wounded and a skirmish line was formed under the command of Colonel Benteen to protect the volunteers. Water was obtained, but one of them was killed and six were wounded. The Indians rushed us occasionally and annoyed us all through the day, but something must have disturbed them for I saw them making a big fire in the valley, raising great clouds of dust and smoke. About six o'clock we saw them moving out of the smoke and heading in the direction of the Big Horn Mountains. At first, we thought it was the return of Custer that had startled the Indians." Reno smiled without humor. "But he was long dead and so were those poor fuckers who had followed him so gaily. You know, I do not give a fuck about Custer, his fucking family or that damned newspaperman. But I cannot help thinking about those poor young boys who must have shit themselves in fear as they died...I think about Keogh...I think about Cooke. Did you know they scalped his whiskers?"

Collins shook his head. It was such a tragic little piece of news it almost made him laugh, but one look at Reno's face drove all mirth away. The man was tortured by his memories. It was plain to see.

"The whites went with the Indians then?" he asked his companion.

"Must have. All that night, we cared for the wounded and kept watch, thinking those red bastards might sneak back to finish us off. Dr. Porter proved himself to be invaluable and quite competent. DeWolfe, our senior surgeon, had been killed just east of the river on the 25th. Again, Custer was discussed. Benteen referred to him as the Murat of the American Army. Considering that Custer was dead at the time, I guess his reference to the French Revolution was not far from the truth, for the massacre at the Little Big Horn was indeed Custer's Waterloo. Most of the men were vitriolic and one of them predicted Custer's inevitable court-martial, the mention of which did not dampen my spirits. The question was settled the next morning by General Terry, bringing aid and the first news of Custer's disaster. Lieutenant Bradley had discovered the battlefield while scouting ahead of the column."

"What was the total of your losses?"

"Some of the fellows we had lost in our retreat across the river sneaked back to us at intervals. Our final count was three officers and forty-seven men, including the scouts. When Gibbon's men arrived, we moved all the wounded down the hill and across the river to their camp, fifty-two wounded all told. I ordered the rest of the men to bivouac with Gibbon's men."

"When did you view the field?"

"Not until the 29th, when it was deemed that we would let the wounded recuperate one more day before transporting them to the mouth of the Little Big Horn to the steamboat. We went in a body to explore the battlefield."

"They had lain in the hot sun for four days?"

"Near enough."

"My god," said Collins, who was not unfamiliar with battlefield corpses. "The stench must have been horrific."

Reno's mouth twisted. "I truly cannot understand how so many were supposedly identified. Christ, the bodies had bloated beyond recognition...some of them had exploded from internal gasses, sending their entrails everywhere. It was a scene of unspeakable destruction. Remember the Wilderness?"

Collins nodded, remembering that hellish piece of ground from the war and the unburied corpses, the stench, the predation of birds and animals.

"It was like that," Reno told him. "The animals had been at many of them. The eyes were gone, the faces, rectums, genitals picked apart. The flies were in huge, black clouds. That bullshit about Custer not being scalped out of respect...hell he was going bald and had cut his hair so short no self-respecting savage would have wanted it. I will tell you one thing. Bradley, Benteen and I had a private council over Custer's body. It sure as hell looked as if he had shot himself in the side of his head."

"That would not be inconceivable," C.W. said.

"Hell no, the fucking coward. It looked as if he may have taken cover behind a couple of his men, but I guess we will never know." He paused. "Now I feel the ground moving under my feet and know I will be held accountable in every way."

"Perhaps Grant can help. He wants to."

Reno smiled wryly. "He is on shaky ground himself."

Collins steered him back to the topic at hand. "Any untoward bodies evident?"

"Difficult to say, given the state of the bodies and their nudity, but there were a couple of corpses that caught my attention. They were down closer to the camp and the river. They were not stripped of their clothing and had been sort of laid out in the manner of the Indians. One had a red stone placed on his chest. The animals had mostly left the bodies alone, I guess because of the clothing being left on, and it seemed clear to me these men had been with the Indians. It was then that I decided to make a report to Terry."

"Anything distinctive about them?" C.W. asked.

"Both were beardless, in the way of the savages, and one had red hair. That was queer as well. They both had full heads of hair left untouched. The darker one wore braids, but I am certain he was as white as you or me." Reno looked furtive a moment, then seemed to come to a decision. "I took a watch off of one of them."

"You what?" Collins asked incredulously.

"I took a watch off the redhead. Hell, he was not one of ours."

"Do you still possess this watch?"

"I have kept it, wondering what to do with it."

"I will need to see it. It could be very important." Collins paused. "What about Myles? You mentioned Cooke...did you see Myles?"

Reno looked at him. "Keogh?"

Collins nodded. "Did you see him?"

Reno sighed. "Yeah, we found him. You saw his horse on the parade grounds. He is now the pet of the fort. He drinks buckets of beer. I think he is fast becoming a dipsomaniac."

"And Myles?"

"He had holed up behind a small hummock and it

looked as if he had held his own for quite some time. There were piles of shell casings in front of him and a couple of dead Indian ponies. He was lying naked except for his socks, a sight that had a peculiar effect on all of us who viewed the body. There was a bad wound in his knee, which corresponded with a wound on his horse. They must have been shot at the same time. He was badly bloated, but I could see he had not been mutilated. We knew for sure it was him because he was still wearing that sheep medal the Pope had given him."

"His Agnus Dei. What about his pistol?"

"Pistol?"

"His engraved English pistol. Hell, he showed it off to everyone. You must have seen it."

"I had forgotten. It was not on him or around him, but one of the other soldiers might have taken it. I saw quite a bit of looting."

Collins looked at him askance, thinking about the watch. Reno shrugged.

"Any whites found in the encampment?" C.W. asked him.

"There were quite a few tepees left intact. I learned from one of my Crow scouts, Goes Ahead, that it was a custom to abandon the tepee of someone killed. Some of the standing tepees contained dead bodies of warriors. One of them held three bodies, laid out with all of their personal belongings and costumings. All three were white, I swear it."

"Did you show them to anyone else?"

"I attempted to get General Terry to come, but although he expressed interest, he could not find the time, given all his responsibilities. I was loath to bring anyone else into it, due to emotions running so high. I witnessed one soldier taking his rifle butt to a dead Indian's head, bludgeoning it into a reeking mash."

"Any clues as to who they were?"

"There were some blacksmithing tools with them. Oddly enough, I found a grindstone on its frame nearby. That was all. The men were clean-shaven, wearing a bizarre ensemble of white and Indian clothing. One even wore a breechclout."

Collins stood up and stretched and Reno followed suit. They shook out their jackets. Reno finished the whiskey and flung the bottle into the Missouri. The sun was going down and the air was noticeably cooler.

"Tell no one of our conversation," C.W. told Reno.

Reno smiled wryly. "You think me an idiot?"

Collins put a hand on his shoulder. "I am sorry you had to revisit all of it again."

Reno stared at the opposite bank of the river. Collins noted that Reno had the damaged look about him he had frequently witnessed in soldiers during the war...soldiers who had reached their limit of unspeakable memories.

"I go through it every day and every night," Reno told him. "It will never be over. It will have no ending."

Collins had a gnawing gut feeling he was right.

# 5

Walking again down the rowdy main street of Bismarck, Collins did not see the storefronts, wagons or piles of merchandise lining the dirt roadway. He was still on the Little Big Horn, with the dust, the screaming, the smells of blood and corruption. He had been in enough battles that the reality of Reno's descriptions had created vivid images within which he now dwelled. A close call with a mound of canvas tarps brought him back to his immediate surroundings and the need to find a room for the night. He looked around and located what appeared be a hotel. The interior of the building was slightly cooler than the heat outside, but the odor of unwashed bodies and greasy food was overwhelming. Collins retreated swiftly and wandered around until he found a livery stable. An old man in a derby hat, trousers, and suspenders was forking out a stall inside. The naked skin of the man's saggy torso was grimy and slick with sweat. The smell of manure was strong. Collins was not repulsed, however, as the fragrance of the stable was far preferable to the lobby of the hotel.

"Got a moment?" he asked the man, who stopped and turned around.

"Mebbe."

"Need a horse."

"Got a few here. How long?" The old man spit a stream of tobacco onto his pile of manure and straw.

"Not sure. I would prefer to purchase one rather than

let it."

Greed replaced apathy in the man's demeanor. "Got one good gelding. Cost you though."

"How much?"

"Forty. Gold, not paper."

"Need to ride him first. Can you fetch my saddle and other trappings from the train station while I eat? It is held under the name of Collins." He flipped a dime at the man who caught it deftly.

"One other thing," C.W. said, as the man headed for the door.

"Yeah?"

"I will want to bunk here for the night. Have you any objections to that?"

The man shrugged. "Not if you buy the gelding," he told him.

C.W. walked back into the late afternoon of Bismarck's main street, having stashed his carpetbag behind a pile of straw. He wandered aimlessly, looking for a place to eat and finally chose to go into one of the quieter saloons. He went over to the bar.

"Got any eats?" he asked a friendly looking man behind the bar who was chatting up one of the resident girls.

"We got a cook, such as he is. Let me see if he is sober enough to be trusted."

The man came out from behind the bar and went through a door in the back of the spacious and sparsely furnished room. A variety of antlers seemed to be the greater balance of the decorations. Predictably, the saloon girl turned her attention to Collins. Apparently, none of the other girls were out and about yet, it being too early for real trade. She was heavy set, her face pockmarked and slack. Her velvet and lacy clothing was ill fitting and rank with sweat stains and her teeth were bad.

"Howdy mister," she said, coming around the corner of the bar in his direction.

"Good evening."

She tittered idiotically. "Good evening," she repeated, moving closer.

Collins was relieved to see the barman returning. "Cook is sober enough. Says he can get you some steak and eggs."

"Excellent," C.W. told him, moving away from the girl and taking a seat at a nearby table. "Any chance of some coffee?"

"Sure. We always have coffee. The later in the day, the stronger it gets." He grabbed a cup from behind the bar and went over to a potbellied stove topped by a large enamel coffeepot. He poured a cupful and brought it over. "This would take the hair off'n a dog," he told C.W., who took a swig of the hot brew.

"Tastes like buffalo chips," he said, wondering if it was indeed coffee.

The barman chuckled and went back behind the bar. The girl was sidling nearer again and Collins caught a good whiff of her. "Go on, you," he told her. "Not interested."

"Leave the man alone, Jenny," said the man behind the bar.

"Screw you, Barney. I do what I please," she answered.

"Then please take a bath," Collins advised her, flatly.

"Fuck you, mister. I am clean enough for the likes of you."

Barney came out from behind the bar and dragged her away. "You will ruin the man's appetite. You really do goddamn stink like old jism."

Jenny went off in a huff to both men's relief. A scruffy one-armed man in a dirty apron brought out a plate of food and Barney refilled his cup. The eggs were overdone, but the steak was not bad and there was fresh cornbread.  Collins ate hungrily while Barney hummed a tune and thumped out a rhythm on the bar.

"Where you from?" he asked after a while.

Collins hated small talk.  "Just recently, San Francisco."

"No shit?"

"No shit."

They shared views about the Barbary Coast and gold strikes until the saloon filled up with patrons and Barney was too busy to chat.  Collins helped himself to a couple more cups of coffee, then paid and walked back to the stable.  There was still sufficient light to see well and he found the old man sitting just inside the door holding the reins of a stout looking gelding already sporting C.W.'s saddle.

"Took you long enough," the old man said without rancor.

C.W. walked over, patted the horse's shoulder and tightened the cinch.  The dun gelding side-stepped a little.  He went to his head and examined the set of the bit.  "What is your name?" he asked the tattered old man, now wearing a shirt that had once been white.

"Jenkins"

"Well, Jenkins, I appreciate you saddling him up for me.  I believe I will take him for a stretch. Anything I should know?"

"You should know how to ride," he answered and grinned with the few teeth left in his mouth.

Collins grinned back.  "Anything else?"

"He is a five year old I got in last week.  He is healthy and I do not believe he is fit for children."

"Fair enough," Collins said and led the horse out in front of the stables. He swung aboard and held the horse in. The animal was paying attention, with its ears turned back and an alert stiffness in its stance.  Collins eased up on the reins and squeezed its sides with his legs.  The horse responded by moving forward and Collins guided it down a dirt track that led south.  Soon he was out of town and trotting through open ground.  He stopped the horse, then let it go again, turning it left then right and finally opening up into a gallop. At first the horse tried to get its head down to buck, but Collins pressured the left rein, picking its head up, and the horse changed its mind.  The animal had a good, ground-eating lope that was comfortable and smooth.  He slowed the horse to a walk and began to talk to it.  C.W. enjoyed the evening air and his solitude after the crowded train, Reno's anguished tale, and the bustling town.  He toyed with names for the animal, deciding on Ulysses as a minor nod to Grant.  Smiling to himself, he let the gelding wander leisurely back to town and it was almost completely dark when he returned to the stable.  Jenkins was sitting by a hurricane lamp on a small table, reading the *Bismarck Tribune.*

"I thought maybe you had stolen the beast," he said, without looking up.

Collins swung down, unsaddled the gelding and led him to a trough to drink.

"Put him in one of the back stalls," Jenkins told him when he returned.  "There is already hay in the feeder bunks and enough clean straw for you to make a bed.  I threw your satchel back there too."

Collins raised his eyebrows in inquiry.

"Oh go on," Jenkins said, "I am no thief.  By the way, you got my money?"

C.W. fished two twenty-dollar double eagles out of his pocket and handed them over. "Got a receipt?" he asked.

The old man got up and walked into an adjoining room that apparently functioned as an office.  He licked the end of a pencil stub and wrote on a pad of paper.  Coming back, he held out a slip to Collins, who had to admit that it was more than sufficient and written in an amazingly tidy hand.

"Nice fist," he said.

"Thanks.  I was not always the vagabond you see before you," Jenkins told him, resuming his seat by the lamp.

"You own this place?"  Collins' curiosity was up.

"I do now."

"What in the hell does that mean?"

"The fella I worked for was killed in a bar brawl last April.  I just naturally took over."

"Naturally," C.W. said. Ulysses shifted his weight and stuck his nose in Collins' armpit. "Is there more to your story?"

"Came west for the California gold strike.  From Cincinnati.  Quite a town dandy and no goddamn sense.  What you see now is the wreckage of gold, booze and a taste for opium."

"Glad you found a place to come to rest," Collins told him.

"You and me both, pal," Jenkins said, resuming his reading.

Collins led Ulysses to the back of the stable, finding that Jenkins had lit a railroad lantern for him and had actually laid out a kind of pallet of straw.  As he sat down and pulled off his boots, he ruminated on the outlandish brew of humanity that peopled the West.

# 6

Collins woke early, as was his habit, and organized his belongings between carpetbag, saddlebags and bedroll.  He exchanged his suit for a sturdy shirt, denim trousers, twill vest and a roomy linsey-woolsey coat with big pockets.  His black, short-brimmed Stetson was always a constant.  He strapped on his belt and holster for the first time, checking his .45 Colt revolver and sliding it home.  He carefully secured the watch that Reno had given him in an inside pocket of the vest.  Collins took a moment to greet Ulysses in his stall, scratching behind his ears and rubbing his eyes, already liking the horse's intelligence and even temperament.  He then walked to the front of the stable and found Jenkins sitting on the cluttered desk in the office, drinking coffee.  He wordlessly took in the change in Collins' appearance and pointed to a coffeepot on a small stove in the corner.  Finding a cup nearby, he poured coffee and leaned against the wall opposite to Jenkins.

"Need a telegraph office," he said, after a while.

"One down the street to the west.  Next to the Bismarck Hotel."

Collins dug out four bits and tossed the coins onto the desk next to Jenkins.  "For the lodging," he said.

"No need for that.  Already overcharged you for the horse, even at the present inflation rates."

"Just the same.  Beat the hell out of the hotel I encountered."

"Most of them are pretty rough.  Couple of good ones though.  Could have directed you."

Collins shrugged.  "I like the clientele here better."

Jenkins grinned.  "I see your point."

"I need to buy a rifle."

"There is a dry goods store down near the telegraph office.  Might cost you, though."  Jenkins took off his grimy hat and scratched his head vigorously.  "What sort of rifle you looking for?  Buffalo gun?"

"Naw, no need for a buffalo gun.  Looking for a Model 73."

"Well now, I happen to have a Winchester 73 I inherited from my dead boss.  I  got no use for it."

C.W. smiled.  "How much?"

"Forty...in gold."

"Does everything around here cost forty dollars?"

Jenkins bared his scanty teeth in a smile.  "It do for you," he answered.

"Let me see it."

Jenkins went to a cluttered corner of the office and dug behind a coat rack piled with moth-eaten saddle blankets, scraps of leather strapping and ratty clothing. He brought out the rifle and handed it to Collins.  It was wrapped in a piece of oilcloth.  C.W. unwrapped it and examined the gun.

"It is in fine shape," the old man told him.

"It looks to be in good condition.  Have any cartridges?"

"Nope.  Those you will have to purchase."

Collins leaned the gun against the desk.  "I will send my telegram and buy some shells.  I will also have to stop at the bank."

"Wells Fargo is on the opposite side of the street and down a ways toward the river from the telegraph office and hotel."

Collins went out into the morning light.  The roadway

was already bustling with activity and, occasionally, a victim of the previous night's debauchery could be seen sleeping it off in an odd position against piles of goods, under a water trough or, in one instance, in the middle of the street.  Horses and wagons avoided running over him and Collins thought this to be rather extraordinary, given the general callousness of a gold hungry town.  He did, however, walk over and encourage the man to relocate, which he did protestingly.  C.W. found the Bismarck Hotel and the Western Union office next door.  The operator was impertinent and officious, traits that seemed to Collins to be shared with all telegraph operators. He gave Collins paper on which to write his message.  He wrote, "Found friend stop have trail stop must see buford stop will visit grave stop send funds to Helena stop very odd stop," and signed it "*fa'g an bealach*," the old Gaelic war cry from the Irish Brigade, meaning "clear the way."  By signing the telegram in this way, Grant would know that all was confidence.

The operator examined the strange message.  "To whom shall this be sent?" he asked.

"To Hiram at the White House in Washington D.C."

"You are joking."

"I am not.  Please send it as I have instructed."

"You have friends in the White House?"

"Please send the telegram."  Collins placed the cost of the telegram on the man's counter.  "Thank you," he said, walking out the door.

He took a letter of credit issued to him by Grant's personal secretary into the Wells Fargo office.  He received paper notes and gold pieces. Another letter of credit would await him in Helena.  He then found the dry goods store and purchased .44-40 cartridges for the rifle, jerked meat, salt pork, dried apples, hard tack, and a sack of coffee.  Back at the livery, he found Jenkins napping in the sun against the east wall of the building.

"I will try out the rifle.  I have cartridges."

"It is where you left it," Jenkins told him.

Collins retrieved the rifle and loaded it.  He then carried it out back and walked a little ways out of town.  Choosing a dirt bank as a backdrop, he shot several rounds at a rock, hitting it almost every time.  Seeing that the rifle was sufficient for his purposes, he carried it back and handed Jenkins two more double eagles.

"Pleasure doing business with you," Jenkins told him, pocketing the gold pieces.

"No doubt."

"Ready to push on?" the old man asked.

"Need passage on a steamship."

"I have heard that the *Far West* is still being used to travel as far as the Rosebud in the service of the military."

"Then I had best make arrangements."

Collins headed down the street to where he had noted the location of the Coulson Line Missouri River Transportation Company.  He found out that the *Key West*, a sister boat to the *Far West*, was being resupplied and would be headed out to carry reinforcements and supplies to military personnel waiting on the Tongue River the very next day.  Pleased at his luck, he purchased passage for Ulysses and himself.  He returned to the livery.  Jenkins had disappeared, so he saddled Ulysses, slipped his new rifle through the offside billet, and set out for a long ride into the countryside.

# 7

The coffee colored water of the Missouri shouldered sluggishly past the *Key West*. Collins felt stupefied by the featureless landscape and monotonous thumping of the paddle wheel. The soldiers and civilian support personnel on the boat were of singularly dull dispositions and limited wit, so the journey was unrelieved by the company he kept. He grew especially weary of the unremitting racialism and blood lust expressed *ad infinitum* in almost all the conversations of which he was within earshot. He found that the only passable and reasonably intelligent conversation to be had was with Captain Buesen. Buesen was originally from Massachusetts and had actually attended Harvard for a year. Their shared interest in paleontology served to fuel the exchange of theories and friendly scientific arguments. Unfortunately, the captain was prone to unexpected and inexplicable periods of morose depression, during which he was uncommunicative and somnolent. As a result, C.W. spent long hours watching the shoreline slide by, smoking his pipe and concocting vague theories as to the identity of the white men he sought. Occasionally, he went below to visit Ulysses, who seemed as bored and restless as he was. Whenever the steamboat stopped to take on wood, C.W. managed to take a stroll through endless grasslands, but there was never sufficient time to exercise his horse.

When the *Key West* arrived at Fort Buford, at the

head of the Yellowstone River, the first order of business for Collins was to retrieve his horse and take him for a long ride along the northern banks of the Missouri. Ulysses was recalcitrant for much of the outing, so Collins put him into a long lope through hilly country until he leveled out into a restrained walk. Collins then headed him back to the fort, reestablishing the bond they began in Bismarck. Having placed him in the care of the stables, Collins went in search of General Terry. He had heard Terry was stationed at Fort Buford after a fruitless chase up the Yellowstone following a cold trail. The Indians he sought, thought to be some of the participants in Custer's demise, had slipped away to the north, probably taking refuge on the Milk River. Meanwhile, Colonel Miles and the 5th Infantry were harassing bands of Sioux in the vicinity of the Tongue River, while Crook was launching another expedition from Fort Fetterman. At the moment, Terry was a bit in disgrace for having waited a full month before he and Crook engaged in pursuing the Indians from the Little Big Horn, the result of waiting for substantial reinforcements.

Collins found General Terry in his quarters, writing letters at a small roll top desk. He knocked on the doorframe, the door being open, and went in at a gruff invitation from the general. Standing patiently while Terry finished writing, Collins took in the man's appearance. He was tidy, but seemed a trifle beaten. The general carefully blotted the writing, lay down his quill, corked the inkbottle and turned to look at his visitor.

"Yes?" he asked, simply.

"My name is Charles Collins. I have been sent at the behest of President Grant to look into...shall we say, sensitive information provided to you by Major Reno."

Terry's eyebrows furrowed. "I have received a cryptic telegram from the Adjutant General. I was to expect a visitor. Are you he?"

"Indeed."

"Very well. Sit down." Terry indicated a wooden chair nearby.

Collins sat. "Any other news?"

"No. Just the visitor."

"Very well. I will get right to business."

Terry nodded. "Proceed."

"I have heard Reno's complete story from his own lips. Is there any reason to doubt his veracity in any way?"

Terry digested this information and weighed it. "No," he said after a while. "I do not believe so. It is true that he has been drinking inordinate amounts of alcohol, but the man is so intrinsically honest, I do not believe this would affect his recounting of the events on the Little Big Horn. Benteen has born out everything he has told me."

"Did you, in fact, see any sign of white men having fought alongside the Indians?"

Again, Terry was pensive. "Yes," he said at last. "I do not want this repeated to anyone but the President."

"My discretion is my livelihood."

"Of course. Although I did not tell Reno, I, too, saw the dead white men he reported to be in the tepees. I also saw other bodies that were white and obviously on the side of the Indians. This is the real reason I made the report to the Adjutant General. There was enough evidence to warrant concern. Apparently President Grant thinks so as well?" He looked at Collins quizzically.

"Apparently."

Terry sighed and scratched his chin through a thick beard. "I do not know, Collins. The violence is reaching its peak and I must confess a certain empathy for the red men. Have you heard that Congress will soon pass the Sioux appropriation bill? Now they will be forced to cede all their remaining lands and withdraw to a strictly delineated reservation on the west bank of the Missouri. I wonder how we would react to a relentless conqueror of another race?  Would we be as forbearing as the Plains Indians have been for the past fifty years?"

Collins was surprised at hearing these sentiments expressed by Terry.  "I fear their demise is imminent. I could have taken their part, if given the opportunity. Although to make such statements would be infinitely fatal in most company."

Terry smiled the faintest of smiles.  "Do we suppose these white men are fighting from a sense of solidarity with the Indians?"

"Perhaps."

"If not, then why?  It is quite puzzling."

"I hesitate to conjecture as to the motives of these men. My theories may cloud my investigation."

Terry examined him for a moment.  "You spied for Baker in the war," he finally said, meaning Lafayette C. Baker, the head of the secret service after 1862.

"For a time."

" Never cared for him, but I heard you were reliable and...not ungentlemanly."

"I embrace honor in all endeavors."

"So I have heard.  What does Grant intend to do with the information you provide him?"

"I cannot say for I do not know.  I believe he is concerned about political ramifications."

"There are certainly a number of Métis or half breeds in Montana Territory.  No cause for concern there."

"Did the bodies you saw appear to be mixed bloods?"

Terry examined the toe of his right boot. "No," he said slowly.  "They were definitely white...really very white."

"Then that, sir, is the mystery and the conundrum."

"Indeed."  Terry shifted in his chair.  "Did you need lodging for the night?"

"No, thank you very much.  I will bunk on the steamboat."

"Drink?"

"No thank you, unless it is soft."

"Coffee?"

"Yes."

When Terry left, Collins perused the room. It was furnished with a potbellied stove, desk, a small assortment of wooden chairs, one stuffed chair near a window, and a hanging shelf with books. No pictures adorned the walls. A large map of Montana Territory was the sole ornament in the room. Terry obviously was not intending a prolonged stay. He returned with two large steaming mugs.

"I always have coffee. It is one luxury I cannot do without."

Collins accepted a cup and blew on the surface. "Smells good."

"How far are you willing to go?" Terry asked, retaking his seat at the desk.

"How do you mean?" C.W. asked, not quite certain of the import of the question.

"Did the President give you a time limit? I am merely curious."

Collins sipped his coffee. "I do not believe there is a time limit, no. I received the impression that the President wanted an answer no matter the time or distance involved."

"Then the trail may be long. There will be a presidential election soon."

"I am aware of that," he said, attempting to discern whether Terry knew more than he was willing to say. C.W. paused and drank more coffee. "Did you see Keogh?" he asked abruptly.

Terry's face saddened. "I did."

"I am interested in his pistol. It was quite distinctive and I may be able to trace it."

"I remember it. It was a beautiful weapon. Now that you bring it to mind, I do not recall seeing it on the battleground...nor did I see it in the possession of any of the soldiers."

"Not looted?"

"I do not believe so. I attempted to limit the looting to Indian bodies only. Of course, I could not be everywhere at once."

"Of course."

Terry picked up the inkbottle and pointlessly examined the contents. "I have had a thought," he said, after a while. "Perhaps a way to pick up a trail."

Collins was interested. "Yes?"

"There is a fellow in Deer Lodge...at least that is where I last heard he was residing...his name is Stuart. There were two of them, but I believe the older of the two died a couple of years ago at Fort Peck. The brother in Deer Lodge is named Garver, or some such, but I have heard that he is quite a shot and loves to collect novelty guns. He is also married to an Indian and may have dealings with them beyond most of the white men in Montana Territory."

"Sounds promising."

"Deer Lodge lies just south of the Clark Fork River to the southwest of Helena."

"Could this Stuart fellow have been in at the Little Big Horn?"

"I doubt it. I heard his brother had been involved in stealing revenue from the Milk River Indian Agency in order to line his own pockets. He was also an erstwhile buffalo hunter. I doubt that his younger brother's sympathies lie too much with the Indians. He is an early settler and has, no doubt, had his share of conflicts with the red men. And he has, I believe, political aspirations."

"Worth looking into, though."

"I agree. Where will you proceed next, if I may inquire?"

"I will travel to the Cantonment on the Tongue River

to see General Miles.  That is the end of the line for the steamer anyhow.  From there I plan to proceed to the battlefield."

"Well then, brace yourself, for it will not be pleasant. I have little doubt that scavengers have made short work of our weak attempts at burial.  Honestly, Collins, the stench and destruction were daunting."

"Reno imparted such."

"Will Reno survive this debacle, do you think?"  Terry asked.

Collins sighed.  "It is doubtful, in my opinion.  Too many factions want to use him as a scapegoat.  Elizabeth Custer must have an excuse for George."

Terry looked ill.  "There is a stinking black cloud emanating from the Little Big Horn that will not dissipate for many years."

"That reminds me.  I need to clarify a point, if I may."

"About the Little Big Horn?"

"Yes"

"Go ahead.  I will answer if I am able."

Collins paused to drink from his cup.  "What exactly *were* your orders to Custer?" he asked, cradling the mug in both his hands.

Terry stroked his beard and shifted in his chair. "What did Reno tell you?" he asked.

"I would rather that you shared your own recollections," Collins said, tactfully.

"Aw hell, Collins," Terry said, suddenly looking him in the eye and dropping all pretense, "Officially or unofficially, I told him *not* to engage the Indians on his own. I ordered him to report back before committing to any action. I offered him Gatling guns for his own protection. I *believed* Reno's report about the possible number of Indians out there."  He paused.  "In all honesty, however, I knew he could never resist forging ahead."  He dropped his eyes to the floor.  "I sacrificed those young men who rode with him."

"If Crook had not been pinned down on the Rosebud and all three columns of soldiers had been able to converge on the Powder River country as planned, do you believe the campaign would have been a success?"

The question hung in the silence of the room. Collins sat quietly, hearing the distant voices of men through the open door. Terry seemed to be weighing his answer carefully.

"This is for the ear of the President?" he asked.

"Not necessarily. I am attempting to puzzle together a stronger sense of last summer's events."

"Well, then I can answer confidently that all three columns would have been decidedly insufficient to guarantee success against the masses of Indians concentrated on the Little Big Horn. Of course, this would not be a popular opinion and one I choose to keep predominantly to myself."

"Then, truthfully, many soldiers' lives were saved by your decision to send Custer out on reconnaissance, especially if you suspected he would engage the enemy on his own."

"I tell you, Collins, it was an ill-conceived endeavor from its inception. I find I regret much...especially letting Sheridan talk me into taking Custer with me in the first place. The man was ever a thorn in my side."

"In that, I do not believe you are alone." Collins finished his coffee and stood. "Thank you for the coffee and the information."

Terry stood as well. "Do find me on your return journey if possible," he said, extending a hand to shake.

"I will, sir," Collins said, and took his leave of the general, stepping through the door into the noonday heat.

# 8

Although tempted to ride Ulysses down the Yellowstone to meet Colonel Miles, Collins opted to stay on the *Key West*, as there were supposedly many bands of marauding Sioux and Cheyenne along the river. Collins doubted this to be true, conjecturing that the Indians were more likely to be evading marauding bands of soldiers and civilians out to avenge the losses on the Little Big Horn. Nonetheless, Collins figured that his mission would be seriously thwarted if he was mistaken and Captain Buesen seemed to have slipped free from all evidence of depression and so was jovial company as the boat steamed its way south. When rain drove Collins to the solitary shelter of his cabin, he fished out his beloved volume of Shakespeare from his saddlebags.

For years, Shakespeare had been a companion on long winter nights, in lonesome solitude, during a brief stint in jail due to mistaken identity, and by campfires from one coast to the other. His mother had considered Shakespeare to be the only Englishman who was worth his salt and had used him almost exclusively to teach young Charles to read. It seemed to him that every human experience was to be found within those ancient words and he found comfort in the idea. The texts also offered an unbroken connection with his beloved mother, dead these many years.

When the rain subsided, Collins joined Captain Buesen in the pilothouse. Water dogs floated out across meadows in the distance and the air was rich with dank earth and the wet bark of deciduous trees. With a full head of steam, the boat was seemingly flying past small islands. Open grasslands stretched endlessly on either side of the river and small herds of antelope could be seen at intervals. Collins imagined that great herds of buffalo would have been a common sight along the same route not many years before. He knew that the annihilation of these impressive animals had driven the Indians into violence more surely that any previous insult at the hands of the white men. Now that plagues of miners had overrun their precious Black Hills, they truly had nothing to lose.

"River is too shallow for this time of year, in spite of this rain," Buesen observed.

"Does it ever become too shallow for the boat?" Collins asked.

"Sometimes."

"What is that over there?" C.W. asked Buesen when they rounded a bend in the river.

The captain squinted, looking in the direction his companion was pointing. "Trees?" Buesen asked.

"I do not believe so."

As the steamer drew closer, they could make out scaffolds on which the Indians often placed their dead. Shreds of clothing hung down and flapped in a slight breeze, eerily appearing as if the dead were waving at them.

"Gives me the willies, that," Buesen said as they steamed by. "Bury their dead in the air, damn savages."

"I wonder what they make of us, burying our dead in vast plots of earth as if planting a crop?"

"A damn sight more civilized than what they do, I will warrant," the captain said stubbornly.

"Come now," Collins challenged, "As an amateur scientist, one must keep one's mind unfettered by prejudices."

"Well, if you had heard the wounded soldiers' stories from Captain Marsh, as I did, you might have some prejudices same as me."

"Perhaps, and yet I had a friend who was on the Washita. There are no true heroes in this conflict."

An enormous blue heron arose from the reeds nearby and sailed over their heads.

"I suppose there have never been true heroes in any conflict," Buesen observed, watching the bird fly away. "Humans do not make awfully reliable heroes. Our sentiments are impure."

"What of our intentions?" Collins asked, bemused.

"Also impure. Greed, lust, gluttony...always interwoven with intentions."

"Now you sound like so much fire and brimstone."

"Do I? What about your Shakespeare? He seems to be of a similar opinion, unless I am mistaken."

"Touché. You really should have stayed at Yale," Collins said, intentionally making a grievous error. "You have a professorial style."

"Harvard, damn it, Harvard. I cannot abide a Yale man. Well, which am I? Preacher or professor?"

"Both, much the same as your favorite Harvard scholar."

"Emerson? I cannot abide him."

"I would have pegged you for a transcendentalist."

"Ha! Then you would be mistaken, indeed."

Collins smiled, enjoying the man's wit. His attention was abruptly diverted. In the far distance, there seemed to be many horses with riders. He pointed.

"I see them," the captain said. "Probably Indians. Staying out of rifle range."

Just as he spoke, some of the passengers below began firing in the direction of the horses.

"Damn fools," Buesen observed. "They are wasting

their bullets and shooting at god knows what."

The distant riders grouped up and stopped their horses. Buesen handed him a spyglass. He scanned the terrain. "They are Indians," he told the captain. "Not sure what they are doing."

The passengers had ceased shooting, seeing that their gunfire was having no effect. The Indians resumed their journey and the steamboat soon passed around another bend. Chalky colored banks rose on either side of the river.

"Always suspected there would be fossils here," Buesen said, changing the subject.

"Ever stopped to see?" C.W. asked.

"Never had the opportunity. Now I have to be careful of Indian attacks."

"Do you really believe that this was all once ocean?"

"I have seen enough crustacean type fossils in eastern Montana Territory to believe it."

"What of the English bishop claiming that the earth is only six thousand years old?"

The captain dismissed his question with a wave of his hand. "Now you are truly goading me. Such talk is ridiculous."

"And Darwin?"

"Have you read the book?"

"I have," Collins told him.

"Then you know his scholarship is sound. We must embrace science, not archaic belief systems."

"Do you expound your theories in all types of company?" Collins asked.

Buesen gave him a deprecating look. "Hell no. It would not be safe in certain company."

"I can imagine that tar and feathers would be a genuine concern."

"The West is changing, Collins, but discretion is the better part of valor, after all." Captain Buesen grinned mischievously and steered the boat around a snag.

Collins smiled and returned to his perusal of the landscape. Dark clouds squatted upon the distant western horizon and a breeze blowing from their direction brought a teasing scent of wet sagebrush, mint-like in its freshness. "So you talked to Captain Marsh after he had transported the wounded men back from the battle of the Little Big Horn?" he asked abruptly.

"Yes."

"Did he say aught regarding the culpability of Major Reno in the battle?"

"He said much regarding how well the Major looked after his wounded." The captain's face narrowed in sudden anger. "Are you yet another who seeks to lay all blame at the poor man's feet? I have had dealings with Custer. Do dead men take no share of blame in this weary world?"

"I believe Reno to be an honorable man and soldier, in answer to your first question. In answer to your second, there will be short blame for Custer if his widow has her way."

"What course is his widow pursuing?"

"Newspapers, books, rabble-rousing...anything to place the blame on Reno."

"Damn. The man endured hell. He saved most of his command."

"Justice is a rare commodity, Captain. I seek it often and seldom find it."

Buesen eyed Collins. "What exactly are you doing out here, Mr. Collins? What are you seeking at the moment?"

"Reconnaissance, Captain Buesen."

"Reconnaissance? Military reconnaissance?"

"Let us say... reconnaissance."

The captain snorted. "It is clandestine, then."

"Clandestine. Yes."

"May you have success, Mr. Collins. May you pursue

justice to Major Reno's advantage."

"God willing and the creeks do not rise."

Collins said no more and Buesen retreated into silence.  The river rolled along its chalky banks as the boat bore slowly westward.

# 9

As Collins led Ulysses from the *Key West* into the gathering crowd of soldiers, he was overwhelmed by mingled odors of sweaty woolen uniforms, wood smoke, bruised sagebrush and dust.  Colonel Miles' new headquarters, known as the Cantonment on Tongue River, was situated on the mouth of the Tongue in the heart of Sioux territory.  Canvas tents as well as crude log and mud huts created a busy hub of military activity and Collins asked around until he found a larger tent with a rudimentary wooden porch upon which sat a table with chairs and several men.  Collins recognized the narrow-shouldered man, with colonel's insignia on his immaculate uniform, sitting in the center behind the table.  C.W. tied Ulysses, laden with his entire outfit, to a nearby tree and walked over.  He stepped onto the porch and waited to be noticed.  His plain civilian clothing was enough to announce his presence in the surrounding sea of uniforms.  After a bit, the lively conversation revolving around the latest scouting foray dwindled to a halt.  The colonel studied Collins, waiting in his relaxed stance and unmilitary manner.

"You sir.  Why are you here?  Peterson," he said, turning to his orderly, "why is this man here?"

"Why are you here?" Peterson asked.

"I have come to speak to Colonel Miles on a matter of importance."

"What matter of importance can you have to speak

of?" the colonel asked rudely.

Collins sighed, "A matter involving the White House. Have you not received a communiqué?"

"Peterson? Did I receive word about an ill-kempt civilian from the White House?" Colonel Miles asked and the five men around the table began to laugh.

"Uh, sir..." Peterson began tentatively, "you did, in point of fact, receive word that the Adjutant General was sending a man to see you."

The laughter died. Collins had already stepped off the porch, untied his horse and was walking away. He had had a belly full of officious bullies and their lackeys. The sound of running feet came up behind him and a breathless Peterson clapped a hand on his shoulder. Ulysses swung around, startled.

"Wait," he said. "The colonel wants to see you."

C.W. removed the hand from his shoulder and turned. "Do not touch me, son."

"The colonel..."

"I heard you," Collins told him. "I will make camp down by the river over by that far cottonwood. After which, at my own convenience, I will attend to your colonel. Is that understood?"

"But..."

"That is all." C.W. led his horse toward the river and Peterson was left behind. He unloaded his trappings, unsaddled and hobbled Ulysses, and lay out his bedroll. He gathered enough wood for a cooking fire and made a rock ring for a hearth. When a comfortable camp was ensured and attended to, Collins made his way back up the bank to find Peterson had been waiting for him all the while. He burst out laughing.

"I was not to return without you," Peterson told him, red-faced.

"Well, here I am. Let us proceed."

The two men walked back to the colonel's tent. By

this time, the other men had departed and Miles sat at the table alone.  He motioned to a chair across from him.  Collins mounted the porch and sat.

"I had forgotten the message concerning your visit.  I have much on my mind."

Here was a man with no apology in him, thought Collins.  He had not altered for the better since the war. "I see," he said and sat waiting for the colonel to advance the conversation.

"Peterson, you may go."  Miles packed a pipe and lit it carefully.  "I take it you are here about the Sioux campaign," he said, finally coming to the point.

"In a way.  I am en route to the Little Big Horn."

"Then you will certainly be killed by Sioux or Cheyenne warriors."

"I sincerely hope not."

Miles examined him, puffing furiously on his pipe. "I know who you are.  I recognize you.  Why are you proceeding to the battlefield?  What are you seeking...or should I say, what does Grant wish to know?"

"I am not at liberty to say what information President Grant seeks.  I am only here for the most recent and reliable information regarding the whereabouts of hostile bands of Indians so that I may avoid them in my journey west."

"They are on the move at all times.  We are seeking them and they know it.  All hell is about to rain down on their heads."

"No doubt.  So then, you cannot aid me?"

"I can assign a troop to protect you... as you are so apparently dear to the President," Miles said sarcastically.

"I believe the presence of green troops would put me in infinitely more danger than if I were to sojourn on my own."

"I care not either way," Miles told him, dismissively.

"Do you need supplies?"

"A few items. And I need a pack animal."

The colonel wrote briefly on a scrap of paper and fairly tossed it at Collins. "Take this to the supply tent. Get what you need. But know this, my friend...I will not be sending troops to search for you or bail your truant ass out of any trouble you may stumble into," he said, unpleasantly. "No matter how many messages I receive from Washington."

Collins stood, picked up the piece of paper and turned to walk away without response to the colonel's final riposte. He made his way to the supply tent and made the most of his ability to fill out his meager stores of tobacco, coffee, and other provisions. He acquired a battered sawbuck packsaddle, some rope, and a couple of used panniers and was subsequently sent to a makeshift stable to see about an animal. A barrel-chested and very Irish corporal was the first friendly interaction Collins had found since arriving in the cantonment.

"A pack mule, you say?" the corporal asked.

"Or horse. Whatever will not fold on me the first day out."

"Where might you be headed? We are not often asked to supply valuable animals to civilians, you know."

"I am headed west on official business, boyo," he replied in a strong Irish brogue. "Not that it is any of your affair."

"Well then, I have a very official mule that would be more than happy to give you service."

Collins raised his eyebrows. "I suspect that you are about to be rid of an obstreperous beast who has caused you unending woe."

The corporal laughed heartily. "Not a bad wager, but I am in fact most fond of the animal and fear for its safety in this military campaign. If you swear to keep her near and dear to your heart, I will send her off with you."

At this, the Irishman disappeared around back of the brush arbors and pole corrals that made up the stables. Collins had the premonition of being mightily played upon. After a few minutes, the corporal returned leading a pretty red mule that was tall and well proportioned.

"Meet Molly," he said, handing the lead to Collins.

Molly looked at Collins with large and doleful brown eyes. He tied her to a hitching rail and threw a blanket on her back, followed by the sawbuck. She stood patiently while he fitted the breeching, cinches and breast band to her muscled frame. "Are you not setting me up after all?" he asked.

"No sir, I am not. She is a lady all in all. You must treat her as such and lavish her with loving kindness. I am sad to see her go, but fear the redskins will kill her or steal her if she stays in the service of the U.S. Army. We lost forty-seven mules in a damn Indian raid around a month ago. I hear they eat mules, perish the thought."

Collins stowed his flour sacks full of sundry items in the panniers. The mule stood steadily without a turn of the ear. "By god," he said, "I believe you are in earnest."

The corporal smiled sweetly. "Is she not a darling? If ever you decide to be rid of her, I would take it kindly if you would find a safe haven for her. Or else ask around Montana Territory for Corporal Patrick Murphy and bring her back to me."

"Corporal Patrick Murphy? How many do suppose there are of you in the U.S. Army?" Collins asked, grinning.

"There may be a few go by the same moniker, my fine friend, but there be only one of me," Murphy said, puffing out his bulky chest.

"No doubt," Collins said, "No doubt at all."

The corporal bid Molly farewell with a catch in his throat and Collins led her to his camp. Ulysses came over and Collins shooed him away until he had unloaded the panniers and unsaddled the mule.  Then he hobbled her and sent her off to engage in the usual equine rituals of greeting.  He watched, amused, as it soon became obvious that Molly would be the dominant of the two. He lit a fire and made coffee and fried some bacon.  As he sat by the fire, eating bacon wrapped in stale bread, Peterson walked into his camp.

"The colonel wishes to see you," he said, standing stiff as a ramrod.

"What about?"

"I know not, sir.  Only that he bid me fetch you."

"Where do you hail from, boy?"

"Boston."

"Same as Miles."

"Yes, sir.  The same as Colonel Miles."

"Related?"

"Distantly."

Collins finished eating and drank down a cup of coffee.  He placed a large hunk of cottonwood on the fire to keep it and stood up.  Brushing dried grass off his trousers, he walked over to Peterson.

"Off we go," he said and took the lead toward where Miles' command center stood.

Colonel Miles was seated in the tent by a small wood stove smoking his pipe when Peterson announced Collins' arrival.  Miles nodded to a chair opposite the stove and asked Collins if he would sit.  Collins sat.

"I was a bit brusque earlier.  Perhaps you had more information to impart to me?"

Still no apology forthcoming, thought C.W.  "No," he said simply.

"I recalled that you handled certain rather sensitive missions during the war.  I have heard rumors that you continue such work from time to time."

"Perhaps."

"Is this such an occasion?"

"Perhaps."

"And you have no further information to impart to me?"

"No." Collins imagined he could see the machinery working in the man's head.

"I have heard that you visited with General Terry at Fort Buford."

"I did."

"He has failed in his mission. I am now in command of this campaign."

C.W. sat uncommunicatively. He had never cared for Miles. He was cut from the same cloth as Custer; all ambition and machination.

"I will round up the Sioux and force them onto the reservations," Miles stated. "If you are here representing Grant, then perhaps you can be of service to me."

"I have my own purpose. I will go my own way." Collins' suspicions were aroused.

"You may go your own way, according to your purpose. I merely wish to know what you discussed with Terry."

"If you attempt to restrict my movements in any way, I will resist most adamantly," C.W. said very quietly.

"What? What did you say to me? Exactly what are you implying, Mr. Collins?" Miles asked belligerently.

"I am implying nothing." He stood. "And now, if you will excuse me, I shall return to my camp and the remainder of my supper."

"I have not dismissed you."

"I did not ask to be dismissed," Collins said, stepping off the porch of the tent and walking away.

GRANT'S INDIAN POLICY

# 10

Collins woke after a couple of hours' sleep and began packing his outfit by the light of a half moon. He caught his animals and saddled each one quickly. He loaded the panniers on the sawbuck, placed his bedding and other "possibles" on top and roped the load using a diamond hitch for security. After kicking dirt on his fire, he climbed into the saddle, snagged Molly's lead rope and faded quietly away from the cantonment.

Fording the Tongue River and following the Yellowstone westward, Collins had the vague sense of a narrow escape. He had not cared for Miles' proprietary manner and had suspected that, until he was more forthcoming about his mission, the colonel was contemplating forcibly holding him in the camp. Ulysses snorted at a deer bounding out of the river bottom a small distance ahead, but Molly showed no reaction. C.W. felt a real fondness for Corporal Murphy in regards to the mule. He needed reliable animals where he was going and had no complaints on that score.

It would be dodgy going for the next few days, thought Collins, sneaking through country where soldiers and Indians alike were stirred up like a newly excavated anthill. He judged it would take about three days hard riding to get to the site of the battlefield, barring inclement weather or detours due to roving bands of Indians. He hoped they would all be up north, avoiding Miles and General Crook, whom he had heard was still patrolling the Yellowstone country.

Staying in the open and skirting groves of cottonwoods, he rode until daybreak. He stopped briefly to eat some hard tack and tighten the cinches on the animals, then continued on. The landscape was monotonous, the high grasses and patches of sage stretching unbroken to the north. He carefully perused every dust devil to be certain it was not precipitated by human sources. Collins was forced to admit to himself that he was more anxious than he had been for many a day and momentarily wished he were safely ensconced in Jenkins' livery stable. He knew from experience, however, that he would settle into solitude quickly and find comfort there.

As the sun rose in the sky, the day warmed considerably. Around noon, Collins stopped to let the animals rest. He hobbled them to graze a bit, then dug out some jerked meat to chew on as he studied the horizon. Far to the south there appeared to be a dark line of scattered brush or, perhaps, buffalo. He rather doubted buffalo, as so many of them had been slaughtered over recent years. Again, he felt the stirring of sympathy for the Indians and the loss of their way of life. Still, he mused, he had no wish to meet up with any of them while on his own and deep into the borderlands between Sioux and Crow territories. Wanting to cover as much distance as possible, as quickly as possible, he traveled without stopping until reaching Rosebud Creek, just as the sun was setting in the west.

The next day, as Collins covered mile after mile of prairie, he began to be able to make out distant mountains to the southwest. Once, he spotted smoke far off to the south, but he felt no need for concern. A solitary wolf shadowed him for several hours, but the animals took small notice. The large gray beast had disappeared by mid afternoon. Collins marked a small group of antelope and supposed the wolf had become interested in better prospects.  Fresh antelope meat was tempting to him, as well, but shooting his rifle was not an option for a lone traveler in the heart of Indian country.

Collins made camp that night along the Big Horn River and figured that the next day would bring him to the battlefield.  He did not relish the prospect of being faced with the chaos of human remains, mauled by animals and stinking of tragic death.  He slept poorly and packed up early, pushing south along the east side of the river.  Ulysses and Molly were restless and irritable, as if sensing what was ahead.

About midday, he espied a group of horses with riders in the east that seemed to be moving in his direction.  They were creating a plume of dust as they rode and Collins retreated into a clump of trees and brush on the river, dismounting and tying his animals in the thick of some alder brush.  He did not loose their cinches in anticipation of a possible and desperate flight if they were discovered.  C.W. took his rifle and bellied to a small rise from which he could track the riders' progress.  He pulled out his old military field glasses and watched as they drew closer. He could make out that they were Indian warriors, riding bareback and armed with lances, bows and some with rifles.  Their hair told him they were Sioux or Cheyenne, being worn long.  One of them wore a cavalry officer's hat and Collins had a definite idea about where the Indian might have recently acquired it, heightening his discomfort.

To his surprise and relief, the ten or so warriors veered off to the north before reaching the river.  He lay low for some time after they had ridden out of sight, then made his way carefully back to his animals, which stood patiently and quietly in their grove of yellow and orange leaves.  He mounted up and headed south, goading Ulysses into a fast walk and keeping close to cover.  Not long after, he reached the fork of the Little Big Horn and followed it back toward the southeast, making his way closer to his destination.

The delay caused by the encounter forced him to camp before reaching the battlefield. Collins was grateful for a respite prior to facing an unpleasant investigation of the field of carnage. Molly and Ulysses were in sore need of rest and feed, so he hobbled and turned them loose before tending to his own comfort. The river was trickling desultorily through high banks and he had chosen a camping spot that offered cover as well as a path down to water. The horses found their way down and Collins followed them with a canvas bucket to fetch water for himself. He stood for a moment, talking to the animals in low tones and scratching behind their ears. As he was studying his surroundings, out of both caution and curiosity, he noticed a queer looking object down river. On closer examination, the anomaly revealed itself to be the remains of a man encased in blue wool, the remnants of an army uniform.

Glancing instinctively around, he knelt by the corpse and rolled it over. From the appearance of the flesh, he could see it had been in the water for at least part of the time. A broken arrow shaft extruded from the shoulder and another from what remained of the belly. His scalp had been taken. The man had been a lowly private and how he had come to die alone, down by the river, was a mystery. Collins was certain he was still a good distance from the battlefield and this fellow was well out of its periphery. Not being particularly sentimental about such things, Collins left him where he lay, knowing that nature would dispose of him in the way of all rotting flesh. Somewhere in the vastness of America, he mused, there must be a relative waiting for news that would never come.

Collins took his bucket some way upstream from the corpse to get his water. He climbed back to his campsite and the animals followed him up.  They wandered off to graze among the still green grasses protected by the shade of aged cottonwoods that surrounded them.  Collins looked at the setting sun sending its light through the golden dying leaves across the river and was saddened at the thought of the hapless victim of cowardice or mischance lying below him.  In true Celtic humor, his mood darkened into melancholy, pondering the useless end of so many other men who would never see another autumn, another winter, another spring.  His gorge rose at the thought of Custer with his cocksure manner, disregard for honor and complete disregard for the welfare of his men.  Oddly, his friend Myles had been coming more and more into Custer's orbit over the past years and C.W. had been dismayed to see him do so.  Not previously ambitious, Myles had seemed to be seeking advancement through his association with Custer and notoriety through his escapades.  Unfortunately, Collins had not found the opportunity to speak with Keogh for more than a year and now the issue was moot.  Collins morbidly wondered whether Myles had had an epiphany regarding Custer as he was desperately fighting for his life.

He did not sleep that night, keeping watch in his cold camp, chewing on hard tack and jerky and keeping a close eye on the whereabouts of his horses.  He smoked his pipe, shielding its glow with his hands.  As soon as he could see in dim predawn light, he packed up his outfit, saddled the animals and headed along the river.  As was his wont, an unpleasant task that had been dreaded would now be boldly faced.

G. A. CUSTER - HERO OF THE CIVIL WAR

# 11

After a good two hours of riding, Collins began to notice detritus from the battlefield. A broken arrow with fletching was cast off nearby, a few feet away lay a moccasin and what looked like a wad of human hair. He followed the ridgeline above the river, having been thoroughly briefed by Reno. Further along he looked down at a scene of complete destruction. White bones, clothing, drying meat, and military buttons glittering in the sunlight bespoke the site of Custer's end. He dismounted and left his animals to graze while he perused the area. Moving down slope, Collins began to pick up the scent of death, permeating the soil and air around mounds of bones and shallow graves excavated by coyotes, bears and wolves. By the time he was in the thick of it, the stench was overpowering, especially as the dead had been somewhat reconstituted by autumn rains. The animals and men were gathered in clumps, according to where they had died, the balance of them being just down from a small knoll, on the west side. Toward the river, there was another area of scattered bones and hardened flesh, where others must have met their end.

As used to death as he had become during the war, Collins felt his throat contract walking alone among the soldiers' remains all littered with desiccated horse carcasses, dry grass and twisted pieces of clothing. Melted fat from disintegrated bodies permeated the soil and gave off a musty and foul odor. A shallow grave nearby had been dug enough to expose a skull that had been chewed upon vigorously by strong teeth. He could see a few coyotes skulking in the tall grass here and there; no doubt permanent residents of the battlefield until all marrow was extracted from the last bone or deep winter snows made their scrounging impracticable. Magpies, crows, ravens, even the occasional eagle, also boldly inhabited the surroundings. Ribs, pelvic bones, legs stuck in boots, curled hands, with just enough sinew remaining to bind them together, lay haphazardly all around. C.W. searched the ground for clues among the carnage. Perhaps just an inkling of who the white warriors had been or, possibly, Myles' fancy English pistol.

Collins retrieved his animals and led them down to the river, where he unsaddled and hobbled them. He stowed his outfit nearby in some brush, but he was not overly concerned about Indians, knowing they would probably be giving this scene of their spectacular victory a wide berth. Across the river, he could see the skeletons of lodge poles and piles of nondescript garbage. He climbed back up to wander among the dead, bending to examine an object here and there. On one occasion, he picked up a Green River knife, most probably lost by one of the Indian warriors. It was worn from many sharpenings and of an older style, the type favored by trappers prior to '49. Collins stuck it in his belt, thinking it would either be of practical use or a valuable bit of information if he could discover its provenance. The ground was littered with spent shells and he was stunned to find guns lying around in profusion, many of them the standard issue Springfield carbines and Army Colts, but also Henry repeaters, Winchesters and the occasional antiquated muzzleloader from the days of the fur traders. These guns, he surmised, must have been abandoned by the Indians. He thought it was queer that they would abandon any weapon in their current plight.

Collins stopped to gaze around him, making certain he remained alone.  The sound of scolding magpies rose from a mound of decay below him, but all else was silent and solitary.  He set himself to examine the hill as systematically as was possible, given the chaos of clothing, hats, boots and coats jumbled with the pieces of bodies that strewed the field.  One quite disintegrated head, recently exhumed by animals, appeared to bear dirty reddish blonde curls and remnants of similarly colored facial hair.  He was momentarily tempted to boot the thing, but abstained.  He did not bother to investigate further, as its identification was singularly unimportant to his mission.  The manner of the man's death would, no doubt, become fodder for lies and legend.

As the day wore on, he stumbled onto a disinterred corpse, twisted in a grotesque position by scavengers.  An arm was detached, some rib bones lay about and the skull was hanging on by a shred of jerked skin. Something made him look closer at the grisly form and his guts tightened as he noticed the Agnus Dei medal torn loose and lying nearby.  The sock on one emaciated foot was enough to convince him he had found his erstwhile friend, Myles Keogh.  Some of his thick mustaches remained on the crust of an upper lip, but most of the flesh had been eaten from his face and form.  A few tufts of hair showed on an unscalped pate and unholy beetles inhabited the skull, crawling from his eye sockets and ears.  Collins found a crude stake close at hand with the name of "Keogh" carved faintly upon it. He caught a movement from the corner of his eye and was momentarily spooked, kneeling as he was beside abject death, but he turned to see a pair of ravens rising from a pile of bones, one with a piece of hide carried in its black beak. These men would truly be scattered to the four winds, he thought morbidly, and turned to carefully gather up and rearrange his friend's earthly remains.  Going in search of and finding the shoulder blade of a horse, he used it as a digging tool to re-excavate Keogh's modest grave. After having worked energetically for quite some time, he placed the body inside its new home and carefully laid the distinctive medal in its place upon his breast. He packed and rammed the dirt with the heels of his hands as a defense against further marauders and, using the Green River knife he had found, carved Keogh's name definitively on the wooden stake and hammered it deep into the soil with a rock. As he mournfully turned to take his leave, he said in the Irish, "*Ni dhiolann dearmad fiacha,*" and walked deliberately away. A debt is still unpaid, even if forgotten. The remainder of the day was taken up by further wanderings among the horrors of the field, producing little but dark thoughts and depressed spirits.

As Collins prepared his camp for the evening, the wind came up and thunder could be heard approaching with clouds from the west. A violent storm blew in by dark, rain mixed with a gravelly hail, stinging his face and chilling him to the bone. He huddled with the animals in a tight copse of willows, fancying he heard the terrified screams of men and horses and the hell raising battle cries of Sioux and Cheyenne. When the storm had passed, he hunted for dry wood under the cottonwoods and lit a fire. His morale was at bottom, so he dug out his Shakespeare and began to read by the firelight. Night wore on sleeplessly until, exhausted, Collins wrapped himself in his bedroll. Wolves and coyotes sang to the dead in the stillness. When Ulysses wandered over to blow warm breath his face, he told him, "'True is it that we have seen better days,'" and shooed him away. A favorite quote could always console him.

The day broke through fog and C.W. rekindled the fire to make coffee. He sat, enveloped by a secure blanket of moisture, and savored the hot liquid. He broke out a bit of oats for the animals, wanting to save most of the grain for harsher conditions. He rubbed both of them down with a saddle blanket, talking quiet nonsense to them, grateful for their stoical company. As the sun began to burn through the mist, Collins climbed down to cross a narrow place on the Little Big Horn and went into the remains of the Indian camp.

G. A CUSTER'S FUNERAL

# 12

The camp was as eerie as the battlefield, even though the smell of death did not permeate its environs as strongly. Lodge poles rose in formation on either side of him, following the river to the south amid piles of old buffalo robes, as far as he could see. Reno had not been exaggerating when he had told him the camp was several miles long. It stretched to the west as well, spreading through the groves of cottonwoods toward low hills and open prairie. Brush wickiups, used by young warriors without families, lined the riverbanks. Collins wandered through the debris, poking at piles of garbage with his foot and examining the contents of burned lodges. Reno had told him that Terry had ordered several men to burn the village, but mostly they had burned the tepees still covered in hides and holding the bodies of the Indian dead. In several lodges, he found the charred remains of bodies, but it was impossible to tell if they had been white or red.

He walked through the village, following the river south. There were fewer discarded weapons, but other rubbish was plentiful. Near a gnarled old tree, Collins picked up a fabric doll, obviously of white manufacture, and wondered about its provenance, surmising the worst. On a pole nearby was a human head, picked nearly clean by birds, and he remembered Reno's story about the soldier whose horse had run away with him. He wondered why no one had bothered to take it down and bury it.  Intricately beaded moccasins, hardened by rains, pieces of buckskin, metal pots, horn ladles, parfleches, wool blankets, and other debris made up the piles of refuse left behind by the Indians.

They had to have known that all hell would follow on the heels of such a victory and news of Terry's column approaching must have put them to reckless flight.  Ironically, they could have taken out Terry's command, as well, if their numbers had been as vast as Reno and Terry had reported.  The camp was certainly large enough to have accommodated innumerable family groups and warriors.  In their precipitous flight, the Indians had left behind much that would have been sentimental, practical, even essential.  Collins was sure that the coming winter would finish off the free ranging Sioux and Cheyenne.  Starvation, inclement weather and the implacable Nelson Miles with his 5th Infantry would flog them onto reservations without mercy.

Curious to see the site of Reno's retreat and the bluffs where he took a defensive position, Collins continued through the camp until he came out of the scattered tepee sites and began to find signs of pitched battle among the drying grasses.  Horse carcasses, bits of clothing, spent cartridges, arrows and hats were strewn about and he followed the trail into the cottonwood thicket as described by Reno.  There he found what must have been the scattered remains of Bloody Knife, still partially attired in an array of soldier and Indian clothing.  He had not been scalped, for his braids remained somewhat attached to the exploded abomination that had once been his head.  A Winchester repeater lay hard by, its stock decorated with the brass tacks so favored by Indians in adorning their weapons.  No other bodies were visible and Collins assumed they must have been dispersed somewhere nearby.

He moved on toward the river and found the ford

used by Reno in retreat. Narrow and unspeakably steep on the opposite side, he grimaced at the thought of attempting a crossing at full gallop under fire with a predominance of unseasoned soldiers. To save as many as he did, Reno must have nearly beaten them across. His respect for the man increased palpably. Too bad Reno's critics could not be forced to journey to the battlefield, Collins thought. They may not be so bold in their accusations thereafter.

Not wanting to cross the deep ford on foot, he continued along its west side, looking for signs of the hills where Reno had made a stand. The river curved sharply a couple of times and then, as he scanned the bluffs to the east, he spotted a metal object glittering in the sun. Having brought his field glasses, he pulled them out of his shirt and scanned the hillside. Plain enough, he could see the earthworks, the packsaddles, the dead animal remains, all used to secure a defensive position. He did not need to inspect it further, as it appeared much as Reno had described it. C.W. stood in the peaceful noonday sun and imagined he could hear the defensive battle raging above him in blistering summer heat. It seemed truly amazing to him that anyone had survived the gross miscalculations of Terry and Custer on those last days of June. Amazing indeed.

Taking a direct route back to the Indian camp, he proceeded to examine more of the lodges. Behind one thoroughly charred tepee rested a grindstone. Collins used a stout branch to dig through the scorched garbage in its center. He found a couple of skulls, burnt clothing, plenty of bones, some tools and little else. If this had been the lodge containing dead white men, then Terry had seen to it that all evidence had been thoroughly destroyed. Odd, thought C.W., not for the first time, that Terry had reported Reno's information at all. There was nothing to be learned from the conflagration, so he moved on, searching for anything that might provide illumination regarding the white warriors.

As he wandered through the village back toward his camp, he espied something white fluttering under some brush.  He went over to it and picked up what appeared to be a book.  As he thumbed through it, he could see it was handwritten in pencil, much of it blurred with wear, water damage and the pages rubbing together.  Its cover was of burgundy leather and it had once sported gilded ornamentation on the spine, but very little was left.  The words were written in fairly illiterate English and Collins figured it would take some time to decipher.  He stuck it in his coat pocket for later study.  He followed the river back to the spot where he had crossed in the morning and returned to his camp. He knew there was little more he could learn from this tragic site. It was time for the next stage of his journey.

Ulysses and Molly were nowhere in sight.  His gear was all present and intact, so he surmised they had wandered off on their own, having foraged enough nearby to be moving further afield.  He cursed them under his breath and, retrieving his rifle, began tracking them through the trees and brush along a northerly route. They were still hobbled, he could tell from the tracks, but he had known many a mule or horse that could cover several miles when similarly restrained.  It was getting on to dusk when he finally found them, cropping lush grass in a meadow by a small spring.  They offered no resistance when he looped ropes around their necks and began leading them back.  He verbally berated them as they walked, calling them heartless ingrates, motherless children, the devil's own, and they bore up under his calumniations with fortitude.

About halfway back to camp, he jumped a large white wolf chewing on something in a patch of tall grass.  Ulysses snorted and shied, but C.W. held on and he settled down next to Molly as the wolf silently faded into the river bottom like a wraith.  He went over to see what had been so absorbing to the animal.  Three or four human carcasses in indiscriminate anatomical disarray were lying in a hollow.  Tatters of blue fabric told him they had been more soldiers who had died separately from their fellows on the battlefield or with Reno.  Maybe they had run for it and tried to hide in this sheltered place.  Perhaps they had deserted the night before the battle and had been overrun by the Indians all the same.  Their Army-issue carbines and pistols lay dispersed among the gnawed rib cages, dried morsels of flesh and shredded uniforms.  No one would ever identify these soldiers and their mystery would remain inviolate.

Weary of death and its accoutrements, Collins picketed the horses against further adventures, decided he did not need a fire, ate some hard tack and rolled up in his bedroll before full night had fallen.  Before dawn, he was up and preparing for the trail.  He watered the animals, gave them a handful of oats each, and saddled and loaded them.  As the sun was appearing on a cloud streaked eastern sky, he forded the Little Big Horn headed cross-country toward Fort C.F. Smith and the Bozeman Trail.  The farther he moved away from the battlefield, the more his natural equilibrium returned and the nagging melancholy that had accompanied him for several days lifted.  In spite of his constant wariness of Indian activity, Collins began to enjoy traveling through the wild, untrammeled prairie with two obliging beasts of pleasant disposition.

FETTERMAN MASSACRE

# 13

The abandoned fort offered shelter. Its crumbling walls provided shade and a windbreak, though small protection from rain or snow. C.W. thought the weather might be turning for the worse, so he had made Fort C.F. Smith his destination for the night. Dismounting, he poked around where some of the houses had been before the angry Sioux had set fire to them. The wooden cross beams had thoroughly burned, but not the adobe walls. Collins chose a spot with three walls that would block the piercing and escalating wind coming from the northwest. He unsaddled and secured the animals and organized his gear. Scrounging for cottonwood limbs along the river bottom, he passed through the post's old burial ground with faded and worn markers. With dark and ominous clouds filling the skies, the cemetery seemed as sad and desolate as the battlefield had been. He built a lean-to large enough for him and the horses and piled brush as a further barrier, leaving plenty of room for a fire. By the time he had his camp set to his liking, a genuine blizzard was blowing in.

Sitting by a warm blaze, watching Ulysses and Molly browsing on a pile of branches he had brought in for them, Collins drank coffee and ate a tin of beans. The storm howled and cried among the fort's ruins and he tried to remember the history of the abandoned military installation. Built sometime in the 1860's to protect travelers on the Bozeman Trail, it had been constructed almost entirely of adobe. With a formidable stockade around the perimeter, it would have been fairly secure, except for the fact that soldiers had to hunt, gather wood and cut hay for the winter. The men at Fort Phil Kearny, to the south, had experienced similar difficulties with such duties. The Sioux consistently waited until a detachment of soldiers left the fort, then attacked, harassing the work details until the forts were severely constrained in any activity beyond the safety of the immediate vicinity.

On the winter solstice of 1866, a woodcutting party out of Fort Phil Kearny was attacked, causing the fort's commander, Colonel Carrington, to send a large detachment to the rescue. As C.W. remembered the report of the event, Carrington had given explicit orders not to pursue the Indians over a nearby ridge. As it turned out, the Indians had become quite adept at taunting the soldiers into combat through decoys and outright insults. The end result became known as the Fetterman Massacre, named after the commanding officer of the military detail that had been lured to its death, Captain William J. Fetterman. Word of mouth had led Collins to believe that Fetterman had been eager to make a name for himself, much the same as Custer. Now, it seemed the two men would share the ignominious fame of dual massacres within a decade of conflict with the Sioux.

Fort C.F. Smith, also constructed by a detail under Carrington's command, was frequently harried by war parties. Finally, in 1867, a haying detail consisting of a handful of soldiers and civilians held off approximately seven hundred Cheyenne and Sioux warriors by taking refuge behind a log corral. They withstood hours of prolonged attack until relieved by soldiers from the fort. In response, the government had decided to withdraw from the Powder River country and close the Bozeman Trail in return for an agreement from the Indians to allow unmolested travel on roads south of the Platte River. The forts had been forfeited and were destroyed shortly thereafter by the Sioux, outraged at the duplicitous maneuverings of the white men.

Ten years later, there would be no further agreements, exchanges, treaties or compromises with Indians anywhere in U.S. territories. The death knell had rung with this last disaster. Despite the righteousness of the Sioux in protecting their interests, no quarter would be given now that the U.S. Army had the justification it needed for abject slaughter. Odd, thought Collins, that seeing his friend Myles in such a sad and disintegrated state had not filled his breast with the desire for vengeance and hatred of the red men. The English had ever earned his ire, but the plight of the Indians seemed to be so similar to that of the Irish, he could only see them in the role of the oppressed. Their acts of violence were those of a conquered people fighting for autonomy and independence. It was due to this similarity that Collins had never been tempted to engage in the military activities of the western territories nor join Keogh in his adventures on the frontier. Myles had always marched to a different drummer.

Banking his fire against the falling temperatures and rolling snugly into his bedding, C.W. pulled out his Shakespeare to read by the dim light. He chose *Macbeth*, amusing himself by drawing comparisons between the Macbeths and Custers. The blizzard increased in fury and Ulysses pawed the ground with seeming anxiety while Molly stood in serene patience. Collins spoke to his companions in a low voice, imparting to them that all would be well come morning and hoped he was not in error. Already his future travels seemed daunting now that the weather had turned and he was perforce headed north to further his investigations. His next stop would be Fort Ellis, where he could resupply and rest up a bit before going to Deer Lodge in search of the gun-collecting pioneer suggested by General Terry.

The following morning was bitterly cold. Snow was still falling, but the wind had died down. Collins stirred up the fire and added wood. Soon he had coffee and some bacon frying. He hobbled the animals and turned them loose to forage for grass in the foot deep snow. With flour, water, a little baking powder and grease, he made crude biscuits and cooked them on a flat rock. It was a tasty breakfast and he took his time with it, given the weather. Come noonday, he would know better whether it was prudent to push on or not. He cleaned up his camp and went out to check on the animals. They had wandered down into the river bottom and were finding grass under the trees. He climbed back up to the fort and onto what remained of the lookout tower in a corner of its disintegrating ramparts, surveying the blanched landscape surrounding him.

Far away to the west and south rose mountains that appeared to be of grand proportions. Nearer to the south lay the Big Horn mountain range, the western border of the Powder River country. He would soon be passing out of Crow, Sioux and Cheyenne lands and into the region of Montana Territory that was safer for travel. Snow blanketed the terrain in all directions and the temperatures remained stubbornly low. It would be slow going, but the sun appeared to be burning through the clouds in the eastern sky and he decided to move on. As he was turning to climb down, he caught sight of several columns of smoke on the northern horizon. C.W. pulled out his glasses and scanned the area. He could not see much, but there appeared to be a camp in the trees along the Big Horn River a couple of miles to the north. Suddenly roused, he jumped down to fetch his animals back to camp and safety.

Eager now to depart the area, Collins saddled and

packed Molly and Ulysses as swiftly as possible. He dumped snow on his fire to eliminate any residual smoke and climbed into the saddle, heading down from the fort, across a shallow ford in the river and across the open grasslands to the west. He glanced behind frequently, wary of being followed, but to his relief he could espy no movement anywhere on the vast whiteness of fallen snow surrounding him.

Once certain that he was clear of danger, Collins angled north toward the Yellowstone, for the first time on his journey referring to the military issue map he had acquired from the sutler's store on the Tongue River. He wanted to cross the great river using a ford just above Pryor's Fork, supposedly one of the safest crossings and the one most employed by the army when passing through the region. The sun did, indeed, burn through the clouds, lending some warmth to the day. The snow was deep but light, and little hindered the progress of his strong and healthy animals across the undulating prairie. Becoming concerned about snow blindness, he stopped in a coulee and dug his fire blackened coffee pot from a pannier. Using his index finger, he rubbed black soot from the pot and smeared it around his eyes as a prophylactic measure that had proven its worth in the past.

Due to his late start, C.W. did not cover as much ground as he would have liked. There was spare cover for a secure camp on the bleak landscape and the sun was rapidly departing the sky. He was worried that another storm could blow in and that he and his companions would not survive without shelter. Loath to stop, he continued to ride and was heartened by the reflected light afforded by a splinter of moon. Sparing his animals with a moderate pace, he made his way across the seemingly endless expanse before him. A dark line of trees finally appeared in the distance. He figured he must have reached the eastern banks of Pryor's Fork and was heartily grateful.

Collins estimated the time to be well after midnight when he had tended to his stock with rubdowns, water and grain and finally prepared a comfortable camp. He was exhausted and quite hungry. Having chosen a spot under a spreading cottonwood that would undoubtedly disperse all trace of smoke, he built a fire and heated a tin of beef and toasted stale bread. A long smoke with his favorite pipe followed and then he was ready for a well-earned sleep. He checked on the animals and bid them a good rest, secure in their shelter of willow brush. As he rolled himself into his bedding, he smiled at his own contentedness, alone in a wasteland of snow and hostile Indians with only a horse and mule for company. Sometimes very little could seem to be more than sufficient.

# 14

Ulysses shifted his weight uneasily as C.W. surveyed the land below. All the snow from previous days had melted into greasy mud, making their trail rather treacherous in places. Having crossed the Bozeman Pass, they were overlooking the Gallatin River Valley, Fort Ellis and the town of Bozeman, named after the founder of the Bozeman Trail, John Bozeman. Bozeman had been killed in 1867, either by a partner or the Blackfoot Indians. Oh well, thought C.W., the west was a dangerous place, especially for those who were predators themselves. He nudged Ulysses into a walk, gave Molly a little tug, and descended into the valley below.

The military post of Fort Ellis was spread out like a small town, making no use of any type of stockade such as those deep in Indian territory. The Gallatin Valley had long ceased to worry about attack. The unremitting influx of miners and the strategic disposition of military garrisons over the past decade had pushed the Crow and Blackfoot into more remote areas. As a result, the community prospered, especially after Nelson Story had brought a great cattle herd into the valley. Back in the 1860's, Story had armed his men with Spencer's Repeaters and fought off jayhawkers, Indians and had even outwitted Colonel Carrington at Fort Phil Kearny to bring a herd of three thousand head of cattle to the meat hungry market of the Montana gold fields.

Collins rode into the center of the fort. He would

not receive further funds until Helena, but had retained enough means to purchase adequate supplies for the time being. He found the sutler's and tied his animals to a rail outside. It was a well-built structure of wood, with a porch, several windows and a shingled roof. As he mounted the steps, a soldier bounded out of the door above him and nearly knocked him down. After so many days of solitude, his temper was raised in an instant.

"See here," he began, regaining his balance, "Have you taken leave of all courtesy?"

The man steadied himself against the porch railing and appeared mortified by the encounter. C.W. could see from his bars that he was a first lieutenant, but was unable to discern whether he had been drinking or not.

"Good god, man. I *am* sorry. I just did not see you there and was ...wait a minute. I know you. Wait..." The young lieutenant scrutinized him. "You are Captain Charles Collins. You were in Atlanta."

As was common to his nature, Collins had ceased being angry at the moment of apology and was engaged in looking the man over in an attempt to place him. He had already decided the lieutenant was not inebriated, just energetic. "I was in Atlanta after the siege," he concurred. There really was something familiar about the fellow.

"Right. Captain Collins. You were in the Secret Service. I remember you from the trials of the Confederate raiders, the ones who were burning Negro encampments."

"Yes." Collins stepped up onto the porch. He held out his hand. "I am sorry. I do not recall your name, much as I try."

"Bradley. Lieutenant James Bradley, at your service," he said, shaking hands.

"Of course. Of course. It has been a long time."

"It has indeed. Much has transpired since then."

Collins detected a shadow falling over Bradley's mood and suddenly remembered that here was the man who had first discovered the hideous carnage of the Little Big Horn battlefield. He took his pipe out and began packing it with tobacco. Bradley followed suit with a cigar and they propped themselves amiably on the porch railing.

"You were with Gibbon and Terry at the Little Big Horn," C.W. said after a bit.

"I was." Bradley's cigar sent out a pleasing scent on the cool air. His face was now impassive.

"May we speak candidly?"

The lieutenant surveyed him closely. "Yes."

"I remain in a similar… employment as when we knew each other in Atlanta."

The other man cocked an eyebrow. "Really? What brings you to Fort Ellis?"

"Nothing particularly to Fort Ellis except as a stopping point, although I must admit, if I had known you were here, I would have made it a more particular destination."

A look of growing comprehension came to the lieutenant. "You are here in regards to the battle. You are investigating the military disaster of last summer."

Collins puffed on his pipe for a moment, considering. "May I have your word that what we discuss will remain between us alone?"

"You may," came the answer without hesitation.

"Then perhaps we can retire to the privacy of your lodgings? Do you have pressing duties to attend to?"

"I am currently on temporary leave. I will be leaving for Fort Shaw in a few days"

"Excellent. Then I may occupy some of your time?"

"Of course, Captain. Whatever you require."

Collins smiled, banging the ashes from his pipe against the railing. "I am no longer in the military. I am a civilian."

The lieutenant seemed puzzled. "But you said..."

"Yes, still in a similar employment, but outside military parameters."

"Then for whom are you investigating, if I may ask?"

"Well, not to put too fine a point on it, for the highest authority that may come to mind."

C.W. watched as the lieutenant disentangled his meaning. "You cannot mean...?"

"I do. Now, where may I billet my stock? They are in sore need of rest and fodder."

"I will take you to the stables and authorize their care." Bradley stamped out his cigar.

"We are most grateful," Collins said, climbing down the steps to untie their leads.

Bradley led the way to the stables and gave the private on duty clear instruction to take excellent care of the animals. Collins and Bradley unsaddled them and stowed his gear in a corner stall.

"Please do me the honor of being my guest," Bradley suggested. "My quarters are modest, but I have an extra cot. You will need blankets, but little else."

Collins gladly accepted, digging out his bedroll and the carpetbag, which held the sum total of his personal items. The men walked together through the muddy main street of the fort to the officers' quarters. Bradley's rooms were on the first floor of a two-story clapboard building with peeling white paint. His lodgings were modest, with sparse furniture. Three planks stretched across two carpenter's horses served as writing desk and dining area, but the woodstove emitted welcome warmth. A shelf and pegs on the wall hung with a variety of bridles and headstalls, cinches, latigos, and other odds and ends. C.W. dumped his load on an empty cot in the corner.

"I seem to remember you were married in Atlanta," he said and took a seat at the table.

"My wife and daughter are at Fort Shaw.  Mary is expecting another child and chooses not to travel at this time." Bradley fetched two cups from the kitchen and poured coffee from a pot on the stove.

"Thank you," said Collins, eagerly reaching for a cup and blowing on the steaming surface.

Bradley sat across from him and picked up his coffee. He sipped it and winced. "Not very good, I am afraid." He studied Collins.  "What information are you seeking?"

"Well, I am unable to be completely frank with you regarding the exact nature of my investigation.  I would be grateful for a synopsis of what you found on the 27th of June, this year.  I would especially appreciate any details previously unremarked in your reports or any anomaly observed by you on the battlefield."

C.W recalled that this fellow had had a reputation in Atlanta for keen observation and retention of information.  He was an avid scholar of history and possessed an active and tireless nature.  Above all, he remembered Bradley as a scrupulous man of honor and integrity.  His unplanned encounter with this man could prove invaluable to his mission.

The lieutenant appeared to be uneasy.  "But you cannot hint at what details you require?"

"I am afraid not... Be reassured, Lieutenant.  This is not a test to catch you up."

Bradley rubbed a finger behind his ear.  "I did not think it so.  But as you can imagine, I do not relish the recollection of my discoveries, nor do I know how to make them succinct for your usage."

"Merely relate them.  I will discern their usefulness to my purposes."

"Very well.  I will endeavor to do you a service." Bradley drank some coffee.  "Where do you wish me to begin?"

"At the moment when you knew you had discovered an irreparable disaster."

Bradley sighed, studying the surface of the planking. He seemed to be able to view the field of battle on the battered plane of wood. "I was riding in advance of the column as usual, on the morning of the 27th of June. I was scouting some three miles ahead and on the other side of the Little Big Horn River. I espied what appeared to be a number of skinned buffalo, but as we drew nearer, we found Custer's entire command in the embrace of death." The lieutenant closed his eyes. "The stench was appalling. What I had thought to be buffalo were naked bodies so bloated that many of them had...exploded. As you know, I am no stranger to the vagaries of war, but this scene was abysmal in its grisly reckoning."

"I have seen it. Even at this late hour it remains a ghastly vista." C.W. finished his coffee. "What of Custer?"

Bradley smiled sardonically. "Later, Colonel Benteen, myself and two other officers identified what we thought to be him. Although I reported in a Helena newspaper that his body, while naked, appeared to be unmarked, I can report to you now that the only apparently fatal wound must have been self-inflicted."

"Are you sure?"

"All the bodies were horribly misshapen and distended. You can imagine after days in the hot sun. But I swear, and questioned Benteen about it again later with his concurrence, the wound I observed was a bullet wound in the left temple. Have you ever known a red devil to execute a man in the head at close range? There were powder burns."

C.W. shook his head. "Were you certain it was him?"

"The odd tint of his hair was enough. Most of the others were more difficult."

"Was Major Reno one of the officers who viewed the body?"

Bradley looked surprised. "Yes...he was. Is that important?"

"Not particularly, except that I had similar information from him."

"But I assume that this is not the information you are seeking?"

"No," answered Collins. "Go on."

"There is not much else to relate. We attempted burials in the hard, dry ground, knowing the scavengers, already at work, would continue their ministrations." Bradley looked at him questioningly.

Collins decided to trust the man. "Did you find evidence of white men who fought alongside of the Indians?"

Comprehension crossed the man's face. "You have spoken to Major Reno."

"I have. I was unaware that you were in his confidence."

The lieutenant shrugged. "I was not. I brought some...intelligence to General Terry. *He* took me into his confidence."

"Intelligence?" C.W. was intently focused and Bradley seemed to again become uncomfortable.

"I do not know if it is something I should relate to you."

"Lieutenant, I urge you to share what you know with me and me alone. If it is what I suspect, then it is central to my investigation. Do you require proof of my credentials?"

"On my honor, sir, I have never had cause to doubt you and do not do so now." He rubbed his hands together contemplatively. "It is that...it haunts me. It is... difficult to revisit."

"This is no small mission I am pursuing. Much importance has been placed upon it."

Bradley picked up the cups and went to refill them. Collins was baffled by the man's reluctance. He readily accepted the full cup and sipped it, studying the lieutenant as he regained his chair.

"Perhaps it will help to reveal what I know," Bradley said.

"Help whom?"

"Me."

Collins waited, his interest further piqued.

"As you probably know, I was made Commander of the Scouts, placing me in charge of the Crow Indians. Prior to us making the horrific discovery of June 27th, many of the Crows had gone back to the agency after speaking with three of their tribe who had escaped Custer's fate by fleeing the battle. Several stayed with us, however, sworn enemies of the Sioux and hoping for an opportunity to engage them, despite their tendency to believe that Custer had been 'wiped out.'" Bradley picked at his mustaches nervously. "After we had made our... discovery and reunited Terry's, Reno's and Gibbon's commands, my Crows went roving about, looting the dead. I reprimanded them several times, but to no avail. We needed their services and their allegiance to us was wearing thin. Thankfully, they spent more time in the Indian encampment than looting the bodies of soldiers above. At some time during the 28th, they came upon a wounded man and brought him to me."

"Why you?" Collins asked.

Bradley shrugged. "I suppose because I was their commander. Not that it mattered much most of the time."

"Who was the man?"

"Well, there is the oddity. It was a white man, but speaking the Sioux language and wearing the trappings of a Sioux warrior."

"A white man?"

"I swear to you, this man was tanned, but unmistakably white. He had dirty blonde hair and blue eyes."

"Many of the Sioux have lighter skin, hair and eyes," Collins told him.

"Yes, I am aware of this fact. I have seen them. This man was white, very tall and, I would hazard a guess, from Nordic extraction."

"Did you attempt to speak to him in English?"

"Repeatedly, but he would speak no other tongue than Sioux or use the basic sign language of the plains. One of my scouts spoke some of the language. According to him, the man's communication consisted mainly of insults and defiance."

Collins toyed with his cup. "What happened to him?"

Bradley's face became grim. "I tried to protect him. I wanted to get him to Terry. Those damned Crow kept goading the man and poking him with the tips of their knives. One hit him rather hard with a coup stick upside the head. He went crazy and before I could intervene, Little Hand gutted him as you would a fish. Yellow Dog threw him down and scalped him. It occurred very quickly. Then they all had their knives at him and I could see he was somehow still alive through part of it. When they were finished, they jumped on their horses and rode off whooping as if they had achieved a great deed, instead of tearing apart an unarmed man. I went through his blood soaked clothing to see if there was a clue to his identity and all I found was this." Bradley stood and walked over to a camel back trunk in the corner. He took something from a small pouch and handed a gold ring to Collins.

"It is a claddagh," he told the lieutenant, turning the ring and looking for an inscription inside.

"A claddagh?"

"Your man was not Scandinavian. He was Irish."

"But surely..."

"'My Beloved 1836'" C.W. read aloud. "It is the inscription."

"I will be damned to hell. Irish. Does that mean that he could not speak English, only Sioux and Irish?"

"No. The Irish tongue has been outlawed for so long that all Irish perforce speak English."

"Then why would not the man speak to me?"

"You were the enemy. As much so as the Crow."

"But my god, he was white. Why would he see another white man as the enemy?"

"It is plain," said Collins, smiling politely, "that you know little of the centuries long strife between the Irish and English. Besides, he had been fighting against the U.S. Army. What do you suppose would have happened if you had led him to Terry? Would all the soldiers along the way not have behaved similarly to the Crow?"

"I had not considered..." Bradley trailed off.

"The man died fighting his enemy. It is the Indian way. It is the Celtic way as well. Do not berate yourself. May I keep the ring?"

The lieutenant looked astonished. "Of course. I kept it only because it seemed to matter. It is difficult to explain. I do not loot the dead."

"Good god, Lieutenant, that never crossed my mind. It is a clue and it may have significance." C.W. put the ring in a pocket of his vest. "May I smoke?"

"Yes, please do."

Collins took out his pipe and filled it. Bradley struck a match and held it for him.

"Thank you. You have been of great assistance. I have two more questions." He looked at the lieutenant questioningly.

"Yes."

"What happened to the body?"

"I hid it beneath some brush, then went to find General Terry. He refused to accompany me back to the site, but acknowledged the information. That is when he shared the observations made by Major Reno. He swore me to secrecy regarding the dead man and Reno's intelligence."

"No doubt," said Collins, wondering why the general had not confided Bradley's story to him at Fort Buford.

"I later buried the body as best I could.  What was the other question?" Bradley asked without enthusiasm.

"Did you at any time see aught of Captain Keogh's famous English pistol?"

"Well, yes.  I had heard about it and asked to see it in camp on the Rosebud."

"Did you see it after?  Did your scouts loot it?"

"No.  I would have taken it from them by force."

"I see."  C.W. puffed on his pipe.  "What do you know of a man named Stuart in Deer Lodge?"

"Another question?" Bradley inquired wryly.

"Another, I fear."

"I know a Granville Stuart.  He is presently employed in a bank in Helena, but he recently resided in Deer Lodge."

"Does he collect guns?"

"Yes he does."

"He has an Indian wife?"

"He does.  She is Shoshone."

"You know him well?"

"Well enough.  We are both interested in early history of the west."

"I see," said Collins and stood to bang out his pipe in the wood stove.  Bradley followed him over and added wood.  They stood warming themselves.

"A word of warning, however," Bradley said.

"Regarding?"

"Regarding Mr. Stuart.  He is decidedly against the Irish."

"And why is this?"  C.W. asked.

The lieutenant shook his head. "No idea."

"Well, he will have to overcome his prejudices for a wee bit," Collins said with a strong accent and they both laughed.

A wind came up and rattled the roof shingles.  The

room darkened as the sun went behind a cloud.

"What shall the future hold for the west when the Indians have all been confined to reservations?" Bradley asked after a while.

"Towns and churches," Collins answered. "It will soon be unrecognizable."

"You say it with regret."

"I do, Lieutenant. I say it with much regret. You will regret it too, when the time comes," he said, and stared out the window at the snowy mountains looming over the prosperous river valley.

# 15

The lamplight flickered slightly as he strove to decipher the poorly written words smeared across the pages.  Collins rubbed his fatigued eyes and stretched a moment.  The cot creaked.  He winced, not wanting to wake Bradley across the room.  Returning to the journal recovered from the camp on the Little Big Horn, he thought he could make out the name of General Meagher and Antietam.  He searched his memory of the battle and recalled that the Irish Brigade had suffered terrible losses under Meagher's command.  C.W. also remembered that the general had been accused of drunkenness during the conflict, after falling off his horse.

He read the words, "*dam the man to hell and all purdishun,*" and assumed this sentiment had been penned by a personage who had lost a friend in the battle or had been a soldier of the brigade.  There were many passages he could not make out, then "*drunk agin and god help us on the marrow.*"  The next passages were definitively dated 1862, but the penciled words were lost beyond all recognition.  He scrutinized the pages until his head ached and all he could discern were "*Fredericksberg*" and "*Canonball killed the basterd.*"  C.W. knew that Meagher was not killed, but merely wounded by a cannonball in the Battle of Fredericksburg, so perhaps the diarist had only been conjecturing.  What followed appeared to be an unending list of names and he assumed that, given the tragic destruction of the Irish Brigade at the Battle of

Fredericksburg, it was a partial roll of those killed in action. Almost 4,000 men of the brigade had marched into the battle and a mere 280 soldiers survived. General Meagher had returned to duty four months later, but he soon resigned due to the fact that so few combat-ready soldiers remained in his Irish Brigade. Concomitantly, few of his men still trusted him and most blamed him for the dire losses. Meagher had later been reinstated, but his military career had been distinctly uneventful for the rest of the war.

Too fatigued to continue, Collins put the diary back among his belongings, blew out the lamp and fell asleep. Almost at once, it seemed, Bradley was standing over him with a cup of coffee and sunlight was streaming in the window.

"Good morning," he said, sitting up and accepting the coffee.

"Good morning. Sleep well?" Bradley sat at the table.

"Not really," Collins answered, rubbing his head. "What do you know of General Meagher?"

"General Meagher?" The lieutenant was plainly confused.

"You remember…the Irish Brigade and all."

"Oh, yes of course. He has been dead many years. He fell off a steamboat back in '67. He was the acting governor of Montana Territory."

Collins sipped his coffee. "I had heard he had died. I was unaware of the circumstances."

"Most suspicious. His body was never found."

"What is your opinion about his drinking?"

"I always believed the rumors. I, myself, witnessed his drunkenness on two occasions."

Rubbing his eyes, Collins stood. "Damnable strange," he said, walking over to the table and taking a chair.

"What?"

"He is somehow related to this business. The fog

bank thickens."

Bradley frowned. "But he has been dead these nine years."

"'There are more things in heaven and earth, Horatio, than are dreamt of in your philosophy.'"

"Then enlighten me."

Collins walked over and retrieved the journal. He handed it to Bradley.

"What is this?" asked the lieutenant, riffling the pages.

"A diary I found in the camp on the Little Big Horn."

"What camp?" His eyes widened in incredulity. The *Indian* camp?"

"Precisely."

Bradley examined a page closely. "It is impossible to read. The pencil markings are all rubbed together."

"That may be, but I have made out the names of Meagher, Antietam, and Fredericksburg."

"Fredericksburg? Was not that the battle where Meagher lost most of the Brigade?"

"It is."

Bradley fetched the coffee pot and refilled their cups. "Fredericksburg and Meagher are mentioned in a journal found at the Little Big Horn? More than passing strange."

Collins pulled out his pipe and carefully packed the bowl. "What were the theories surrounding Meagher's disappearance?"

"There was conjecture of murder. Or that he had fallen off the steamboat while drunk."

Striking a match, C.W. lit his pipe. "If murder, then who?"

"Political rivals. Some hinted that there was trouble between him and the Vigilantes. Some have even put forth the opinion that an ex-confederate soldier had sent him to his death."

Laying the book on the table, Collins turned to the

place where he had stopped reading the night before. In the bright room, full of sunlight, the writing was easier to see. He puffed on the pipe and studied the pages.

"Breakfast?" Bradley asked.

"With pleasure."

"I have some venison and a few potatoes."

"That would be most welcome."

The lieutenant went into the alcove that housed a small sheet-iron cook stove. Collins continued to pour over the journal. He could read enough to understand the author had embarked upon a journey west with some other men. There were many pages that seemed to be about hunting, fighting Indians and building rafts to float the Mississippi. He read the words "*fredom to make meat*" then "*fight as most fit fer lim an lif.*" The writer was clearly unlettered. There were several pages ripped out. Then he made out Meagher's name again. He struggled to unravel the words and, not for the first time, silently damned the man for using pencil and not quill. The name *Thompson* showed more than once in conjunction with Meagher's. There seemed to be an allusion to Fort Benton as *Ft Bintin.*

Collins called out to Bradley, "What do you know of a fellow named Thompson from Fort Benton?"

Walking to the door with a carving-fork in hand, he shrugged. "Thompson, you say?"

"This mentions Meagher again, Fort Benton and someone named Thompson."

Bradley frowned, then his eyebrows raised. "No. Now I remember. It is not a man named Thompson that is mentioned. The steamboat from which Meagher disappeared was named the *G.A. Thompson.*" He stepped back to his stove.

C.W. pored over the pages with little effect. Then he read a passage stating, "*rot in watry grave fer F.burg an frends ded ivermor.*"

The lieutenant brought in plates mounded with meat and fried potatoes. He set them on the table and Collins put his book aside. "I suspect my diarist may have had a hand in Meagher's demise," he said.

Bradley paused as he was taking a seat. "You are joking."

"No, I am not. What would 'rot in watery grave for Fredericksburg and friends dead evermore' impart to you? Especially after references to Meagher and the steamboat?" C.W. filled a fork with meat and began eating.

"I guess it is plausible," Bradley agreed.

"Although what this fact has to do with our other mystery is beyond my ken."

Bradley wiped his mouth with the back of his hand and drank some coffee. "For all the world I would bet some Indian took that journal off a dead man. No doubt one he had killed and scalped himself."

"Perhaps," Collins said, setting down his fork. "But why would a red man carry around an item of no earthly use to him?"

"On our march along the Yellowstone last May, I shamelessly vandalized a Sioux scaffold. It held the remains of a warrior dead some two years. Among his effects, we found a packet of letters from a soldier's wife accompanied by a soldier's hymn book, no doubt relieved from the same poor fellow as had supplied the letters. Among the same burial goods, we found a letter from Fannie Kelly, the white woman captured and long since released several years before the discovery. I am certain the dead man who possessed these items, and held them in such esteem as to be buried with them, could not read English."

C.W. frowned. "I was not aware that Indians valued such keepsakes. Your point is well taken." He proceeded to finish his breakfast, frustrated that this most recent clue had been effectively refuted.

"Did you have enough to eat?" Bradley asked, as he ate the last of his own meal.

"Plenty. It was quite good."

"Fine," the lieutenant said and stood to clear the dishes. "Will you be staying on?" he asked. "You are most welcome."

"Winter is upon us and I cannot take the chance of being snowed in. I must to Helena to see this fellow Stuart about Keogh's gun." He retrieved his pipe and stepped out into the chilly morning. Smoke lay low across the valley. A horse whinnied in the distance.

"I suppose I will never know the result of your inquiry," Bradley said, joining him.

"I fear not. I may see you later at Fort Shaw, however. Upon which event I promise an update."

"I, too, will seek news. Most discreetly, of course."

Collins puffed on his pipe. "At this moment, I am convinced I am following a red herring. How in the hell will I find the truth without wading into certain demise in a Sioux stronghold?" he asked, rhetorically. "I care not for my chances."

Bradley sat on the top step of the low stoop. "I wish I could accompany you," he said. "It is a most intriguing mystery."

"Perhaps," C.W. agreed. "But one that I may not survive."

# 16

Having resupplied at Fort Ellis, C.W. neglected to visit the neighborhood of straggling houses known as Gallatin City near the three forks of the Missouri River. Being entirely self-sufficient and loath to account for himself to curious frontier settlers, he chose to avoid contact. As the Madison Bridge was under repair, he crossed the Missouri at a ferry just below the junction of the Jefferson and Madison rivers. Beyond him to the north lay an open valley created by millennia of the great river's wanderings.

Collins was camped on the Missouri and dusk was coming on swiftly, when he heard a voice seemingly from nowhere. Ulysses snorted and blew and even Molly circled her picket restlessly.

"Hello there," came the voice again, closer now.

C.W. retrieved his rifle from its resting place among his gear and walked forward. He had chosen a remove among thick alder and trees along the Missouri, assuming his camp would be obscured. He stood at the ready as a muscled bay horse wended its way into his camp. A rather diminutive man perched upon the mighty beast, looking slightly ridiculous.

"Smelled your smoke," he said, dismounting. He eyed Collins' Winchester and held out this hand. "Beidler's the name. Deputy Marshal."

"Good evening," Collins said, formally, and shook hands while looking the man over. Beidler appeared to be forty some years of age, with bushy mustaches, broad shoulders, remarkably small hands and a shrewd look about his eyes. "My name is C.W. Collins."

"Well howdy, C.W. Collins," Beidler said. "I was hoping I might bunk here for the night. Like some company and you might possibly have news I could savvy." He had a bluffness about him that Collins had not yet penetrated as being hearty in nature or pure chicanery.

"I doubt I would have information useful to you, but you are welcome to camp, if you have a mind to."

"Good enough, then. Good enough." Beidler set about unsaddling his horse. He picketed the brute near Collins' pair, fetched his saddlebags and proceeded to unwrap a bloody package of newspaper and canvas from which he extracted a large hunk of meat. "Hope you favor antelope. Many a man refuse to eat it, but I am not above it, given it is fresh. I shot the beast this morning."

"Fresh meat would be decidedly welcome," Collins told him, leaning his rifle against a rock close to hand, a gesture not unremarked by his guest.

Beidler rigged a spit over Collins' fire pit, carving branches with a fourteen-inch Bowie knife worn in a scabbard on his belt. He speared the meat and set it over the coals.

"Coffee?" C.W. asked when the man was through with his preparations.

"Indeed. Indeed." He accepted a steaming cup and sat on his haunches in the manner of one used to such a posture.

Collins took a seat on his bedroll near the fire and his rifle. "Deputy Marshal?"

"Out of Helena. Under U.S. Marshal Pinney." Beidler fished a wad of chewing tobacco from his mouth, tossed it in the flames and took a noisy swig from the cup. "Am after a fella knifed a whore over Missoula way. Worked on a gambler in one of our houses is why I am after him now. Failed to kill him though he might wish he did."

"Headed south?"

"On his trail along the Missouri. Why I proposed you might know a thing or two."

"I have not encountered a soul other than a ferry operator since departing from Fort Ellis. I am traveling with purpose."

"Purpose?" Beidler's sagacity revealed itself a moment.

"A purpose associated with my employment by the Pinkertons." Collins chose a supportable lie that would bear scrutiny.

"Pinkertons...Seems we are not in unrelated lines of employ. I, myself, did duty guarding stagecoaches between Virginia City and Bannack back in the late 60's and was of some help to the Vigilantes."

Collins recalled hearing the man's name. "John X. Beidler. You are *X. Beidler*."

"Indeed. Indeed I am."

"You are associated with Mr. W.F. Sanders."

"I am indeed. He has not forgotten his old friends from the Vigilante days." Beidler turned the meat, now emitting a most appealing odor. He took a small pouch from a trouser pocket and sprinkled salt on the roast.

"I am presently en route to meet a man named Stuart. Are you familiar with him?"

"James Stuart died in '73 up at Fort Peck, but his younger brother Granville resides now in Helena."

"It is Granville I am seeking."

"Then you will find him at the First National Bank of Helena. I have known him well for years."

Collins placed potatoes, purchased at an exorbitant price from the sutler's at Fort Ellis, in the coals to roast. Beidler attended the meat while regaling his host with stories from Virginia City and its surrounding environs. He was mildly entertaining, but C.W.'s unshakeable mistrust of the man kept him on his guard.

"You should have seen the parade of youngsters following old Bill's gelding, waiting for it to take a shit," Beidler told him. There had been a preceding story about an early miner feeding gold dust to his horse. "Meat is done."

Collins ate in silence while his companion provided further tales, no doubt embellished, of his days cutting wood for steamboats on the upper Missouri River. He claimed that the famed "Liver Eating" Johnson had been his partner for a while in a concern established just above the mouth of the Musselshell.

"Did he, in fact, eat livers from Indians?" Collins asked, in an effort to appear less taciturn.

"Oh yes. Yes indeed. Why I, myself, witnessed such an act up near Captain Hawley's trading post."

"You witnessed him eating a raw liver from the abdomen of an Indian?" Collins was intrigued in spite of himself.

"Indeed. Indeed I did. Right from the belly of a heathen warrior. I confess I did not witness the eating of it in its entirety as I was spewing my last meal into the grass. Bastard made me gag."

"No doubt."

"You see, it was on the occasion of Mrs. Hawley getting herself scalped. A squaw had raised the alarm and we had gone out after her and had found the lady stunned, but very much alive, despite her missing topknot. After seeing her back to the post, a group of us pursued the savages and we cornered them in a washout. We intended to avenge this insult to Mrs. Hawley and we killed nigh on to thirty-two of them. After it was finished, we took their scalps, cut off their heads and cut the rest of them into quarters. Johnson took the liver from one and held it aloft, offering a bite. There were no takers and then he commenced to chaw on the thing. That is when a few of us was sick. We took them heads to the post, boiled the flesh off and put them on display for the folks aboard steamboats plying between St. Louis and Fort Benton."

"And Mrs. Hawley?" C.W. asked.

"Oh she survived the shock and is still living for all I know. Wears a wig though, I would hazard."

Discomfited by this reminder of the brutality engaged in by so many men of the west, Collins made more coffee and smoked his pipe. Beidler took an enormous bite of tobacco from a plug housed in the breast pocket of his shirt.

"What news might Granville Stuart have for the Pinkertons?" he asked, spitting a stream of brown juice into the fire.

"I am, unfortunately, not at liberty to divulge such information."

An artful aspect passed over the man's face, which was quickly replaced by his general expression of joviality. "Indeed. Indeed. I merely had pondered I might be of use to you, seeing as I have been around Montana Territory more than old Granville of late."

"Much obliged to you, but I fear I require specific intelligence from Mr. Stuart regarding a minor matter."

"Indeed. Indeed." Beidler stood, stretched and retrieved his bedroll from his gear, returning to spread it open near the fire ring and proceeding to arrange himself in a half reclining position upon it. "Fine animals you have there. Fine, indeed," he remarked, again spitting into the flames.

C.W. stared into the fire and smoked. He had decided that perhaps this man was not a danger, precisely, but warranted watching due to an overweening curiosity as well as an obviously overdeveloped need to tell stories. He required that Beidler not ferret out even a hint of his mission or at whose behest he had embarked upon it.

"I am afeared that I trod upon your good will, C.W. Collins. I implore that you will forgive my prying as it was meant in all effort to be of aid." Beidler was looking at him circumspectly.

Collins removed the pipe from his mouth and knocked out its contents on a rock. "Not at all, Mr. Beidler. But I am weary and will now retire. I thank you for your company and the antelope roast, which was delicious."

"My pleasure. My pleasure indeed, especially after being welcomed into so commodious a campsite."

Beidler stood and walked into the darkness. Collins could hear him urinating copiously. He checked on Ulysses and Molly, running a friendly hand over Beidler's bay as he passed. He removed his boots and climbed into his bedroll. His companion followed suit and engaged again in telling tales of lynching Clubfoot George, Jack Slade and other villains who had purportedly disrupted the legitimate denizens of Virginia City's heyday. C.W. drifted to sleep with a hand on his Colt while the man's voice droned on in the firelight.

## 17

Helena had flourished since his last visit. No trace of the fire of '72 remained along Main Street. Collins walked leisurely toward the Gulch, his animals safely boarded and his gear stowed in the International Hotel. He entered the red light district between Wood and Bridge Street and found a two-story brownstone building with a mansard roof and elaborate chimneys. A beveled oak door with leaded opaque windowpanes stood above a polished marble stoop. He cranked the brass doorbell. Almost at once a Chinese maid opened the door and stood back to allow his entry into a perfumed and gilded foyer.

"May I help you sir?" the unfamiliar maid inquired.

"I wish to see Josephine."

"Miss Hensley is still asleep, sir. It is early yet."

"It is after the noon hour. Please inform her that Charles Collins is here."

"But sir…"

"Tell her or I promise she shall be quite cross with you."

The girl reluctantly left him standing in the foyer and was gone for some time. When she returned, her manner was apologetic. She led him through an elaborate parlor filled with velveteen draperies, glittering chandeliers, flamboyant tables and "S" shaped *tete a tete* chairs, a colossal grand piano and waggish paintings of partially clothed women. The mingled scents, however, of sweaty perfume, stale alcohol and lingering tobacco smoke were less exalted. He followed the maid up a stairway and into a wallpapered corridor of several doors. She guided him to the last one and knocked lightly.

"Come in," came a soft and throaty voice from within.

The maid opened the door and ushered Collins into a spacious set of rooms. She then exited and closed the door behind her. He could make out an enormous bed in the dim light. Heavy curtains effectively inhibited any sunlight from invading the suite. On the bed sat a figure in a dressing gown, brushing her hair and emitting a most tantalizing scent.

"Hello Charles," she said, with the faint but exotic accent he always found suspect.

"Hello Joe." His eyes adjusted to the dimness and he walked over to sit beside her. He leaned and kissed her on the back of the neck. "You have been a busy girl, I observe."

"Is this not grand? It cost sacks of money, but I made it back the first year."

"Quite grand indeed. Any coffee?"

"Over on the side board. You can serve yourself."

Collins smiled and walked over to a silver coffee set. He poured some into a dainty china cup and sipped it. "Delicious," he said.

"Of course," the woman said, got up and moved over to a small divan. She arranged herself upon it in a pose reminiscent of some of the paintings hanging in the downstairs parlor.

C.W. finished the diminutive portion of coffee and walked over to her. She coyly pretended not to notice him, but he pulled her onto her feet, embracing her and kissing her deeply on the mouth. Then he released her and draped her back onto the divan in a grandiose gesture. Her thick and bountiful tresses framed her pale and doll-like face. It was a face that masked a forceful character and puissant business acumen. She was studying him as he stood over her.

"Why are you here?" she asked with an air of disinterest.

"To see you." He perched on the side of the divan next to her. He took her hand and examined it as if it were an item of supreme value and rarity.

Josephine laughed richly. "You came all the way to Montana Territory to see me? It is not possible."

He kissed her palm. She took back her hand and lightly slapped his face.

"I came all the way to the tenderloin, which was quite out of my way," he told her.

"Heartless wretch. Wait until The Duke hears you have arrived. He will shoot you, no doubt."

"Have you hired the dandy again? Silly wench. He will rob you blind."

"He will shoot you. That is all I care about."

Collins leaned down and kissed her, moving his hand under her dressing gown, finding warm flesh. She moaned and pushed against him. He carried her to the bed and undressed swiftly while she lay watching him. He pulled open the frills of silk that draped about her petite and compact figure and lay down beside her, stroking and kissing her until neither of them could exert further control. He was a thorough lover and it was quite some time before they leaned back in the sweat soaked bed, satiated and comfortable.

"I should charge you for my services," Josephine said, as she rolled over to look at him.

He stroked her silken cheek, unmarred by the powder she would, no doubt, apply later in the day. "I should charge you, my dear," he said, then arose and began dressing.

"You are not staying?"

"I will return later for some of your fine victuals, but

no, I am not staying. I have a room at the International."

She sat up and made a rude noise. "That benighted dump. Why not here?"

"I am on official business. It would not be seemly to my employer if I boarded in your establishment."

"Fine." She waved her hand dismissively. "Then do not expect a warm welcome when you return."

Collins sat on the bed to put on his boots, then pulled her into another concupiscent embrace. He released her after a bit, then said, "I will return for oysters, steak and delicate pastries. If you do not wish to be friendly, so be it."

Joe dropped all pretense and pulled him down for one more kiss. "Very well, my sweet. Return for food and whatever else strikes your fancy. I am really quite pleased to see you after so prolonged an absence.

"There is only one gal for me," he said, smiled his best gallant smile, and left the room in a most gratified humor. Passing through the downstairs, he saw that some of the girls were already beginning to grace the parlor. All were dressed impeccably as this was the strict rule at any of Chicago Joe's establishments. He greeted them cordially and went out into the street as a light snow was beginning to fall.

# 18

On the corner of Grand and Main stood a financial edifice of impressive proportions. A turret and several gables crowned the commanding brownstone bank, set in the midst of Montana Territory's new capital city. Collins climbed the steps, newly swept of snow, and entered the lobby. At once a tidy clerk inquired after his business and he asked to see Mr. Granville Stuart. He was ushered toward the back of the building past the line of tellers behind ornate brass cages. An office door stood ajar.

"Your name, sir?" the clerk asked prior to knocking.

"Charles Collins."

He tapped somewhat timidly upon the oak door.

"What is it?" the voice resonated.

"A gentleman to see you, Mr. Stuart. A Mr. Collins."

"Send him in."

The clerk opened the door for Collins and left them. A large man with graying hair and beard sat behind a desk leaning over a stack of account books. C.W. noted he wore the type of beard that was too thin and straight to ever appear groomed. Normally clean-shaven, with trim mustaches, he was disdainful of townsmen wearing beards. It hinted at laziness. The President, of course, was an exception.

The man made a notation in a ledger book and placed his pen in a brass holder. He scrutinized Collins a moment.

"Mr. Collins," he said slowly. "Please take a seat." C.W. removed his Stetson hat, placed it on the edge of the desk and sat in the proffered chair. It was significantly low, placing the person seated in a disadvantaged position so as to be easily intimidated, almost as if the desk could plow right over the top of financial supplicants. Such tactics rarely had any effect upon Collins and he crossed his legs nonchalantly. Stuart paused again, then asked, "Do you wish to open an account?"

"No. I have come about two matters. The first is that there should be a letter of credit waiting for me in this bank. The second is regarding a rare weapon. My understanding is that you collect unusual firearms."

"Do you wish me to check on the letter?" Stuart's air was supercilious.

"Not yet. If you are willing to spare a bit of your valuable time, I would rather discuss the gun."

Stuart adjusted himself in his chair and appeared to be contemplating whether or not to give Collins the time of day. He stroked his beard. Collins sat comfortably, perfectly willing to endure this man's pretentiousness.

"Collins. Is that Irish?"

"Decidedly so." Now we will see, thought C.W.

Stuart's manner became increasingly peremptory. "Do you mind enlightening me as to why I may have some information regarding a weapon that interests you?"

"Lieutenant Bradley suggested you might."

"Is that so?"

"It is." Collins was actually enjoying himself. The prejudices of others amused him. He fixed his best humorous gaze upon the banker.

"What is the gun?" Stuart asked, dropping his eyes and arranging the ledgers on his desk.

"A .45 caliber over and under officer's pistol made by J. Manton and Company of London and Calcutta." C.W. watched as the man struggled to conceal his interest.

He purposely omitted the fact that the Keogh's name had been delicately carved into the grip.

"Percussion cap?"

"Yes."

"This is indeed a rare weapon." Stuart picked up his pen and turned it between his fingers.

"It is."

"What is its provenance?"

"I know not. I only know that it is missing and thought perhaps that you, being a known collector, may have happened upon it."

"Mr. Collins, it not my habit to broker stolen items."

C.W. was ever annoyed by those who scrupulously contrived opportunities to protect their questionable honor. Still, he retained his good humor and said, "It is not stolen. Only missing."

"You are most cryptic," said Stuart, raising his tone and leaning forward. "You come to me for help and proceed to bob and weave. I do not appreciate it."

Keeping an even manner, C.W. said, "I take it you have not encountered the pistol?"

"Whether I have or have not, this interview has come to its conclusion." Stuart rose to his feet. "I suggest you check at a teller's window for your letter."

Keeping his seat, Collins looked up with aplomb at the tall man standing behind the desk. His voice became very quiet. "I suggest you sit down and extend a bit more courtesy. I am not here on a whim. Nor am I someone to be trifled with."

"What?"

"Please sit. My business is associated with the disaster on the Little Big Horn last June. You will find that the letter of credit is issued from Washington D.C. More I cannot say."

As Collins had suspected, the man was all too easily impressed by the mere mention of power and authority.

He sat and placed folded hands upon the desktop. "This gun is connected to the battle?"

"It is."

"I have not seen nor heard of it. It is unusual enough to have caught my attention had it been circulating. My friend and employer, Mr. Samuel Hauser, also collects rare weapons. I can inquire as to whether he has been approached with such a pistol."

"That would be most helpful, Mr. Stuart," Collins said, standing and picking up his hat. "I will now go to retrieve my letter of credit, as you suggested. Tomorrow I will return to ascertain whether Mr. Hauser provided any information regarding the gun."

"May I be of further service? Do you require lodging?" asked Granville Stuart, regaining his feet and walking around the desk to shake hands.

"Thank you, no," Collins said, accepting Stuart's extended hand. "I am quite familiar with Helena and am comfortably situated in a hotel. Good day to you, Mr. Stuart." Collins left the room and the man, making for an unengaged teller. He was disgruntled that his visit bore no fruit. The trail was circuitous and unrewarding, but persistence had frequently paid dividends in former cases. He would not weaken.

# 19

Collins sat in a private dining room with fine linens upon a mahogany table. An elaborate silver candelabrum provided warm light by which he could equally admire the delicate viands upon the fine china plate before him and the silk and jewel sheathed Joe in a chair across from him. Despite the exaggerated powder and paint she habitually employed for evening hours, the woman presented a beautiful vision of deep burgundy silks and glittering diamonds, crowned by her exquisitely coiffed tresses of reddish hue. She picked delicately at her own plate, while Collins ate heartily, delighting in the rich flavors so in opposition to the plain nourishment he had been depending upon for many days. The piano player was adept and he found the music emanating from the parlor quite enjoyable.

"Charles...you cannot hint further at your business in Helena?" Josephine inquired, by way of making conversation.

C.W. swallowed and wiped his mouth on an impeccable white napkin. "Not much. I have some items, however, that I would like to submit for your perusal. Given your...how shall I say? Intimacy...with so many Montana residents, I was hoping perhaps you may have seen these items before."

Joe smiled artificially. "Intimacy? That is what you call it? You know I have not been on that end of the trade for many years. I am a business woman."

Collins took a sip of water from a crystal goblet. "I know, my dear. I only meant that you possess a comprehensive knowledge of many people from a great many social classes. And you have been in Helena for quite some time. 'What is the city but the people?'" he quoted.

"Of course I am willing to help you in any way I may. What are these items?"

Collins finished his meal, wiped his mouth again and settled back in the thickly padded chair. He reached into his suit jacket, somewhat rumpled from its long journey in his carpetbag, and placed the watch he had gotten from Reno, the ring he had acquired from Bradley and the diary found at the battlefield upon the white linen table cloth before him. Joe arose, with much rustling of silk and petticoats, and swept closer. Her perfume was seductive. She picked up the ring.

"What a cunning little piece. It seems I have seen something similar before."

"It is of Irish design. Common among some of the miners, I would imagine."

" 'My Beloved 1836.' How came you by this?"

"No questions, if you recall."

She grimaced and replaced the ring on the table. She picked up the watch. "Does it open?"

Collins shrugged. "I have not been able to master the catch."

Joe sat and began toying with the casing. In a few moments it sprang open. She gave him a dazzling smile.

"Yes," he said, holding out his hand. "You are wonderfully clever."

"Oh no. I want to look first." She studied the watch. "There is a daguerreotype here. Of a uniquely plain woman."

"May I examine it?"

"Not yet...Oh look, there is an inscription."

"What does it say?" C.W. asked, smiling patiently.

She remained obstinate for a bit, then sighed loudly and handed it over.  Collins examined the image.

"She is decidedly plain. Someone's sweetheart? Mother?"

"Mother.  With such a physiognomy, it could only belong to a beloved matriarch."

"You are a snob."

"Of course.  That is why I employ the loveliest girls in all Montana Territory."

"Love is blind. Perhaps it is a cherished wife"

"Then I pity the fellow.  Can you read the inscription?"

"It is in the Irish. *'De reir a cheile a thogtar na caisleain.'*"

"And what does it mean?"

"'It takes time to build castles.' An appropriate sentiment for a timepiece."

Joe rang for the maid.  She came in and deftly cleared the dishes, then offered coffee and brandy.  C.W accepted coffee and Joe had a snifter of brandy.

"Odd the watch and ring both seem to be Irish," she said when they were alone again.

"Odd indeed."

"And this battered little book?" she asked picking it up. "Psssh.  It is unreadable."  She tossed it down.

"Not quite.  So none of these articles are recognizable?"

"Only the design of the ring.  What are you pursuing?" she asked and walked over to a sideboard.  She brought back a silver cigar box.  He accepted one, cut the end with a penknife and lit it.

"You are perfectly aware that I cannot apprise you of my doings," he told her, puffing on the expensive tobacco, amused by her persistence.

Joe took a seat beside him and swirled her brandy. "It is all very intriguing."

"Yes, I know.  Perhaps I will tell you about it in our

dotage.”

She moved over to his lap.  He put down his cigar and played with a coppery ringlet of her hair.

“The watch is silver with gold inlay.  Must have been quite dear.”

“Yes, my thoughts as well.”  He kissed the shell of her ear and stroked her throat.

There was a knock on the door.  Joe pulled free of his embrace and walked over.  Collins could see “The Duke” over her shoulder.  He recognized Collins as well.  There was a muffled conversation, then Joe shut the door on him.

“The Duke is going to shoot you,” she said, coming back and taking a chair.

“What a tragedy it will be.”

“What?” she asked.

“His sudden demise.”

“Amusing.”  Joe sipped her brandy.  “I should go in soon.  My clients miss me.  And we have had a problem with knives lately.”

“Knives?”

“Some john from Missoula cut up one of my girls last week.”

“Did he also slice up a gambler?”

“Yes.  How did you know?”

He drank some coffee.  “I ran into X. Beidler on the trail.”

“*That* fool.  He and his boss, Pinney, cared nothing about poor Lizzie despite all the taxes and fines I pay.  Only some no account gambler from over at one of Couselle’s houses.”

“How *is* Louisa?” Collins asked.

Joe cut her eyes at him.  “Never mind.”  She got to her feet and drained her snifter.  “Tell me, why is any man’s life worth more than a scarlet woman’s?”

“It is not.”

"Liar." She leaned down to kiss him on the mouth. "I must go. You may retire to my suite and Lola, my maid, will fulfill any requirement...with some exceptions. I should not be long."

"I will wait here for a bit, but then I must return to my hotel."

"It is snowing."

"I have faith I will survive the journey."

Joe stopped with her hand on the doorknob and looked at him. "I hope they find you frozen in a snow-drift come spring."

"I adore you my darling," he said, blowing her a kiss.

The door slammed. C.W. smiled, pocketed the ring and watch and picked up the diary. He opened it to the page that referenced Fort Benton. The candelabrum on the table held many candles of good quality and, therefore, provided excellent light. He was able to divine more of the contents than in his prior endeavors. Again, there were several references to the G.A. Thompson, then he read, *"dolan wer quik in lernin wither he wer the won."* There were several passages wherein he could only decipher a word here and there then, *"tripp to camp cook on stembot fer sartin"* some blurring, and, *"mak good job of it fer good en all."* After this came two smeared and stained pages. Then Collins could read, *"dolan fedd plinty blerny and wisky   old man ravin bowt them as wer wantin to kill him  in ft bintin    hed bak to stembot tomson ravin    wf sandrs and them othrs wint to    tek duds and ly him on bed    go way."*

The next lines he could penetrate were those referring to Fredericksburg and a watery grave. Collins picked up his cigar and relit it from a candle. It seemed to him as if the author of the diary had, indeed, been up to some mischief in regards to General Meagher. His instincts told him the Irish thread that appeared to be weaving through all tangible clues could hardly be ignored. He hoped that, given common and virulent prejudices regarding so-called "Papists," the answer he sought could not be laid at the door of Irish immigrants.

He smoked his cigar and deliberated on how unsatisfactory his investigation had been to date. Knowing he must surely send another telegram to Grant in the morning, C.W. was at a loss as to what particulars he should report. The only salient information he had acquired thus far was that there were, without doubt, white men fighting with the Indians. How many, who they were, their motives, all remained a mystery. The diary's mention of Meagher and Fredericksburg might suggest a connection to the war, but not definitively, especially given Lieutenant Bradley's assertion that an Indian had most probably been in possession of the diary at the Little Big Horn.

He was returning to his study of the journal when the door opened. He looked up, expecting Josephine. Instead a slim, wiry man in an oddly foppish suit entered.

"Hello Hamilton," Collins said.

"Collins." The Duke came to the table and stood over him.

Neglecting to look up at the man, he snuffed his cigar and sipped his cup of coffee, even though it had gone quite cold.

"How long will you be staying?" The Duke inquired.

"I am just leaving," Collins said and stood, forcing Hamilton back a step. He was at least a head taller than the bordello dandy before him. "Excuse me, please," he added politely and, picking up the diary from the table, made to exit the room.

"Just a minute, Collins." The Duke said, blocking his way.

"Yes?"

"My position in this house demands that you answer to me regarding your plans."

C.W. looked down at him, noting the risible nature of his facial hair and the calculating ice in his pale gray eyes. "Hamilton, if you are palming one of your little whore pistols, I bid you remember the last time you braced me. Now get out the road." Collins pushed past him and went out the door.

"I will not be disregarded," The Duke said and followed him.

Joe appeared in the hallway without. "Ham...Get back to the parlor and do your job," she said, imperiously. "Charles is none of your business."

Hamilton went past them without a glance or word.

"You are leaving," Joe said.

"I must, *acushla*." He bent and kissed her forehead.

"Tomorrow?"

"Perhaps. A most profound thank you for a lovely evening," he said and turned to leave in the opposite direction than that taken by The Duke.

Stepping out a side door into snow driven by a fierce wind, he contemplated returning to the warm gaiety of the house and the satisfactions of Josephine's bed, but thought better of it. Putting up his collar, he oriented himself and set off in the direction of the International Hotel. Best to disengage himself. It was a lesson learned long years before.

# 20

There was at least half a foot of snow on the ground in the morning. The sun, however, was brilliant and Collins felt positively ebullient as he proceeded along partially cleared walks to the telegraph office. Inside, he penciled a terse message to Grant.

"On trail saw lincoln saw buford saw tongue cantonment stop visited grave most unpleasant some clues stop helena may offer aid nothing definitive stop no presumptions please stop action is eloquence stop." He omitted the Irish war cry that he had included in his last telegram, as he felt that his investigation was somewhat stalled at the moment. Instead he had added the minor quote from Shakespeare that he used on occasion as code to inform the president he was not yet discouraged. A bit of a prevarication, but not much.

Collins incurred predictable incredulity from the telegraph operator at the destination given for the telegram, paid the fee and stepped back into the dazzling morning. He found a hotel serving breakfast and stepped in. While perusing the *Weekly Herald*, he partook of a quite acceptable plate of eggs and ham. The coffee was weak, but he had come to expect this in most public establishments.

An item in the newspaper caught his attention. A few days before there had been a drunken Irishman arrested for creating a public nuisance. When the man had been searched prior to incarceration, a white man's scalp had been found in his possession. An investigation had ensued to no avail and Thomas Cronin had been anything but forthcoming. C.W. instantly considered that an interview with Mr. Cronin might prove beneficial. Finishing his meal, he paid and made his way back to the bank in order to discover whether Mr.'s. Stuart or Hauser had any useful intelligence regarding Keogh's pistol.

Granville Stuart was engaged in reviewing a loan application with a fellow who was apparently a local butcher. Collins sat in an overstuffed leather chair and waited, occupying himself by admiring a young woman in a stylish costume standing at a teller window. Her clothing attested to wealth and position, at least according to Helena's frontier standards. He caught her eye as she finished her business and turned to leave. Startled, she paused to examine him with patent appreciation then, blushing furiously, she dropped her gaze and hurriedly exited the building. Collins smiled, truly enjoying the effect his blue eyes, black hair and stolid countenance had upon some women.

The butcher passed by, having conducted his affair to satisfaction, according to his general air of complacency. C.W. arose and knocked lightly on the open door, finding Stuart preoccupied with collating paperwork from the previous transaction. Stuart looked up and assumed an unctuous manner.

"Mr. Collins. Do come in and sit down."

"I prefer to stand," C.W. answered, not intending to stay long nor sink below the prow of the man's desk. "Any information from Mr. Samuel Hauser?"

"I am afraid I have nothing to add. Sam has never encountered such a pistol, although its existence certainly caught his interest. He was quite intrigued by its provenance and how it came to be connected with the calamity on the Little Big Horn."

"I am afraid that I cannot illuminate you gentlemen

further.  As it is, I appreciate your efforts on my behalf."

"You are in receipt of sufficient funds necessary to your continued inquiry?" Stuart asked, standing to shake Collins' hand.

"I am, in fact.  Thank you for your kind concern," he said, taking the man's hand and turning abruptly to leave before he could be detained by persistent questioning.

Outside, the snow was beginning to melt in rivulets that trickled from rooftops and walkways and turned the streets to mud.  C.W. wandered the town deep in thought.  If the pistol had been taken by one of the Indians, it would most probably be lost to posterity, unless traded to a white man or turned in to an Indian agent.  Its usefulness as a clue was therefore negligible excepting the off chance it was retained by one of the Indians' white allies and he could actually run them to ground.  The likelihood of such an eventuality was trifling.  He gazed into various shop windows without seeing the goods therein.

Montana Territory was home to approximately 15,000 souls at present.  In spite of considerable distance between communities, and wide stretches of unoccupied country, the residents tended to be mutually aware and figures such as Beidler, W.F. Sanders, Bradley, Stuart and pivotal military gentlemen tended to be well known.  Also, there was an almost constant flow of residency from one town to another, as employment and opportunity were sought.  Given this, it was not unthinkable that if ready knowledge were available as to the existence or identity of white men fighting with the Indians on the Little Big Horn, he would have caught wind of it.  There was no profit in denying that he was thus far palpably thwarted in his search.

With a reluctance born of legitimate trepidation, Collins finally came to the definite conclusion he had been avoiding for days.  On the assumption that Cronin would constitute another dead end, he would be forced to seek further answers among the Indian population of the territory.   Here he would be severely handicapped, as he spoke no northern plains dialects nor could claim acquaintance among the various Siouan tribes.   As it stood, he did not entertain confident anticipation of either success or survival.

Coming out of his reverie, C.W. asked directions of a local grocer.   Proceeding toward the courthouse, he allowed himself to appreciate the recent growth of Helena and its coming into itself as the newly appointed capital of Montana Territory.   Since the fire of '72, the population had been building with a permanence that bespoke of entrenchment.   Here was mineral wealth, abundance in natural resources and room for expansion.   Respectability was already invading, witnessed by the spread of churches and schools.   As he made his way into the courthouse square, C.W. was forced to dodge a luxurious barouche pulled by a team of matching blacks.   It seemed to him that incivility was elemental to nascent civilization.

# 21

A uniformed turnkey led Collins into the bowels of the courthouse where four primitive jail cells were housed. He suspected the man probably doubled as the janitor. The deputy sheriff had been surprisingly uninquisitive as to his reasons for wishing to visit Thomas Cronin and he was admitted without formality. The rather medieval cellar reeked of damp earth, urine and mildew. The jailer unlocked the only occupied cell.

"Give a yelp when you are ready to leave or if he makes a play for you," the man said and disappeared up the stairs.

Collins turned to examine the occupant of the cell. He was large with a rim of wiry red hair surrounding a bald pate, resembling a clerical tonsure. The man's face was pasty from lack of sun and he sat hunched on a miserable cot staring at the palms of his hands. He appeared to be oblivious or indifferent to Collins' presence at the door. A bucket brimming with human excrement occupied an opposite corner to the cot and a dank wetness coated the raw rock of the retaining walls. C.W. leaned easily against the doorjamb of rough iron. It, too, was damp.

"Thomas Cronin?" he asked.

No answer.

"I take it you have not made friends with the good people of Montana Territory."

Cronin snorted derisively.

"I need information. I can do nothing to improve your plight."

"They will hang me. Or I will expire down here. It is no matter." Cronin said gruffly, in a heavy Northern Irish brogue.

"The drink can lead to many an unpleasant adventure," C.W. responded, allowing his native accent some latitude.

Again, the man snorted expressively.

"Why the scalp?" C.W. asked. "Was it what they claim it to be?"

"Aye. But who are you to be wondering?"

"My name is Charles Wolfe Collins."

Cronin looked at him for the first time. "It is a fine name."

"It is a name to live with."

The man nodded solemnly, returning his gaze to his filthy hands, held palm upward on his lap in a slack and hopeless pose.

"I am going to ask a question. Know that whatever your answer, it will not depart with me nor be added to the spite that is heaped upon your head. Will you take my word on that?"

Again, Cronin nodded.

"Did you engage in the terrible fray on the Little Big Horn last summer?"

Another nod, more tentative.

"Were you fighting *with* the Indians or against them?"

Cronin turned his eyes toward Collins with a mingled expression of disbelief, fear and perplexity.

Collins took it as an answer. "How many of you were there?"

The brawny Irishman looked away. "Me mother dinna rear informers," he said, slowly.

"This is not Dublin Castle."

"No, but the strife be the same."

"Is it now?" Collins could sense the man slipping away. He decided on a different tack. He reached into his vest pocket and produced the claddagh. "Well then, have you laid eyes on this fine thing before?" he asked, handing it to him.

The remaining color drained from Cronin's face. "Daniel," was all he said as he turned the ring in his beefy hands.

"You recognize it then?"

No response.

"If he was a comrade of yours I am most sorry to inform you that he is dead."

Cronin glanced at him with tears in his eyes. "I feared as much," he said, handing back the ring.

C.W. took two cigars from a jacket pocket and offered one to Cronin. He accepted it sullenly, biting off the end. C.W. lit a match and held it for him. They smoked silently for a bit and the fragrant smoke did much to improve the putrid atmosphere of their surroundings.

"If I were to seek your confederates, how would I proceed?" asked Collins.

"To what purpose?"

"A purpose that bodes no evil. For my part, anyway."

"For your part?" Cronin eyed him suspiciously through a cloud of smoke. "Who are the others what seek us then?"

"I, too, must have my secrets, Mr. Cronin. But if my word as a fellow countryman is enough, I give it and state that whatever intelligence you provide shall not be used for ill intent."

Cronin retreated into silence for quite some time. Collins puffed his cigar patiently, understanding that this man held grave importance to his continued investigation.

"Your word is not enough for one such as me. I have abandoned my past, kith and kin to become an altered creature." Cronin looked at him in defiance. "With no regrets, mind you. No regrets, for I love my chosen brothers, old and new, and that is God's own truth. But you have dealt with me as more human than anyone in many a while now. I will tell you this and this alone. Those you search for shall be found with the great *Tatanka Iyotaka*."

The man's eyes shone with reverence. Collins noted that his tongue was friendly with the strange language.

"How do I find this great man?"

"The whites know him as Sitting Bull."

C.W. had heard of him, especially as crucial to the Indians' success at the Little Big Horn. "I see."

Cronin stubbed out his cigar on the dirt floor of his cell. "Should you have the chance, tell them this: *Is milis da ol e ach is searbh da ioc e.* Do you understand the Irish?"

"It is a proverb that was oft repeated by my mother, God rest her soul. 'It is sweet to drink but bitter to pay for.'"

"Aye."

Collins threw down the remnant of his smoke and rubbed it out with the toe of his boot. "Many unforeseen eventualities can be most bitter in this life, my friend. *Adh mor ort.*"

"There is no luck left in this world for me," Cronin answered.

C.W. left the man sitting glumly in abject misery and went to the bottom of the stairs, calling to the jailer that he wished to leave. That Cronin would pay dearly for his indiscretions he had no doubt. Political machinery of the new and highly prejudiced capital city would see to that. The fresh winter air outside the courthouse was a blessing and Collins breathed deeply to expel more than just the mere stench of the underground sewer he had recently departed. How the man had come to Helena he would, perhaps, never know.  It was certain he would never leave.

# 22

The sun had once again been obscured by heavy clouds and soft, downy flakes of snow were falling. Despite thoughts of Cronin's pathos dampening Collin's spirits, the trail was now a bit more illuminated and he took heart. He walked in the direction of the livery stable where Molly and Ulysses were boarded. There were few pedestrians about due to the inclement weather and slippery streets thick with mud. He kept to the walkways as much as possible and nodded cordially to infrequent passersby. Arriving at the stables, he waded through muddy slush at the mouth of large sliding doors standing open. His eyes adjusted to the dimness of the interior and he looked around for the proprietor.

He found Mr. Thaddeus Martin in his tidy office going over the weekly accounts. The Franklin stove in the middle of the room was letting off an enormous amount of heat, immediately forcing Collins to shed his coat. He took a chair as far away from the stove as possible and waited for Martin to finish making notations in a diary.

"Charles," he finally said, looking up and removing his spectacles. "Leaving us already?"

"Not yet... Jesus, Mary and Joseph, Thad," Collins said, removing his hat and wiping his brow with a sleeve, "It more resembles hell in here than a stable. Why the blast furnace?"

"I have a chill and the damp is playing misery with my rheumatism. What can I do for you?"

"Merely stopped for a visit with my stock and a wee visit with you."

"Which comes first?"

"You, I suppose. Although I shall be jerked meat in no time."

"It is widely known you are slated for hell, Collins. You might as well become acclimated."

"There may be something in what you say. Meanwhile, do you happen to know anyone who is proficient in the Sioux language or familiar with the people?"

Martin grimaced. "What in god's name are you up to now?"

"Simple reconnaissance."

"Sure. It is always reconnaissance." Martin stuffed and lit his pipe.

"Well?"

"Did you happen to hear of the minor skirmish that took place last summer?"

"Of course." Collins nonchalantly picked up an old newspaper from a nearby table and began fanning himself with it.

"Then why in the name of all that is holy would you plan to go among the Sioux Indians at this point in time? Death wish?"

"Who said I planned to go among them?"

"I did not just fall off the manure pile. Why else would you require an interpreter or guide?"

"Damn," Collins said, lighting a cigar. "How difficult is it to answer a simple question? You are becoming quite an old woman."

"Old woman, my ass. Why would I wish to be complicit in a friend's demise?"

"Allow me more credit than that. I have survived these many years."

"Yes," Martin said, gingerly tamping his pipe with a finger. "But how many times have you had dealings with

Indians? I thought bank robbers and confederate spies were more your métier."

Collins sighed. "I have spent considerable time among southwestern tribes. But truth be told, I am not delighted with the turn my current investigation has taken. Still and all, a hound must follow the scent no matter what the road."

"Then I am sorry. I know of no one who either knows the language or the people... or would admit to it if they did. There are strong feelings among the residents of this territory."

"No doubt."

"I would not make it freely known that your objective lies among the heathen red men."

Collins laughed derisively. "When have I ever made my objectives known, you silly bastard?"

"Yes...and all is safe within my confidences."

"Good." Collins stubbed out his cigar and resumed fanning himself, stifling from the heat. "What about Granville Stuart, the banker? Does he not have an Indian wife?"

"Yes, but I would be wary. Stuart is unwavering in his ambition and the attentions of great men. He cannot be trusted."

"And his wife?"

Martin raised his eyebrows. "That poor soul has yet to be espied in public since their arrival in Helena a few months ago. And she is Shoshone, I believe. Not bosom kin of the Sioux as I understand it."

"Just a thought. I am really against it, my friend. As you say, my strengths do not lie in this arena."

"What of the military?"

"A possibility. Probably my next maneuver." Collins stood, picking up his hat and coat. "I must be on my way. I leave you to your fire and brimstone."

"Your animals are toward the back of the barn on the left

side," Martin said and began sorting through a pile of receipts.

"Have their shoes pulled, will you? I will no doubt be traveling on more ice and snow than terra firma from this point on."

Relieved to be free of the oppressive heat, Collins stepped to the front of the stables and watched the falling snow. When he had cooled a bit, he put on his hat and coat and walked into the interior of the barn. He found Ulysses and Molly sharing a stall as he had requested. They were standing head to tail, chewing each other's manes companionably. He leaned on the gate and watched for while, talking nonsense to them in a low voice. Eventually, Ulysses came to him and, placing his dark velvet muzzle against his collar, snuffed him thoroughly. He scratched the gelding's jaw. Molly watched, aloof as usual. Making sure their hay bunk was full, he left the stables and returned to his hotel.

The resident barber was unoccupied, so Collins went for a shave and bath. The wintry day was waning and he planned to visit Josephine in the evening hours. As he soaked in a steaming copper tub, he considered his next move. Assuming that the current snowy weather would soon abate, he would have to make for Fort Shaw and Lieutenant Bradley, who was to have returned there from Fort Ellis. He had confided sufficiently in the man and he proposed to further enlist his aid in procuring a guide and interpreter. He could think of no alternative.

The elderly Chinese man in charge of the bathhouse brought more hot water, pouring it carefully into Collin's tub. Smiling, he turned his thinking to Joe and the lovely prospects before him. No doubt a tasty dinner would be followed by lively conversation and a satisfactory interlude in a sweet smelling boudoir. The future might well be questionable, but for now he intended to take his pleasures where he may. *Maireann croi eadrom i bhad,* he thought. A light heart lives long.

❧◆❧

# 23

He awoke with a hand wandering through his hair and playing with the lobes of his ears.  C.W. rolled over and embraced the warm and generous body beside him, once again indulging his reawakened enthusiasm with the willing and experienced Josephine.  Morning light was illuminating the room as they finished and he sat up to stretch and relieve himself in the chamber pot.

"Breakfast?" she asked, as he washed with cold water from an ornate porcelain basin.

"Most gratefully," he said, drying and beginning to dress.

Joe pulled the bell and reached for a brocade dressing gown.

C.W. studied her a moment. "Are you still angry about Hamilton?"

She squinted at him in disdain. "Of course.  He will be laid up for days. You broke three of his ribs."

"I warned him not to interfere with me."

The door opened and Lola came in bearing a tray with coffee.

"We will want breakfast," Joe told her.

The maid nodded, set the tray on the sideboard, and discreetly left.  Collins filled cups for both of them and delivered Joe's to where she lounged in the bed, twisting her voluminous hair and pinning it on top of her head. He sat beside her and sipped his coffee.

"Will you not find a reliable and trustworthy man?"

he asked, after a while.

She rolled her eyes. "Where would I find a man such as this for work in a bordello? I need protection and 'trustworthy' men do not apply."

"I am certain there are better men available than 'The Duke,'" he said sarcastically.

"You find me one, I will hire him," she said, draining her cup and holding it out to him.

He got up to refill it. "Well, *acushla*, I must depart soon, but perhaps when I return." He carried the full cup to her.

"When will *that* be?" she asked, taking the cup and blowing on it.

"Where I am heading, maybe never," he said, sitting down again.

Joe abandoned her playful manner and looked at him gravely. "Are you in earnest?"

C.W. smiled at her and stroked her cheek. "Only a bit, my Joe. Only a bit."

"What are you up to now?"

There was a knock on the door. Collins went over and opened it for Lola, who came in bearing a tray loaded with dishes. She set it down.

"Will there be anything else, Miss Josephine?"

"Nothing, thank you. I will ring if I want you."

The pretty Chinese girl curtsied and left, closing the door after.

Collins began exploring the hot dishes arrayed on the tray. He filled a plate with bacon, scrambled eggs and toast. "Would you like for me to prepare you a plate?" he asked.

"No," Joe answered sullenly. "I want you to answer my question. Where are you going?"

He set his plate on a little table near the windows, took a seat and commenced eating. "Now you are worried," he said after a bit. "I was having some sport with you, nothing more."

Josephine got up and refilled her cup. She brought the coffee pot and filled his cup as well. Then she sat across from him and leaned forward. "You were not having sport. You have qualms."

Collins put down his fork, took a sip from his cup and wiped his mouth with a napkin. "Yes, I entertain doubts. I must follow my enterprise into Indian country. I will be vastly out of my element."

"Must you go?"

"Of course. I have yet to cower at the thought of danger and will not begin at this late stage in my evolution."

Joe took a slice of toast from his plate and ate it. "It is always difficult to have you leave me," she said, with tears in her eyes. "Now it is almost unbearable."

He stopped eating and came over to where she sat, bending down and pressing her cheek against his chest. "Now, now," he said, petting her hair. "I make a very poor target."

She smiled, regaining her usual composure. "You are certainly impossible to ensnare."

Collins went over to resume his seat at the table. "You see? Besides, I have already come through the wilderness unscathed just to see you."

"And where *did* you come from?"

He finished his breakfast and drained his cup. "You are such an inquisitive little minx," he said, standing and searching the room for his hat and coat.

"You are not leaving this moment?" she asked.

"I am."

Josephine went over to the bed and propped herself against a mound of pillows. "I have a bad feeling."

He stood looking at her, his hand on the glass doorknob. "You would not have me other than as I am. You would weary of me. And if this be our last encounter, then what more could we ask than the perfection of the past few hours?"

"I want more," she said, as if tossing down a gauntlet.

Collins smiled sweetly. "Why then, can one desire too much of a good thing?'" he quoted and slipped quietly out the door.

# 24

Following the Mullan Road north along the western flood plain of the Missouri River, Collins left Helena early in the morning, making the most of frozen ground. Although much of the snow had melted, there were extensive patches of it spreading across the open plain. In the distance lay a small mountain pass near a wooded ridge called the Sleeping Giant, named for its rather vague resemblance to a man lying on his back. Ulysses was unruly after so long a rest. He spooked and snorted at clumps of dried weeds, rabbits and his own imagination. Molly followed in her usual even manner and Collins thought he sensed in her a slight disdain for the horse's shenanigans.

As the day progressed, a chilly wind arose from the north, but the sun shone brilliantly. Collins rode hard all morning, crossing the timbered ridges and slipping past John's Ranch. He chose not to stop over, as he would rather make time and avoid contact with fellow travelers. A stagecoach passed him around noon, moving at a fair clip, probably headed for Fort Benton. The driver gave him an off-handed nod, his hands full of the lines for a six-up team. The guard beside him held a shotgun in both hands and made no sign. Collins figured the coach carried gold from Helena's fecund gulches. The leather window coverings on the coach were snugged tight against the cold. C.W. had always preferred to journey by horseback than by stage. He disliked paying exorbitant prices only to be packed tightly in a cramped space with strangers who were often of limited hygiene. Ulysses had calmed down and, despite the cold breeze, traveling was not unpleasant. He was glad to be free of town, although it always took him a few days to recover from the charms of Chicago Joe.

The northern days were growing much shorter as the month of October had progressed. The light began to wane sooner than he expected and he began to scout along the sheltered banks of the Missouri for a place to camp. Finding a hollow among thick cottonwoods and willows, C.W. tied his animals and began to unpack his gear. He built a tidy camp, gathered a large pile of firewood against the falling temperatures and hobbled his animals to scrounge among the trees for dried leaves and withered grass. He made a stew of a small piece of beef, purchased in Helena at an extravagant price, some potatoes and one shriveled carrot. With bread and coffee, it was not quite a repast to the standards he had enjoyed for the past few days, but he had found that fresh air and hunger were often adequate condiments for any meal.

Bundled warmly in his bedroll, sleep came slowly as thoughts of Josephine plagued his repose. He dug out Shakespeare and read part of *Henry V* by firelight, revisiting the Battle of Agincourt. A light snow began to filter through his riparian bower and, not for the first time, Collins wished that Grant had sent him upon this mission into northern climes prior to winter setting in. Worries about his future enterprise among the Sioux crept in, leaving him sleepless most of the night. He sincerely hoped that Lieutenant Bradley would, indeed, be at Fort Shaw and that he would have some reasonable suggestion for penetrating into a hornet's nest of desperate Indians struggling for their very survival.

At first light, a grumpy and poorly rested Collins

gathered up Ulysses and Molly and began packing up his camp. He rekindled his fire for coffee, but was not hungry for breakfast. He was saddling Ulysses when the horse began to snort and rear in a show of great agitation. The saddle slipped beneath his belly just as Collins had been in the process of snugging the latigo. This filled the animal with such a degree of terror that he broke the rope securing him to a stout tree and bolted free of the saddle and C.W.'s attempts at calming him. With all the preceding transpiring in short order, it was only after Collins turned to track the direction of his gelding's flight, he saw that Molly, his calm and steady mule, was in such panic to pull loose from her tether that she was sitting on her rear and digging trenches with her front hooves in the half frozen ground, almost choking herself down. Her eyes were rolling in fear.

With the hair standing up on the back of his neck and a sudden inkling of the dangerous nature of their predicament, Collins pulled the old Green River knife from his belt, cut Molly free and dove for his rifle. He rolled to his feet in time to face an enormous blonde bear reared on its hind legs and throwing its head back and side to side with a deafening roar. The enormous grizzly boar came down to all fours and began to pound the ground and cough menacingly, moving closer to C.W. and attempting to focus its meager eyesight while sniffing the air. Knowing that the smell of food was no doubt emanating from his packs and the unwashed pot from the previous evening's stew, he remained motionless with his rifle barrel pointed at the bear while sincerely wishing this brute had already gone into hibernation.

They stood as duelists waiting for the other to make a move, when Molly came crashing out of an alder thicket, charging at the grizzly with ears snaked back. Rearing at the last moment, she struck the beast square in the head in quick succession with both front hooves, then reeling as a well-balanced dancer, she dodged free of the lethal claws as the bear lunged.  Collins chose that opportunity to shoot the beast in the left side of its exposed chest, missing a killing shot, but wounding the animal grievously.  It howled and roared in pain, coming back to all fours and shaking its head. Levering another shell, Collins shot it square in the face to blunt its sense of smell and limited vision.  It charged blindly through the brush along the river and Collins could hear the animal hit the waters of the Missouri, issuing a long deep cry of pain, then silence.

Sitting down on his packs, he reloaded his rifle with shaking hands.  After a few deep breaths and a slug of coffee, he strapped on his holster, picked up the knife and a length of rope and went to look for the bear and his horse.  Molly appeared by his side and he unabashedly kissed her muzzle and stroked her long ears with reverence.  If he ever saw Corporal Patrick Murphy again, he would have quite a tale to tell him.  Collins had heard that mules bore a singular hatred for bear and puma, but the fierce courage he had witnessed had been awe-inspiring. Surely, she had saved his life.

As if aware that their companionship had reached a higher plane, Molly followed him as he picked his way through thick undergrowth to the river's edge.  After a brief search of the area, C.W. spotted the grizzly lying on its side on a gravel bank a hundred feet into the Missouri's waters.  Its sides were heaving slowly and keening groans emitted with each exhale of breath.  Looping a rope over her head and nose, he explained to Molly that she must stay on the bank and tied her to a tree.  Using rocks and patches of ice to keep his feet mostly dry, he gingerly approached the bear with rifle at the ready.  It made a weak struggle to pick up its head, but failed.  Not wanting to see any creature suffer, he placed the barrel of his rifle in the exposed ear and fired.  After a brief peddling of the legs, the bear defecated and its breath eased out with the sound of a distant wail.

Glancing back at the bank, he could see Molly watching, alert and concerned. He was loath to leave the pelt, but doubted that Ulysses would ever stand for the proximity of the hide after his terrible fright. First, he needed to find the damn horse, he thought, and made his way back to where Molly waited. Tugging the rope loose, he walked back to camp, leading his mule and hoping Ulysses might have found his way there. Seeing that he had not, Collins looped the rope around Molly's neck and tied it off to itself. Unsure of what her reaction might be, he jumped onto her back. Predictably, the animal was cooperative and he urged her gently out of the trees and in the direction of Ulysses' escape.

The frozen ground offered no spoor, but tracking his gelding was fairly easy through patches of snow. Collins was not pleased at the thought of wasting an entire day searching for his horse. Even so, he mused, he and his animals were alive and events could have easily precipitated in an alternative and far less advantageous direction. The sun came out of a blanket of gray clouds, cheering the landscape and warming Collins' back. Molly suddenly brayed loudly and shortly thereafter came an answering whinny from a small bunch of evergreens against a low hill. As they headed toward the sound, Ulysses came trotting into the open, still trailing the end of the broken rope.

The gelding followed them docilely back to camp, apparently exhausted from his abrupt flight. Collins hobbled them both and turned them loose to forage and recover. His own rush of adrenaline had left him somnolent. He started another fire, reheated the morning's coffee and fried a bit of bacon. After the small meal, he washed up and stowed the pots away, making certain there was as little an odor of victuals around the camp as possible.

# 25

A light, but stinging snow was blowing sideways from the west, biting Collins' face and making poor Ulysses even more restive.  The horse had yet to recover from his panic of the previous day and, even though Molly had been typically stoical about the heavy grizzly hide that Collins had added to her load, Ulysses had been beside himself with alarm.  His ears had been pinned backward all day, as if he thought the animal would spring back to life and charge him from the rear.  C.W. disliked provoking his horse, but he also felt that leaving the bearskin was tantamount to a criminal act.  He had been unable to abandon it when, at last, he had recovered from his daunting trial with raw nature.

Ulysses' agitation made for a faster journey, however, as the horse endeavored to escape the redolent fur behind him.  As dusk was approaching, they reached Krueger's ranch.  He had decided upon a respite within stout buildings as opposed to another solitary camp along the Missouri. A hired hand met him at the corrals and helped him unload his packs. The middle-aged man hefted down the tied bundle of bearskin and whistled.

"Damn, mister, that must have been a big bear."

"It certainly looked big when I thought it had me," Collins concurred.

They stowed his gear in the barn, brushed down the horse and mule and led them to a lone pen with a lean-to, as Collins did not want his animals in with strange stock.  He gave them some oats and watched them while they ate.  The ranch hand leaned on a rail and waited.

"Nice beasts," he said.

"You do not know the half," C.W. said, smiling at Molly.

"You got a story?"

"Just that this mule saved me from that grizzly," he said, tilting his hat in the direction of the barn.

"You are joshin'"

"Not a bit."

Inside, over a rough dinner of venison liver, boiled potatoes and dried apples, Collins had to recount his tale more than once for the stage travelers, a guard and driver, the ranch owners, their cook and two hands.  He turned down many offers of whiskey and they all trooped outside into a gusty snow to admire the bundled pelt and Molly, the heroic mule.  Given the dearth of entertainment these people stranded on this small isle of civilization enjoyed, Collins, Molly and the grizzly provided much needed diversion.  Collins really was inordinately proud of his darling mule and his Celtic nature was prone to storytelling, in spite of his usual reserve.

The next morning, among much commotion as the team was harnessed and hitched to the stagecoach and travelers and baggage were loaded, Collins saddled his own stock.  He packed his load, including the bearskin much to Ulysses' chagrin, and struck out for Fort Shaw in a northwesterly direction from the stage road to Fort Benton. The landscape was dull and windswept, although the road was plainly marked by travel.  Collins knew that the soldiers of the fort must take their leave in the brothels of Helena as that was the closest bastion of pleasure.  Chicago Joe's establishments were too expensive for noncommissioned military pay, but he had seen the boys in blue along the rows of cribs more within their financial wherewithal.  He whiled away the time reliving luxurious moments spent in Joe's company and forty some miles were broken only by a quick couple of stops for stretching and relieving himself. It was after dark when the faint glow of Fort Shaw appeared in the distance.

Riding exhaustedly into the parade grounds, Collins stopped at the sutler's and asked whether Lieutenant Bradley had returned to the fort. Given an answer in the affirmative, he was much relieved and inquired after the lieutenant's quarters. Back outside, he led his weary animals to an adobe house emitting warm lamplight through floral curtained windows. He tied his horse and mule and stepped onto the porch to knock. Bradley himself answered the door and his welcome was most gratifying.

"By god, Charles, come in, come in," he said, holding the door open and ushering Collins into the warm front parlor. "It is good to see you."

"I really must see to my stock," he told Bradley.

"Of course. Let me accompany you." The lieutenant donned a coat. "Let me tell Mary," he said and went into a back room.

Collins looked around the meticulously decorated parlor, obviously the result of Mrs. Bradley's feminine tastes. A pile of wooden blocks and a doll on the floor attested to the presence of a child, a daughter as he recalled. Muffled voices came from the rear of the house, then Bradley came back appearing a bit flustered.

"Come, Charles. We will get your animals settled, then find a place for you."

They went out into the night. Bradley took Molly and, with C.W. leading Ulysses, they made their way to the stables. Finding and lighting a lamp, they saw to the animals and stowed his packs in an unused corner of a feed shed.

"No one will bother your belongings. I will see to them at first light," Bradley told him.

"I can bunk here.  It is no worry."

Bradley looked relieved.  "I will be frank.  I wished for you to stay with us, but Mary has recently lost a baby and in her delicate condition, does not care for the idea. It is most embarrassing."

"That is nonsense.  What a terrible tragedy for both of you. I would not dream of inconveniencing your family in this crisis and I would feel better watching my trappings and being near my animals.  I am all in and not much for company myself."

"Well then, I will leave this lamp for you and leave you to your rest.  Please do come to the house in the morning.  We have a girl in to help Mary and she makes a wonderful breakfast. Afterward we can find you more commodious quarters."

"I will see you in the morning, then," Collins told him and watched him walk away. Gratefully closing the door of the shed against the growing chill of the night, he rolled out his bedding and unceremoniously lay down to sleep.  The last sound he remembered was the rhythmic tapping of a loose roof shingle played upon by a stiff north wind.

# 26

The cozy kitchen was full of sun as Collins sat across from Bradley and waited for breakfast.  A very young girl was bustling around the large Majestic cook stove, appearing quite capable.  Mary Bradley was still abed, feeling unwell according to her worried husband. The coffee was damn good, thought Collins, as he accepted a refill from the girl.

"This is Henrietta," Bradley told him.  "She is the daughter of one of our corporals and has been a wonderful help to Mary these past few months."

"Hello Henrietta," C.W. said.  The girl gave a shy curtsy and returned to the stove.

"Did I see a bear skin among your packs last night?" the lieutenant asked.

"Grizzly hide.  It was a frighteningly close call."  He proceeded to recount the tale.

"Your mule did that?" Bradley asked, after hearing the story.

"She did, indeed.  Of course she is an Irish mule. That makes all the difference."  He could hear Henrietta giggling in the background.

"What do you plan to do with the pelt?"

"Maybe use it for trade?  I have come for your advice and aid, James.  I have found myself in a bit of a predicament."

Henrietta placed heaping plates of eggs, rashers of bacon and biscuits before them.  She curtsied again at their thanks and left the room.  They paused conversation to eat.

"What predicament?" Bradley asked after a while.  "Is it in relation to the matter in question?"

"It is."

"What does the bear skin have to do with it?"

"The trail leads me into Indian country.  Sioux country, to be exact."

Bradley put down his fork and stared at him.  "You are not in earnest?"

"I must track down Sitting Bull."

"But I have heard he is in the vicinity of the new cantonment on the Tongue River.  He has been harassing Miles' supply trains."

"Truly?"

"That is the talk around the post.  Some of the coffee coolers were making speeches about finding him and exacting revenge for Custer."

Collins used a biscuit to sop up some egg yolk and bacon grease.  "That is a long ride."

"Not to mention dangerous and out of the question."

"Nevertheless, it is where I must go.  I am at a complete loss, however, when it comes to the language and customs.  I was hoping you would recommend a guide and interpreter."

"Charles...you cannot do this.  It is not possible.  If Sitting Bull or Crazy Horse do not kill you, Miles may do the job for interfering in his business."

Collins locked eyes with the well-meaning lieutenant.  "You must believe that I will do what I have to do."

Bradley got up to fetch the coffee pot.  He refilled their cups, put the pot back on the stove and paced the snug little kitchen.  Collins pushed his empty plate away and scooted back his chair to cross his legs.  His companion finally returned to the table, ignoring his unfinished meal.

"There is one possibility," he said.

"Yes?"

"There is someone around the post here who might suit."

"And?"

"You might have some objections."

"I doubt it. Who is this person?" C.W. asked. He saw a glimmer of hope.

"Arbuckles."

"Arbuckles? Like the coffee purveyors?"

"Arbuckles is an Indian that mostly just hunts for the fort."

"What about interpreting?'

"Probably. For pay, of course."

"Of course. When can I meet him? If Sitting Bull is on the Tongue, I must make haste. Miles is rash and may behave precipitously."

Bradley had an odd expression on his face. "We could go now. I believe Arbuckles just got back yesterday with fresh venison."

"That is fine. I will go now to check on my animals and belongings. Can you meet me at the stables?"

"Certainly."

As Collins passed through the parlor, he smiled at Henrietta, who was quietly dusting the various and sundry chromos adorning the walls. Outside, the day had warmed considerably. Someone had tossed a small mound of hay into the pen with Molly and Ulysses. He checked on his goods and all was as he had left it. When he came out of the shed, Bradley was giving instructions to a tall private.

"Take all his property and place it in the empty quarters on the west end of the post. And be certain his horse and mule are well taken care of."

"Yes sir," the private saluted and headed for the feed shed.

"You will be vastly more comfortable with a stove and

some furniture," Bradley told him.

"Thank you."

They walked toward the sutler's store. "I must warn you that Arbuckles may be drunk. That is sometimes the case after a successful hunt and renewed resources."

The store was open and they went inside. A bluff man with a generous belly and thick white beard greeted them heartily.

"Good morning, George," Bradley said. "This is Charles Collins."

They shook hands. "What can I do for you this fine day?" George asked.

"Is Arbuckles about?"

George's friendly posture evaporated. He tipped his head at the rear of the store. "Out back." He turned and began straightening canned goods on a shelf behind him.

"If this fellow is a lush, I do not believe he will suit my purposes at all," Collins said as they went out the back door and down some steps into a slushy yard.

"Arbuckles is not a dipsomaniac. Just drinks on occasion and not that often."

Again, Collins sensed something amiss in Bradley's manner. They approached a small tarpapered shed.

"Look, James. There is something here you are not telling me."

The lieutenant smiled sheepishly. "I told you that you might have some objections. You will see soon enough," he said and tapped on the door.

A muffled voice came from within. "Yes."

"Arbuckles. It is Lieutenant Bradley. I have someone with me who might want to employ you as interpreter and guide. It could be good."

There was a shuffling and thumping. Finally the door creaked open on leather hinges.

"What?"

Collins was stunned.  Standing before him was a tall, muscular Indian woman with salt and pepper braids and a deep scar that pulled down the left side of her mouth. Her eyes were clear and she stood very erect.  She wore a calico shirt and buckskin fringed trousers held up by bright red suspenders.

"Charles.  This is Arbuckles."

The woman shook his hand in a loose, hesitant fashion.

"You have not been drinking whiskey," Bradley said to her.

"No...  I knew there would be someone coming."  Her voice was rich and there was a trace of a peculiar accent.

"May we come in and parlay?" Bradley asked.

Arbuckles stood back to allow them to enter her shack.  Collins followed Bradley into the cramped space. They sat in rickety chairs set at a table made of crating slats across a crude frame of slab lumber.  There was a pleasant musky odor pervading the little shanty. In the dim light, allowed into the one room through oilcloth covered windows, Collins could see a neatly made cot in a corner and nearby, a rude shelf supporting a copy of the 1876 Montgomery Ward Catalog, a U.S. Army manual of cavalry rules and regulations and a worn copy of *Quentin Durward* by Sir Walter Scott.  He was at once intrigued by the sturdy woman who joined them at the table. She pulled up a log stump for a seat and boldly examined Collins, but said nothing.

"Am I mistaken in thinking that you were originally born to the Sioux before being taken captive by the Crows?" Bradley asked.

"That was the reason I gave for not accompanying you on the campaign of last year," she reminded him.

"Yes."

"You were captured by the Crow?" Collins asked.

"Young.  Maybe ten summers."

"She was with Beckwourth for a while," Bradley told him. "That is right, is it not?" he asked Arbuckles.

She sneered. "Beckwith. Not long." She drew a finger down her scar. "Long enough."

Collins noticed she had gone from speaking in complete sentences to speaking in a parody of truncated Indian syntax. He suspected she was trifling with them.

"I need a guide and interpreter to accompany me to the confluence of the Yellowstone and Tongue rivers. I need to find Sitting Bull and his men. I will pay well. Very well. Are you still fluent in the Sioux language?"

She looked him in the eyes and held his gaze, as if reading something deep within him. He found it discomfiting, but endured her contemplation with sang-froid. Bradley fidgeted a bit, but said nothing.

"I speak the language. I speak all dialects," she said, after a long while. "I will not work for you if you intend to kill the Sioux peoples. I will not work for you if you intend to kill any Indian peoples."

"I am not intending to kill anyone, unless it is self defense," C.W. told her.

"Maybe they will kill you," she said flatly. She continued to hold his eyes. "Your name is Charles?"

"Charles Wolfe Collins."

"Wolf?" she looked at him inquisitively.

"Not the animal. After a man who died far away and many years ago."

"A man named Wolf?"

"A clever man. Wolfe Tone... spelled w-o-l-f-e."

She did not respond. Instead, she got up, fetched three tin cups and handed them around. From a tiny stove, she picked up a chipped, enamel coffeepot and poured coffee into the cups. After placing the pot back on the stove, she resumed her seat.

"Thank you," Collins said.

"You are welcome."

They blew on the hot coffee and sipped. Collins could hear the wind whipping up outside as the day neared noontime.

"How much?" Arbuckles asked suddenly.

Collins understood her meaning. "Four bits a day and found for as long as I need you."

"I guide and interpret?"

"Yes."

"I hunt as well?"

"I will purchase plenty of supplies so we do not have to take the time to hunt."

She nodded. "I think we will have to travel fast. I do not think it will be very safe for you."

"That is what *I* told him," Bradley said.

"Young James is right. You should reconsider this journey."

"I cannot. I will not."

Arbuckles read his face and shrugged. "Then I will not try to talk you out of it...But know this, Wolf. I will not lose my life in defense of yours."

"I am not hiring you to be my guard."

"Good."

"Do you have your own horse?" Collins asked.

"Two. I will bring them both."

Collins took a sip of coffee and cradled the warm cup in his hands. "Do you have a name other than Arbuckles?" he asked.

"Not for you." She turned to Bradley. "Do you like this man?"

"Yes. I have great respect for him."

She looked at Collins. "I will work for you."

"Good."

"You do not have an objection to a woman?"

"No."

"I am not that other kind of woman."

"I am hiring a guide and interpreter. That is all."

Arbuckles stood, walked to the door and opened it. "When do we leave?"

The men followed suit and got up.  They walked out the door and stood in the chilly wind in front of the shack.

"We leave tomorrow, at first light.  I will purchase all supplies today.  No whiskey, Arbuckles.  Never any whiskey while you work for me."

She shrugged her square shoulders.  "I never drink whiskey," she said and closed the door.

# 27

Ragged gray clouds skittered overhead as they walked toward C.W.'s new quarters. The private had transferred his belongings, leaving the ripening bear pelt in front of the small row house. He had even lit a fire in the wood stove so that the dwelling was nicely warmed when they arrived. Two worn horsehair stuffed chairs were pulled near the stove and they each took a seat. Collins reached behind him and pushed in some of the coarse stuffing that prickled his back.

"Nothing to say?" Bradley asked at last.

"I am surprised. But she seems well suited. I have not the leisure to be delicate or particular."

"She is really quite a capable hunter. That is why George lends her his shed. I do not, however, believe she will be companionable."

"That is the least of my worries. Is she more loyal to the Crow or the Sioux, I wonder?" Collins mused.

"My guess would be the Sioux. The story is that she went back to live with them as a hunter and warrior for a time and may have been in on Fetterman's Massacre. Of course, she is not liked by most of the soldiers, but they eat the meat she brings in readily enough. A fellow attempted a rape last year and lost his left ear. I would suggest you sleep with one eye open."

"I shall for more reasons than the company of a recalcitrant virago."

The room darkened as more clouds filled the sky in

prescience of a storm.  Collins got up and took a chunk of pine from a nearby box to place in the stove.  He retook his seat and stretched his long legs out before him.

"I am reworking my journal of the Powder River Campaign for publication," Bradley said.

"Really?"

"Perhaps it will generate some revenue."

"Perhaps.  Will you include the incident of the white Sioux warrior?" Collins asked with concern."

Bradley looked at him in consternation.  "Good god man!  Of course not."

"I did not mean to question your integrity.  I hope I may read your account someday.  I am sure it will be compelling."

Bradley shrugged modestly.  "Some may find it interesting."

The wood snapped and cracked in the little stove.

"Your private has taken good care of me," he told Bradley.

"Joseph is a fine lad."

A gust of wind rattled the windows.

"You may have some weather," Bradley said.

"I may."

The lieutenant suddenly sat forward in his chair, much agitated.  "Damn it, Charles.  I am all suspense.  Will you not share the latest intelligence regarding your mission?"

C.W. raised his eyebrows.  "I have not meant to be chary.  We have had other concerns."

"Yes, yes, I know.  But really, Charles, I am most anxious to hear of your latest discoveries."

Collins reached into his jacket pocket to pull out his pipe and tobacco pouch.  He packed the bowl and took out his match safe.  "Granville Stuart is not a very pleasant fellow," he said, lighting his pipe.

"No knowledge of Keogh's pistol?"

"None. Nor had Mr. Samuel Hauser, another collector I was told."

"Yes. Between the two of them they might have run across such an unusual weapon." Bradley picked at some hair poking out the arm of his chair. "What other news then?" he asked.

"A fellow was arrested in Helena for drunken brawling. Unfortunately for him, he was in possession of a white scalp."

"Good god!" exclaimed Bradley. "Was he...*there?*"

"He was. He recognized your ring."

"So you know who those men were. You already have your answers."

"No," Collins said. "That is why I must find Sitting Bull. The man, Cronin, would not tell me much, but he did tell me his companions were allied with the chief."

"The Hunkpapas," the lieutenant said under his breath.

"What?"

"Sitting Bull's band. They are the Hunkpapas."

"And so I must find them to find the answers I seek. Or rather the answers that are sought." He puffed on his pipe.

"And what of the diary?" Bradley asked after a while.

"It is difficult to decipher. It seems as if Meagher was murdered...but whether by Sitting Bull's renegades or by some others, there is no telling." Due to prevailing prejudices he hesitated to share the Irish strand woven throughout, even with Bradley.

Bradley stood. "I must check on Mary. She is certain to be short tempered and so I cannot invite you to dine this evening." His face blushed with embarrassment. "She really is a fine girl when not in such a bereft condition."

Collins nodded. "I quite understand. I will be occupied with supplies and preparations, nonetheless. I will need you to send word to Fort Buford that I may arrive there in a desperate state en route back to Washington. I have no idea what awaits me."

"Of course."

C.W. stood and held out his hand. "I will, no doubt, be off before dawn. It has been a pleasure, James. *Go n-eiri on bothar lat.* May the road rise with you. "

They shook hands. "I will anxiously await news of the safe and successful completion of your enterprise," Bradley said.

"I am most grateful for all your kind aid and best wishes."

Collins stood in the door and watched the lieutenant walk away, giving one final wave before he passed out of sight. Setting aside his spent pipe, he sighed deeply, and turned to unpack and reassemble his gear and supplies. He had much to do and little time for it. As the wind beat persistently against the sides of the building, he felt as bleak as the sky beyond the windows.

# 28

After very little sleep, Collins lit the lamps and made final preparations for departure.  Having purchased a box of salt with other supplies on the previous afternoon, he stepped out the door to unbundle the bear pelt and salt it down so that it would be better preserved for future trading purposes.  He came out onto the small porch to find Arbuckles sitting quietly with her horses, saddled and packed, tied to the railing.  The bearskin was nearby, rolled and secured with rawhide strips.  He walked over to examine it and noticed it now smelled of smoke as opposed to rotting meat.

"You did this?" he asked, nudging the pelt with his foot.

She nodded without looking at him.

"Thank you."

There was no response.

"I must finish packing and fetch my animals.  Do you want coffee?"

Arbuckles stood.  She was wearing a cavalry officer's wool overcoat adorned with beading and buckskin fringe.  He did not want to think where she might have gotten it.  He noticed she did not wear a hat against inclement weather.

"Your animals are here.  I will have a cup of coffee."

Collins stepped off the porch and walked around the corner.  Molly and Ulysses were saddled and tethered to a small tree.  He went back in the house, poured a cup of coffee and brought it out to Arbuckles.  She grunted and accepted the cup.

"Sugar?" he asked.

She shook her head.  C.W. completed his packing. He began hauling the load out the door.  Without being asked, the Indian woman finished her coffee, set the cup on the railing and brought Molly to the front step.  She tightened the cinch and together they packed and secured the load.  Collins was pleased that the wind had died and the sky was filled with stars.  It seemed that the storm had blown over.  He hefted the bearskin onto the top of the packs and tied it down with a bit of rope. There was still no trace of light on the eastern horizon, but the stars and a sliver of moon offered a modicum of illumination.

"Ready?" he asked.

Arbuckles nodded.  Collins went inside to blow out the lamps.  When he came back out, Ulysses was standing with Molly and Arbuckles was checking the cinches of her horses.  He checked his own and swung onto the gelding. Pulling Molly's lead loose from the porch railing, he turned his animals away from the building.

"You will follow," Arbuckles said and rode east, mounted on a big gray and leading a rawboned and roman-nosed red roan loaded with goods and gear.

Collins nudged Ulysses after her.  She set a swift pace and soon the fort was behind them.  He could just barely make out Square Butte on the horizon.  They rode silently, the horses blowing occasionally.  He dug a piece of jerky from his coat pocket and chewed on it, wishing he had taken time for one last cup of coffee.  After a while, the eastern horizon began to lighten and the dawn came into a clear sky.

The sun was barely above the skyline when they came to the Missouri River near its confluence with the Sun River.  It being late in the year, the waters were low, but Collins did not relish the idea of fording the stream, thick with slushy ice. Arbuckles rode south along the river's banks with purpose and they eventually arrived at a wide and shallow stretch, easily accessible on both sides. She led them into the river without pause and without acknowledgement of his continued presence behind her. Ulysses balked a moment, but Collins kicked him hard in the sides and the gelding gingerly stepped into the icy water. Molly followed readily and they had no difficulty with the crossing, as the bottom was firm and mostly even. Arbuckles did not look behind to note their progress, riding east past clumps of willow and breaking out into an open plain of dried grasses and patches of snow. Collins and his animals followed quietly, uneasily making their progress deeper into unfamiliar territory.

When the sun was in mid sky, they came to a small creek. Arbuckles pulled up her horses and dismounted.

"We will stop. Let the horses blow." She loosened the cinches and walked away, disappearing into some brush.

Collins eased the cinches on Ulysses and Molly, scratching them both behind the ears and humming an old Irish ditty. He enjoyed the tangy scent of the wintry copse, warmed by the hesitant sun. He waited for his guide to return, then stepped off into an alder thicket in order to relieve himself and afterward made his way to the edge of the stream to belly down and have a long, cold drink. When he stood, she had all four animals on the creek bank and was letting them water. He came over, nodded thanks and took the reins of his animals, leading them to a lone dead tree and tying them. Digging into his saddlebags, he pulled out hard tack. He held the food up for Arbuckles to see.

"Hungry?"

She walked over and he handed her a good portion. They sat a small distance apart on fallen cottonwood limbs and ate in silence. The woman pocketed a leftover ration of food in her large overcoat and pulled out a briarwood pipe, filling the bowl with a fragrant mixture. Digging into another pocket, she pulled out a steel and flint, striking it onto a cotton twist and using it to light the pipe. C.W. watched her wave some of the smoke back into her face with interest, wondering at her history and doubting she would ever share it with him. He procured his own pipe, packed it and lit it with a match.

"You ruined it, you know," she said, after a long while.

"Ruined what?" he asked, surprised that she had addressed him.

"The hide. You ruined the head and you made a bad job of skinning it out."

"As for shooting the bear in the head, I had small choice. And for the rest, I am no trapper."

The Indian woman puffed on her pipe. "What *are* you then, Wolf?" she asked.

"A tracker." He used a small stick to tamp his pipe.

"A tracker...You are tracking Indians."

"No. I am tracking white men."

"Deserters?"

"Perhaps. We will know when we find them."

"Yet you seek *Tatanka Iyotaka* and his Hunkpapa."

Collins sighed and rubbed the stubble on his chin. "I seek white men who are said to be loyal to Sitting Bull."

Arbuckles frowned. "How do you know of these men?"

"Do *you* know of these men?"

The woman knocked out the contents of her pipe onto her palm. She scraped a shallow indent in the half frozen dirt and buried the spent tobacco. "I know of these men," she said quietly.

Collins stood and banged out his own pipe against the trunk of a nearby tree. "Can you tell me of these men?" he asked. "Will you?"

"I have seen them."

"And?"

"There is nothing more to tell," she said, getting to her feet. "I have never spoken to them. They have always been with the Hunkpapa."

"Always?"

She nodded and walked to her horses. She tightened the cinches, swung onto the gray gelding and forded the small stream. Collins shrugged, checked his saddles and mounted Ulysses. Reaching for Molly's lead, he crossed the creek and followed the taciturn Indian woman across the open country, patched in giddy shadows created by fast moving clouds gathering overhead. He softly sang one of his favorite Irish ballads, *The Minstrel Boy*, seeking to recall all the verses, while his horse shifted his ears back as if pleased by the tune.

UNFAMILIAR TRAILS

# 29

It was nearing dark when Arbuckles pulled up in a small grove of young cottonwoods along a nondescript creek. There was sign of others who had recently camped in the same location and Collins looked questioningly at his guide. She dismounted and poked around the fresh fire ring and shrugged.

"Couple days," she said. "White men...no worry for you."

He stepped off Ulysses and began unsaddling and unpacking before they lost all light. Collins was baffled by Arbuckles' intermittent descent into pidgin English, when it had been made clear to him she was well spoken and rather literate. As he worked, he watched her sort her tack and gear and was surprised to note that the gun she carried appeared to be an old Hawken plains rifle, ornately decorated with brass tacks on the stock. Perhaps she really had been a squaw of the famous mountain man, Jim Beckwourth, after all. He had heard that the Hawken had been the gun of choice for many a trapper back in the days of the fur trade.

The sky remained full of swiftly scuttling clouds, riding invisible currents above their heads, but there was still no sign of a storm. C.W. scouted the area while searching for firewood. Beyond their little coppice along the stream, there was unbroken prairie with only a faint line of distant blue mountains on the horizon. The sun had already set. He came back with an armload of branches to find the woman vigorously grinding coffee that she must have procured from his supplies. A fire was already burning in the ring of stones left by their predecessors in this remote site.

"You found the coffee," he said, piling the wood near the fire.

Typically unresponsive, she set aside the grinder and taking the coffeepot to the stream to fill it, she returned to set it on the fire and pour in the grounds. C.W. went to his packs and saw that all was in order in spite of her helping herself to the coffee. He pulled out cans of beans, a tin of beef and a loaf of bread he had carefully wrapped in an extra shirt. At the fire, Arbuckles was setting a flat rock on the edge of the new coals. She looked at the tin of beef and shook her head.

"Not soldier beef," she said. "Not yet."

From a pile of newspaper beside her, she pulled out two generous steaks of dripping red meat. She laid them tenderly onto the flat rock.

"Perhaps you can take another bear hide," she said, noticing he was looking at the bloody paper. The thought had indeed crossed his mind that the scent of blood might be attractive to unwanted guests.

"You may have that privilege," he told her, smiling.

"Perhaps not right now," she said and threw the paper into the fire.

Collins checked the coffee and saw it was boiling. He used a bit of cold water to settle the grounds and poured a cup for each of them, while Arbuckles tended the steaks and sliced bread to toast near the fire. She had obviously dispensed with the beans and "soldier beef." Taking a seat on the pile of wood, he sipped his coffee.

"I do not believe that 'Arbuckles' is the name you prefer," he said, making conversation.

"Wakalyapi."

"What?"

"Wakalyapi.  That is what you may call me if you do not care for 'Arbuckles.'"

He shook his head.  "It is not that I do not care for 'Arbuckles.' It is just that I assumed it was a name given you out of disrespect."

She poked at the steaks with her skinning knife, pulled from an ornately beaded scabbard worn on her belt.  "It is of no consequence.  You may call me Wakalyapi."

Collins had the vague sense that she was again toying with him, but as he had no basis for his suspicions, he nodded.  "Wakalyapi," he said and got up to find a couple of plates.

The venison steaks were very good and not overcooked.  He ate heartily, suddenly realizing how hungry he really was.  Wakalyapi ate slowly, as if reverentially concentrating on every bite.  Actually, thought Collins, she seemed to perform every task with intent.  It seemed to him to be a profitable manner with which to address the duties of life.  They finished their meal and C.W. took the dishes to the stream to wash up.  On his way back, he stopped to peruse the skyline.  The Milky Way was opaque in the clear night, surrounded by millions of stars.  As always, this evidence of the immensity of the universe and his own diminutive place in its vastness significantly humbled him.  Back at camp, he saw that his companion had disappeared.

After repacking the plates and grinding more coffee in anticipation of an early and abrupt morning departure, he went to see his animals.  Molly placed her head against his chest and held it there for a time.  Since the incident of the bear, she was no longer aloof and often made a show of affection toward him.  Ulysses snuffed his hair and Collins scratched his jaw and neck.  He stayed with them for quite a while, enjoying their company and familiarity.  There was no use in denying that he did not completely trust his guide nor where her loyalties lay. He had ever disliked not having command over his destiny.

All at once, Ulysses balked and snorted and the woman materialized out of some brush nearby.

"I smelled smoke," she told him. "I went to see."

She walked back to camp. Collins followed.

"What did you find?" he asked, sitting by the fire and adding a piece of wood.

Wakalyapi was digging in her outfit. After a bit, she came to the fire with a whetstone and sat down to sharpen her knife.

"Blackfeet, I believe. We will swing south a bit."

He got out his pipe and tobacco and began to smoke. When she was done putting an edge on her blade and had replaced it in its sheath, she put out her hand.

"Give me your knife."

Collins pulled the old Green River from its makeshift scabbard on his belt and gave it to her. She examined it carefully.

"Where did you get this?" she asked.

"I found it."

"It is very old. It is an old style."

"Yes."

She studied him a moment. "You do not trust me," she said.

"No."

She looked at him for a moment longer, then nodded. "It is best...For now, it is for the best," she said and began sharpening his knife.

# 30

Collins and Wakalyapi lay on their bellies in the tall grass and watched as the small band of Indian hunters finished gutting and quartering an antelope and loading it on their horses. The warriors spoke animatedly, subduing their spirited horses and perusing their surroundings at all times. One older man seemed to be sniffing the air in an interested manner. They squatted and ate what appeared to Collins to be the liver and some other organs, then springing onto their mounts, they galloped to the east at top speed, disappearing from sight.

"Cheyenne, not Blackfeet," was all his guide had to say as they made their way back to the coulee where they had hidden their horses. Collins was not reassured.

"Why did you think they were Blackfoot?" he asked quietly as they checked their packs.

"Smell," she said, retreating into her pidgin English. "Blackfeet smell strong."

After two days with her, Collins was convinced she was duplicitous as a matter of course. "Are not the Cheyenne allies to the Sioux?" he asked, as he swung onto Ulysses. "Why hide?"

"Not safe. Not safe for you," she told him from the back of her gray. She headed in a southerly direction from where the Cheyenne had disappeared.

Collins nudged Ulysses to ride parallel with her. He was becoming irritated by her vacillation between illiterate Indian scout to well-spoken companion and guide.

"I do not believe you," he said. "I do not believe you smelled them. I believe this is the southern-most territory of the Blackfoot and it is not common for Cheyenne to be here. That is what I believe," he told her defiantly.

Wakalyapi rubbed her damaged mouth and Collins swore to himself that she was hiding a smile. She said nothing. Thoroughly annoyed, he held up his animals to return to their customary position of following the woman's lead. They were undoubtedly penetrating more deeply into territory where he would have to rely on his guide's experience and knowledge, but her frequent dissimulation did not lend itself to confidence.

They rode through a fierce and bitter wind that beat against their backs from the northwest. There were modest mountain ranges to the north and south and they were passing through what appeared to be a fertile basin of thick grasses and timbered springs. Collins felt certain that the region would someday be thickly peopled with white settlers, seeking more and more land to feed their insatiable appetite for expansion and progress. He watched the erect and proud carriage of the woman riding in front of him and she seemed of a sudden to represent all the Indians of future decades, forever spread-eagled across the chasm of white avarice and ancient cultures. As an Irishman, he was familiar with the angst and displacement that straddling such a schism could generate. He suddenly realized that he probably understood her better than he had thought. No doubt, her mistrust of him and his motives was the source of her subterfuge.

In early afternoon, after many hours of traveling without incident, they came to the bank of a fairly substantial creek. Wakalyapi pulled up and dismounted. She tied her horses to a nearby willow branch and lay on her stomach to drink. Collins followed suit, tying Ulysses and wrapping Molly's lead on the saddle horn, trusting she would not bolt.  After drinking, he stood and stretched, walking up and down and swinging his arms in an attempt to limber his stiff and cold legs and arms. His hands ached from holding the reins and Molly's lead. He wore leather gauntlets, but they were not adequate to the purpose.

"This is your stream," the woman said cryptically.

Having not conversed for most of the day, he was slow to respond.

"What?  It is my what?"

"This stream." She waved her hand in a broad gesture. "It is named *Wakpa Sunkmanitutanka* ...Wolf Creek."

He smiled and shook his head.  "It cannot be mine, if I have never seen it before."

Her eyes twinkled. "Perhaps," she said. "Or perhaps your reputation is so strong it has traveled to this place."

"Perhaps," he said.

The sun was sinking and C.W. wondered whether she intended to camp.  He was grateful to be on the ground and out of the wind, even for a brief recess, and waited for Wakalyapi to inform him of her plans.  Digging into his saddlebags, he pulled out some jerky, left over from a copious supply purchased back at Fort Ellis, and handed her a piece.  They stood silently, chewing the tough meat.

"There is a better place ahead for camping," she said, after she had fastidiously eaten all her portion. "There is a spring and thick brush for cover.  You believe this is the southern-most territory of the Blackfeet and you are correct.  But it is also true that many Lakota and Cheyenne peoples are on the move due to the great retribution sought by the U.S. government after last summer on the Little Horn.  If you are to live long enough to pay me my wages, I must keep you alive.  Therefore, I think it would be best not to camp in this open place."

Temporarily nonplussed by this sudden burst of loquaciousness, he nodded and turned to tighten his cinches and mount up.  By the time he had settled into the saddle and lined out his animals, Wakalyapi had already forded the *Sunkmanitutanka Wakpa* and was riding into the gathering dusk.

# 31

Having built a fire while there remained adequate light to see, they relied on its illumination to unsaddle and unpack their animals, find a couple of cans of beans and the coffeepot and unroll their bedding.  Collins had taken to using the now half-cured bearskin for a back-rest at the fire.  He opened the cans and set them near the fire to heat while Wakalyapi ground coffee and put the pot on.

"You like coffee," he said, weary of the silence that lay between them most of the time.

"It is why the soldier boys named me 'Arbuckles'"

"That is what I had assumed."

Her scar twitched.  "You are not as they are," she said.

"Probably not," he answered, turning the cans with a stick.

"Who was this man you are named for?  This Wolf?"

"Theobald Wolfe Tone.  He was an Irish rebel in the late 1700's.  He had some fine ideas about breaking the oppression of England, but they came to naught. In the end, he cut his own throat."

"Why?"

"So the English could not hang him. 'He perished in a prison alone. His friends unavenged and his country unfreed, '" he said, quoting an old ballad.

"The Irish. They are persecuted by the English."

"Yes.  In a situation very similar to that of the Indian."

"Then why do Irish *wasichu* come as soldier boys to persecute the Indian peoples?"

"Good question."

"You are Irish?" she asked.

"Yes.  I was born in Ireland."

"Why did you leave?"

"It was very bad.  People were starving and my father had died.  My mother and I had no choice."

There was a pause as Wakalyapi took the boiling coffeepot from the fire and poured two cups.  She handed one to Collins.

"When the *blo*...the potato...turned black."

He looked at her curiously.  "Yes.  But how did you know?"

"Irish soldier boys.  I have known many.  Not all of them were bad in their hearts toward Indian peoples."

C.W. used his coat sleeve to pull out a can of beans and set it before Wakalyapi and handed her a fork.  He took the other one out for himself.  They ate in silence and he admitted to himself that this Indian woman held his interest more than any person had in a very long while.

"You read Sir Walter Scott?" he asked, after they had finished eating.

"Yes.  He was English?"

"Yes.  But he was not an enemy of the Irish.  How are you familiar with him?"

"There was a French priest many years ago," she said. "He taught me about reading.  He gave me the book.  The story takes place in France."

"You read and write English?" Collins asked.

"Yes.  And some French."

"Extraordinary."

"Maybe not so much."

He met her steady and slightly challenging gaze. "Maybe not," he said, somewhat chastened.

They each took out their pipes and Wakalyapi offered him her pouch. He accepted it and sniffed the tobacco mixture within. It was pungent with herbs. He stuffed his pipe and handed it back, offering his pouch to her at the same time. She shook her head and filled her pipe from her own pouch. He retrieved a burning stick from the fire and held it out so she could light her pipe from it, then followed suit. They smoked quietly. Collins thought the silence between them might have taken an altered form. He was not certain he cared for the woman's tobacco, but it emitted a pleasant odor and was mild on the tongue. She seemed to be watching him, so he made no comment and gave no sign he was other than pleased.

When they had knocked out their pipes and banked the fire, Collins walked out of their sheltered bower to relieve himself and admire the brilliant night. Once again, they had been spared a stormy day, in spite of the incessant wind. He went over to greet his animals, scratching the woman's old roan as well. Her gray was not amenable to his company and moved away. Molly stuck her nose under his hat and shoved her upper lip around until she had tipped it off. He smiled and bent to pick it up. When he stood, Wakalyapi was nearby, picketing her horses for the night. Not all the hackneyed notions about Indians were wrong, he thought. She could move with great stealth. He suspected she was keeping a watchful eye on him.

Settling himself into his bedding and arranging his saddle and the bear pelt for a backrest, he pulled out his Shakespeare. Opening to the final scenes of *Henry V*, he began reading by firelight.

"That is an Englishman," Wakalyapi observed from her bedroll across the fire.

"Yes."

"You take him everywhere?"

"Yes."

"Perhaps I can look at him sometime?"

"Most certainly.  Have you read him?" he asked.

"Only a little.  He is…difficult."  She seemed to dislike the admission.

"He is very difficult," agreed Collins.  "The language is old."

"Why do you favor him?" she asked, snuggling more deeply into her covers.

"Shakespeare shows me that people have ever been the same.  That human experience never changes."

"It is changing very much for the Indian people," she observed.

"Yes.  No doubt about that," he answered.  "But we still fight battles, fall in love.  We grieve.  We fear death."

There was a pause as Wakalyapi seemed to ponder his statement.  "Perhaps," she said after a bit.  "Or perhaps you will find on this journey that what the Indians now endure is very much worse.  Very much worse than anything Shakespeare could have imagined.  Gold has been found in the *Paha Sapa*, the Black Hills, and all is lost for the Lakota peoples."

Her occasional eloquence never ceased to disconcert him any more than did her sporadic bouts of pidgin English.

"I sincerely hope you are wrong," he said.

"Do you believe I am?"

"No."

"Does your Shakespeare make reference to the Black Hills?" she asked almost angrily.

"No, but he has much to say about gold.  '…Yellow, glittering, precious gold…This yellow slave will knit and break religions…place thieves and give them title…'"

She grunted.  "I am certain there are many Englishmen upon the Thieves Road into the *Paha Sapa*.  And many Irishmen with them."  With that she rolled away from him and was silent.

Collins returned to reading his Shakespeare, saddened by the woman's indignation. He was mystified that she had attached herself to a soldiers' fort when her allegiance seemed patently to remain with the Indians. Perhaps, he thought, between the Crow, Beckwourth, the French priest, brutal experience and reading great literature, she had found no belonging. Perhaps that was one deficiency they shared. Realizing the words before him had momentarily lost their allure, he laid aside the volume and settled down to watch the fire. The wind made a lonely soughing through the surrounding brush, filling him with melancholy until sleep overtook him.

GO AWAY !

# 32

In compliance with Wakalyapi's abrupt dictate, Collins held all four animals within a dense thicket. He watched as she moved silently through weather beaten grasses toward a small band of mule deer, grazing cautiously in the early morning light. She carried a simple bow strung with sinew and a blue beaded quiver slung across her back, stalking down wind. Occasionally, one of the deer would lift its head and she froze as still as an inanimate object. At last, she must have deemed the distance acceptable and standing, pulled an arrow fluidly from her quiver and fired. She hit a large doe as if exerting little or no effort. The animal ran a few paces and dropped.

Responding to her beckoning gesture, Collins led the horses out of cover and made his way to where she was gutting the doe. Ulysses snorted at the blood smell and he spoke to him reassuringly. Wakalyapi deftly decapitated and quartered the deer, split the load between Molly and her old roan, and secured the quarters with cord retrieved from her packs. Collins spent his energies on keeping his horse calm. She handed him a chunk of liver with bloody hands and he accepted it, knowing he had little choice. He chewed the warm flesh, mildly surprised it did not trigger his gag reflex. She watched him as she studiously devoured the rest of the organ.

"Good for your blood," she told him, smiling suddenly, her mouth full of raw liver.

"Nice shot," he told her.

She shrugged. "It is of no consequence."

The woman licked her fingers, secured her bow and quiver behind her saddle and mounted. Collins swung onto Ulysses, who remained jittery around the gut pile and bloody grass. They rode east, the morning light growing stronger and the ever-present wind increasing in intensity. They traveled for several hours until they came upon a well-established trail that cut in a south-easterly direction. Wakalyapi turned to follow it and C. W. rode up beside her.

"What is this?" he asked.

"Carroll Trail."

"To Helena?"

"Yes. From the Missouri River. We will go see Reed. Get news."

He sighed audibly at her foolish manner of speech. "Who is Reed?"

"Alonzo. Trading post. Not far."

Collins refused to ask any more questions as long as she was in the mood to trifle with him. He resented the degree to which she could annoy him. Mostly, he was rather difficult to vex. They rode for a mile or so until they came in sight of a cluster of modest build-ings among some small trees. She led them to the larg-est cabin and dismounted, securing her horses to a rail and loosening her cinches. Collins alighted and saw to Ulysses and Molly, tying them nearby. He wordlessly joined Wakalyapi on the porch and followed her into the cabin.

When his eyes had adjusted to the interior dimness of the building, Collins noted a powerfully built man sitting in a chair beside a pot-bellied stove. The chair was kicked back against a wall and the man was dozing soundly, a fat ginger cat curled in his lap. Wakalya-pi coughed politely and the man opened his eyes and looked at her.

"*Hokahe* Arbuckles," he said as if he had been expecting her.

"*Hoakicipapi* Major Reed."

He looked at C.W. "Who is this?"

"Charles Wolfe Collins," she answered.

Collins glanced over at her, disarmed by her ready response.

"Hello Mr. Collins," the man said and stood to stretch and yawn. The cat slid to the floor and stretched as well. "Glad you folks came along. I was near bored to death."

Reed walked over to a cupboard and pulled out three cups. "Coffee?" he asked.

They both nodded and went over to a table by a small window to sit. Reed set the cups before them and brought the pot from the stove. He poured the coffee, put the pot back on the stove and sat at the table with them.

"Thank you," Collins said, removing his Stetson and setting it on a vacant chair.

"Mind if I ask where you folks are headed?" he asked. The woman shook her head.

"We are traveling to Bismarck," Collins interjected.

"On horseback? With winter coming on?"

Wakalyapi studied Collins then said, "This man is foolish. He wanted to see the country."

Reed looked from one to the other. "I see I should not have asked. It makes no matter." He got up to refill their cups.

Collins looked at the woman. She shrugged. "I want to ask him some questions," she said.

He rubbed his wind burnt cheek and thought about it. Reed sat down again. Collins made up his mind and gave a nod to Wakalyapi.

"We are headed to the Tongue," she said. "There is a new fort there. *Tatanka Iyotaka* is supposed to be somewhere about, causing mischief."

" Miles is there with the 5th and the 22nd.  I do not know about Sitting Bull."

C.W. drank his coffee and said nothing.

"What is the word about bands of Lakota or Cheyenne near here?" Wakalyapi asked.

"None near here," Reed told her.  "Many groups are scattered all over hell and gone since the Little Big Horn, but mostly they are northeast or southeast of here. American Horse caught it near Slim Buttes.  I heard it was bad."

"Yes," the woman said.  "Three Stars Crook murdered him in a cave.  Many women and children were ambushed as well."

Reed shook his head.  "I liked the Horse.  It was a shame.  I was told that Crook has made the claim that white men would never make war on children and women and yet there were many dead and dying in the muddy ground."

"This winter will be hard.  The *wasicun* are out for blood because of the great victory on the Greasy Grass"

Entirely out of his depth, Collins listened to the exchange with interest.

Reed looked at him. "Whose side are you on?" he asked abruptly.

"No side," he answered honestly.  "My private sympathies tend to be with the Indians, however."

"Private sympathies?  What else is there?" Reed observed suspiciously.

Collins made no answer.

"He has given his word he is not working against the people," the woman told Reed.  "I believe him.  That is why I am scouting for him."

"Glad to see you have left the army, Arbuckles."

"Maybe," she said.

"You will stay here tonight," Reed told them both.

"Thank you," Collins said gratefully.  "What do you

think, Wakalyapi?  I could use a night indoors."

Reed looked at him with humor. "Wakalyapi?  That is a good joke. You must speak Sioux."

Collins glanced at the woman.  Once again, she hid her scarred mouth behind a hand and he knew beyond a doubt she had played him.

"What does 'Wakalyapi' mean?" he asked Reed blandly.

"A hot drink...but mostly it is used for coffee. You did not know?"

Collins nodded at his companion.  "What do you think?" he asked.

Reed smiled.  "It is nothing.  It is the Indian way to befuddle.  They come at everything askew."

Collins looked at her.  She returned his gaze soberly, but a trace of mirth remained about her eyes.

"Until you are ready to tell me your name, I will call you Wakalyapi."

She nodded.  "We must see to the horses," she said and got to her feet.

"And you may call me Charles," he added.  "No more 'Wolf'."

She nodded again.  "Okay Charles," she said and went out the door into the gathering night.

Collins looked at Reed.  "Where may we put our animals?"

"Arbuckles will show you."  Reed paused, then said, "Just so you know, I have known her for several years and cannot claim familiarity with her real name."

"It is not important.  If she does not trust me with it, it is for good reason."

"I will get supper," Reed said and went into the back of the cabin.

C.W. stepped outside and found Wakalyapi unloading the animals by a lean-to and a buck and rail corral on the lee side of the barn.  He pitched in to give her a hand without speaking. They piled their belongings in the lee-ward side of the shed and, after securing their bedrolls and personal items, covered the gear with a large buffalo hide the woman carried on her packhorse. The wind was coming up and a bitter chill was creeping into the air. They rubbed down the horses and led them into the corral, Collins filling a makeshift feed bunk with hay from a nearby stack yard.

Standing in the darkening gloom, Wakalyapi sniffed the air. "There is a bad storm coming," she said.

"Blizzard?"

"Yes. I think so."

"Then I am glad we have shelter," C.W. told her.

There was a momentary silence between them. A gust of wind slammed into their faces, whipping them with bits of loose hay. Collins sighed at the thought of more winter weather and hard traveling and picked up his carpetbag and bedroll to go into the cabin.

"Charles," she said in the darkness.

"Yes?" he asked, pausing.

"You can trust Reed. He may have more information."

"Okay," he said, then asked, "Is he a major with the U.S. Army? I heard you call him 'Major.'"

"They call him 'major.' I call him 'major.' I do not know if he is a major."

"Oh," Collins said and stepped onto the porch.

Inside the cabin, the welcoming aroma of food en-veloped him. The door opened and the woman came in with her gear. They placed their belongings in a corner and sat at the table. Reed poked his head out.

"It is almost ready. Help yourself to more coffee," he told them.

C.W. got up, took their cups over to the stove and filled them. He handed Wakalyapi her cup and sat down again. She gave him a singular look.

"What?" he asked, a bit irritably.

"It is of no consequence."

Collins drank his coffee and slumped back in his chair.  He felt enervated.  He was grateful for the stout log walls around them as he heard the wind whirl past the building and shake the windows.

"Thank you," the woman said.

"For what?" he asked.

"The coffee."

"You are welcome."

Reed came into the room bearing plates piled with steaming meat in gravy, boiled potatoes and biscuits. He set a plate in front of each of them and went back to fetch his own.  When Reed sat down, they began to eat and Collins could not remember a meal that tasted quite as good as the one before him.  Not even those eaten at Chicago Joe's, although the evening's entertainment was sure to be remarkably pale in comparison.

"What is this meat?" he asked, when he had consumed a goodly portion of his food.

"Bear," Reed told him.

"Grizzly?" Wakalyapi asked, looking at Collins. Her scar twitched.

"No, just an old black sow I shot when she refused to leave my grain bins alone."

"It is excellent," Collins said, ignoring the woman.

"The trick is to boil it for a long time.  Damn meat is tough and can kill you if you fail to cook it long enough. Tastes like pork."

"Charles shot a grizzly," Wakalyapi told Reed.  "He made a bad job of skinning it, but the pelt is of a color I have not seen for many years."

"Is that so?"

Collins told him the story, well rehearsed from all the previous recounting.

"I will have to go out and see this mule in the morning," Reed said.  "Care to trade the pelt?"

"I thought I might save it to trade later."

"What exactly are you planning to do?  Or is it callow to inquire?"

Collins looked over at Wakalyapi.  She gazed back at him steadily.  He shrugged and said, "I need to find Sitting Bull's band.  I cannot disclose more than that."

"Well, then you had better keep the bear hide, for it may be useful to you in convincing them not to kill you.  I would strongly advise a change of plans as you are unquestionably bent on destruction," Reed told him.

C.W. finished his meal and leaned back in his chair.  "I must do this.  That is all."

The large man studied him.  "Then I suggest you take a supply of tobacco, coffee, and sugar as gifts.  The Hunkpapa are very courtly in their manners and will probably not kill you outright if you bring such offerings."

The woman coughed.  "Do not listen to this *wakanka*."

Reed grinned and stood to begin clearing the plates.  "Still, the gifts would be prudent."

"Yes," Wakalyapi said.  "The gifts would be prudent."

When the table had been cleared and more coffee had been poured all around, they each took out their pipes and smoked the tobacco supplied by Reed.

"Where is Bowles?" the woman asked after a bit.

"Bowles has gone to St. Louis.  He plans to purchase an inventory of farming implements and we are not in accord regarding this venture."

"This is your partner?"  Collins asked.

"Yes.  For now."

"Charles has Shakespeare," Wakalyapi said, changing the topic of conversation.

"Really?  Will you read for us?" the trader asked.

"If you would like." Collins laid aside his spent pipe and went over to his saddlebags.  He pulled out the volume. "What shall it be?" he asked.

"Your choice," Reed told him.

Collins opened the text to the "Crispin Crispinian" speech from *King Henry V.* He began to read with vitality. The irony of the chosen passage struck him as he read. It seemed, of a sudden, to be quite germane to the current experiences of the Sioux.

> *If we are mark'd to die, we are enow*
> *To do our country loss; and if to live,*
> *The fewer men, the greater share of honor.*
> *God's will!  I pray thee, wish not one man more.*
> *By Jove, I am not covetous for gold,*
> *Nor care I who doth feed upon my cost;*
> *It yearns me not if men my garments wear;*
> *Such outward things dwell not in my desires.*
> *But if it be a sin to covet honour,*
> *I am the most offending soul alive.*

When he had finished the speech, his audience applauded enthusiastically.

"You are a thespian, sir," Reed told him as he regained his seat.

"Explain this man who is talking," the woman said.

"Saint Crispian and his brother were…shoemakers actually.  They were killed for their faith many hundreds of years ago.  Later, they were made saints."

"Were they warriors?"

"No."

"Then why did this king call on them before battle?"

"He did not.  Every day has a saint…a holy person… and the day of the battle, October 25, was their day.  The English had a great victory over the French on that day, despite terrible odds."

"It is a good speech," she said.  "I would fight after that speech."

"So would I," Collins said, smiling, and reached to refill his pipe.

"It is almost Saint Crispian's day," she remarked.

"It is," Collins said.

The blizzard began to cuff the sides of the building with great gusts of wind and pelt the windows with icy pebbles of snow. They sat in silence and listened, each wrapped in private thoughts.

TRADING POST

# 33

Collins sat up in his bedroll near the stove, disturbing the ginger cat that had been snuggled in beside him. Faint early morning light filled the room and there was a persistent banging on the door. He heard Reed shuffling around and mumbling in the back of the cabin and then the big man emerged, half dressed, to answer the incessant pounding. Wakalyapi lay burrowed deep in her robes, her eyes alert. A blast of cold penetrated the room as the door opened. Collins could see a small group of indistinct figures on the porch, their breath making white clouds in the frigid air. There was a brief conversation in French before Reed stood back to allow the visitors to enter.

There were four of them, and from what Collins could discern beneath their cocoons of blankets, three adults and one child. He could hear that the blizzard still raged without and this explained the coating of white upon them that was swiftly turning to damp as Reed stirred up the fire. They pulled chairs near the stove and began to unwrap their garments, laying them carefully aside in a pile. Collins rubbed his hair and face to get the blood flowing, stretched and extracted himself from his pile of blankets. As he put on his boots, he was heartened to see that Reed was preparing coffee.

Sitting at the table, C.W. smiled at the newcomers, now having revealed themselves to be a man, two women and a little girl of about six years. They were attractive

people, displaying a distinct combination of strong Indian features and European traits. Wakalyapi joined him
at the table, having moved as silently as was her wont.

"*Slotas*," she said under her breath, fairly spitting out
the word.

The group was now engaged in speaking quietly
among themselves, again in French, with which Collins
had some familiarity. They seemed to him to be discuss-
ing the storm.

"Who?" he asked.

"*Slotas*.    Half-breeds...mostly from Grandmother
Country.  They take game that belongs to Lakota and
Blackfeet peoples. They sell whiskey.  Hunt for gold."

"What are they doing here?"

"Reed knows some of them.  He trades with them.  He
trades with everyone."

Despite their overtly friendly relations, Collins now
observed, his companion was not completely in accord
with the trader

"You do not admire them," he said.

"They have no tribe.  They are between Indian and
white.  They scout and translate for the soldiers against
the people.  They are *oi´lelepi*, good-for-nothings."

"Do not the Lakota trade with them also?" he asked.

"Yes, trade.  When they have to.  When there is no
other choice."

Reed set the coffeepot on the stove and came over to
sit with them.  "They were caught in the storm.  They
are Red River Métis on their way to Frank Chamberlain's
place on McDonald Creek.  The man is Gilbert Salois
and his wives are Genevieve and Marie.  The little girl is
named Belle."

Collins nodded at the family and glanced at Wakalyapi. She was patently ignoring everyone in the room, looking out the window.

"We must go out to see to the livestock," she said as if

aware he was watching her.

They both stood to don coats, gloves, and Wakalyapi produced a beaver fur hat from her pile of belongings. It was cleverly made with blue and red beading along the bottom and strings to tie under her chin.

"Did you make that?" he asked curiously.

"Crow," she said and pushed past the Salois family as if they were so much furniture.

Collins followed, pulling his Stetson firmly down onto his head, and they went out the door together. The wind driven snow hit them as they stepped off the porch. They bent against it to make their way to the dark shape of the barn. Their horses were huddled in the lean-to, nickering at their approach. Collins filled their hay bunk while the woman used a small post to pound at the ice in their trough. Then he went into the neighboring pens to fill the bunks of Reed's horses. When this was done, they stood companionably with their animals for a bit. The horses and mule dug their eager noses into the sweet smelling hay. Ice coated their backs, melting in small rivulets down their sides and their manes and tails were so many strands of icicles. Molly paused a moment to place her nose under C.W.'s arm. He rubbed her off side eye gently with a cupped hand.

"This is an Army mule," Wakalyapi said, looking at the U.S. brand on her haunch.

"Yes."

"Where did you get her?"

"The Cantonment on the Tongue River."

She walked away and came back shortly with a bucket of oats. She poured it out onto the hay. "You have already been there," she said quietly.

"A while back. On my way from Fort Buford to Helena."

She looked at him with mistrust. "I thought you were not working with the army."

Ulysses put his ears back and bit at the roan. Collins

gave him a light tap and he went back to eating.

"I am not."

She studied him closely, in her grave and thorough way. "Will you tell me why you were there?"

He leaned against an interior wall of the shed, out of the wind. "I was on my way to the battlefield."

"You went to the Little Horn?"

"Yes."

"Why?"

"To find my friend. To bury him."

"You had a friend who died at the Greasy Grass?"

Collins nodded.

"Are you then angry with the Lakota?"

"No."

"Why not?"

He watched as the horses rearranged their order at the feed bunk, turning their buttocks toward each other in mock aggression and nipping at each other. They settled back down and began again to eat.

"The Indians were only protecting what belonged to them."

"Why was your friend there?"

"He was a soldier. He went where he was ordered."

"Was he bad in his heart toward the Lakota and Cheyenne peoples?"

Collins smiled. "I do not think so. He had no reason to be."

"Then why fight?" she asked. "I have never understood why these soldiers fight if they are not angry with the people."

"It is difficult to explain. I, too, do not fully understand it."

She looked at him closely again. "Do you fight when you are told to?" she asked. "Even if you are not angry with the...foe?"

Collins suspected she had found the word "foe" in

reading Sir Walter Scott. "I did once. I will not ever again," he told her truthfully.

"Yet you are tracking these white men. These men who are with *Tatanka Iyotaka.*"

"Yes."

"So now we go back to the Tongue to find them."

"Yes."

She shrugged and turned away as if no longer interested in the conversation. "I want coffee," was all she said.

Outside the corral, she cleared the snow and dug in the packs piled alongside the lean-to. She pulled out three frozen quarters of venison and replaced the buffalo hide covering their belongings.

"We will trade these to Reed," she said, handing him two of the quarters. "We can get sugar, coffee and tobacco for trading."

"I have money. You do not need to give up this meat."

"It is of no consequence," she said and headed for the cabin through the swiftly accumulating snow.

Collins watched the woman for a moment and wondered what the days ahead held for both of them. Then he became aware of the chill creeping to his core and, hefting the bulky hindquarters of meat, braced the wind to follow after her.

The next morning, no longer willing to wait for conditions to improve, Collins and Wakalyapi waded through deep snow to dig their belongings out of a drift and begin catching and saddling their animals. Collins made a couple of trips back to the cabin in order to bring the supplies. He felt badly about adding to the weight the animals carried, given the arduous traveling ahead, but Reed and the woman had insisted they bring gifts for the Hunkpapa and he felt obliged to heed their advice. When all was packed and secured, they led their horses to the cabin. Reed was waiting for them on the porch. His guests, the Salois family, did not come out. Wakalyapi had made it manifestly apparent that she was hostile toward them and they chose to stay away.

"Still think you should wait a couple of days," Reed said. "The blizzard may have stopped, but the temperatures are killing cold."

"We have tarried over long already," Collins said. "I must proceed on my journey. I have told Wakalyapi she does not have to continue and I will pay her for her time."

The woman looked at him without expression. "It is not possible. I have given my word."

"Very well. I hope to see you both another time," Reed told them. "It has been a genuine pleasure."

"I agree," Collins said, stepping up to shake Reed's hand.

"*Pilamaya,*" the woman said to Reed. "I will come back."

They mounted their horses and turned to the east with the wind at their backs.

# 34

It seemed to Collins that there had always been bitterly cold wind, endless frozen expanses and the rump of a red roan horse before him. Time had lost meaning and his feet and hands no longer belonged to him in any real sense. Hunched within his heavy coat, he rode mile after mile, Ulysses plowing through chest high drifts and stumbling occasionally over obstacles buried beneath the snow. No longer capable of holding Molly's lead rope with his benumbed hand, he had thrown it over her neck and she followed loyally behind, her dark red coat a splash of color against the featureless landscape behind them. Periodic whiteouts enveloped them in clouds of fine icy dust that found its way into his collar and up his sleeves. Then, as before, the roan horse would incarnate in front of him, leading him inexorably onward.

Slowly, infinitesimally, the daylight was fading. C.W. wondered vaguely if they were to ride through the night and, frankly, could not imagine himself capable of dismounting, or even of any type of locomotion, and so considered the outcome to be moot. He had given himself over to the guidance of the fierce woman just ahead in the glacial wastelands. It was now up to her whether he lived or died and, at the moment, he was not overly concerned. Collins was surprised, therefore, when a line of thick trees appeared in front of them and he soon found himself within the dense shelter of a brushy creek bottom. They had made a dangerous and cautious crossing of the Mussellshell River the day before and he had no idea what this small waterway might be.

Wakalyapi slipped from her gray and walked over to stand beside him.

"How is it, Charles?" she asked, looking up at him.

He tried to get his mouth to work in order to make an answer, but his frozen mustache and stiff lips impeded any response. He merely nodded at her. She reached up and helped him unbend his fingers from around the reins, his leather gloves stiff and inflexible. Slowly, he kicked loose of the stirrups and swung his offside leg over the cantle to slide from the saddle, his legs buckling momentarily. By keeping hold of the saddle horn, he was able to remain standing, feeling blood prickling and biting his feet and lower legs. The woman stood ready to lend him aid, but allowed him to figure his own way back to mobility. Ulysses turned his head to nuzzle Collins' chest as if giving encouragement.

Rubbing a glove over his mustache and mouth to free them, Collins asked, "What is this place?"

"*Phah'in Atha'nkaka Wapala*. Big Porcupine Creek."

He hobbled over to Molly to check on her. She stood with her head low with fatigue, blowing clouds of fog from her nostrils. He began to undo her load with stiff and uncooperative fingers. When, at last, he had pulled all the supplies and saddle from her back, he rubbed her vigorously with a blanket and turned to unsaddle his horse, already much warmer from his exertions. Wakalyapi had already unloaded and picketed her horses and was stripping the inner bark from some of the nearby cottonwoods to use as fodder. Collins fetched some oats from their packs and grained all four of the animals while she made small piles of pungent bark before each of them.

As the light was swiftly fading, they gathered dry dead limbs from standing trees to make a fire. While the woman tended to the blaze, Collins went in search of more wood, wending his way through a labyrinth of willow brush and trees. He stumbled over an obstruction hidden in a drift and fell forward. He came to his hands and knees in the snow and found himself looking into a human face, gray and staring. He let out a cry of surprise and jumped to his feet, looking down at the man's body, frozen and grotesque.

"Charles?" Wakalyapi called, coming through the brush.

"Here," he answered, bending to sweep some of the snow off the stiffened form.

She came to stand next to him. "This will be us if we do not get back to the fire," she said pragmatically.

"It is a white man. I see no wound."

"Probably a thief heading for the Thieves Road. It is of no consequence." She turned to walk back to their camp.

The man seemed to be without a coat. He had not been scalped. Collins wondered if he had strayed from his camp and had gotten lost. The woman was right. There was nothing they could do for this wayfarer now and he was deep into Indian country. Probably a prospector coming to take what was not his to take. Probably a man he would not have cared for with the breath of life within him. He turned to retrieve his load of wood and followed Wakalyapi to their sanctuary by the stream.

She was thawing a remaining hunk of venison near the flames when he placed the wood beside their fire. He fetched the coffee makings and soon they were drinking steaming cups of hot coffee and chewing on strips of roasted meat, content to be sheltered and alive.

"We are not far from the Tongue," Wakalyapi said after they had eaten and were smoking their pipes. "We will follow the *Hehaka Wakpa,* or what you call the Yellowstone River."

"We will have to speak to Miles.  Have you spoken with him?"

"No."

"He is very ambitious.  He is dangerous.  I caution you to stay way from him."

She studied him a moment.  "You warn me of enemies. You show *khola´kichiyapi.*"

"What?"

"You show friendship."

Collins puffed on his pipe, felt the truth of her words and looked for an explanation.  "We have endured much together in a very short time," he said.

"Yes."

"Perhaps you should claim a different heritage.  Perhaps you should say you are Crow or Nez Perce.  Feelings will be strong against the Sioux."

She smiled broadly, which was something C.W. had found to be a rare event. "Some of the soldier boys may know me.  It is no matter."

He leaned to place another branch on the fire.  He found himself to be inordinately concerned.  "You will stay with me?  You will not go off alone?"

Her expression became serious.  "No Charles."  She relit her pipe with a stick from the fire.  "What is within you now?"

Collins watched the flames.  "I had a friend many years ago.  A Mescalero Apache.  He was killed by soldiers while on a mission for me.  They saw the Indian and did not heed the man."

"You have been among Indians before."

He nodded.  "Far south.  It was very different than this."

There was a long pause.  The flames cracked and popped as sap oozed from a hunk of wood.  "You will not tell me why you are looking for the *wasichu* that travel with *Tatanka Iyotaka,*" she said.

"I will tell you. You must tell no one," he said, knocking the ashes from his pipe.

She shrugged. "Who would I tell?"

"I am supposed to find out who these men are and where they came from."

"And why they fight as Lakota," she said.

"Yes. Why they fight with the Indians."

"Is this very important?"

"To my boss in Washington it is."

Wakalyapi grunted derisively. "You are paid for this?"

Collins laughed. "I am paid to find the truth of certain matters. That is all."

"Will these men be punished?"

"I do not think so."

"Do you not want to know why I hunt for the soldiers?"

"I already know."

She looked at him closely. "Tell me."

He sighed. "You do not belong. You have been too many places. Lived too many lives."

She thought about this, then said, "Perhaps. Perhaps I am like the *gnu'gnuska,* the grasshopper. A person can own too many names."

"How long before we get to the Tongue?" Collins asked, aware of her discomfort.

"Two or three days at most."

WARRIORS

# 35

Two days later, in a camp on the Yellowstone, they were about to die. Collins bled from a head wound caused by a blow from a stick, decorated with beading and brass tacks. His hat was on the snowy ground beside him and his animals stirred restively behind him, saddled and partially loaded with gear. Their dying fire smoldered in the chilly morning air. Before him, with Hawken in hand, stood Wakalyapi, the woman who had warned him she would not lay down her life to protect his. As wasps stirred from a nest, Sioux warriors swarmed around them, some mounted, some on foot, all seemingly prepared to deliver a killing blow, either by arrow or bullet. He fancied his hair itched.

Wakalyapi was speaking rapidly in what he assumed was the Sioux tongue. She was gesturing animatedly and in his direction. A young man rushed at them on a small brown horse, yelping, and she raised the rifle. He retreated. She spoke again. An older man, with his left arm in a sling, rode a bony paint up to where they stood and began speaking authoritatively. The other warriors pulled back.

"This is White Bull," she said quietly in English without turning around. "He knows me. He is nephew to *Tatanka Iyotaka.*"

She spoke to the man sitting his horse in front of her. He answered her and looked at Collins. She seemed to relax slightly and lowered her Hawken to a resting position, cradled in her arms.  They spoke at length. Then all hell seemed to break loose again as a trumpet sounded and blue-coated soldiers were suddenly mingled with warriors.  A few shots were fired, but White Bull shouted brusquely and the Sioux disappeared upriver into dense trees and brush.  Collins recognized Colonel Miles riding past with a small cadre of mounted men, followed by infantry pursuing on foot through snow, loaded down with gear and ammunition.  No one seemed to take further notice of their presence.

The noise of pursuit faded and the two of them were left standing in their camp of trampled snow and half-packed gear.  Simultaneously galvanized without an exchanged word, they leapt to loading the remaining equipment and goods, mounted their horses and proceeded down river, away from the Indians and Miles' troopers. Collins carried his hat before him on his saddle horn and he was forced to wipe blood out of his eyes with his sleeve.  After they had ridden some distance, she stopped to turn and look at him.

"How is it, Charles?"

In truth his head throbbed and he had difficulty focusing his eyes.  "I can manage," was all he said.

"You are still losing blood.  We will travel some more, then I will dress your wound.  We are not safe here."

"I understand."

Wakalyapi kicked up her gray and moved off along the mighty river, thick with debris and slush.  Collins fell back into the now familiar routine of following her roan.  Although he had not had much leisure to peruse their attackers, he realized that none of the warriors had appeared to be white nor had he noted the presence of anyone as significant as Sitting Bull.  He supposed that they had been braced by a separate group of Sioux, evidently led by the great chief's nephew.

A couple of hours later, and what felt to Collins as

quarts of blood lost, Wakalyapi pulled up in a dense grove of pines in a coulee some distance from the river. She dismounted and he slid dizzily from Ulysses, collapsing onto the snow, surprised by his own weakness. She knelt beside him.

"I am sorry, Charles. The new fort is just beyond those hills and I thought it would be best for you if we were close before stopping."

He sat up, still holding the reins. His head swam and there was a buzzing in his ears. The woman was gone and he wondered vaguely whether she had left him to make his own way to the cantonment. He noticed in a detached sort of manner that he did not seem to care and that freezing to death was again a viable alternative.

Unsure of the sequence of subsequent events, Collins later found himself wrapped in a buffalo robe, his head bandaged and his bearskin propped behind him. A small fire crackled nearby and he could smell coffee. He looked around and saw that all four animals were tethered nearby and thereby surmised he had not been abandoned after all. Wakalyapi walked to the fire with two ptarmigan in hand. She squatted and began to pluck them deftly.

"Coffee?" he asked, his voice croaking oddly.

She shook her head. "Water first. You have lost much blood from your head."

She fetched his canteen, propped near the fire, and held it out to him. Sitting up, he accepted it and drank. He discovered he was very thirsty.

"How do you feel now?" she asked, taking back the canteen when he was finished.

"Quite wonderful," he said, feeling slightly better. "Why in thunder did that child hit me with a cricket bat?"

She rubbed her mouth tellingly. "He was no child. He was old enough to count coup."

"Please explain that concept."

Her smile showed plainly as she poured a cup of coffee and handed it to him. "It is considered to be more brave to strike your enemy with a coup stick than kill him."

"It is also, apparently, more cruel," he said, gingerly fingering his bandaged wound.

Wakalyapi abruptly stopped smiling and, getting to her feet, she disappeared into the trees. In the distance, Collins could hear the all too recognizable sound of marching soldiers and the occasional blowing of horses. He drank the rest of his coffee and endeavored to get to his feet. Despite the momentary dimming of his vision and a bout of dizziness, he remained erect. Breathing deeply, he made his way to check on the animals and to quiet them should they sense the nearness of other equines. Leaning his forehead against Ulysses neck, he thought his head would split in twain.

Without warning, a hand descended to his shoulder and he spun around.

"Easy, Charles," Wakalyapi told him. "You should not be up."

"What is it?" he asked, walking back to the fire.

"The soldier boys are heading back to the Tongue. There seem to be hostages. White Bull is not among them. I recognize only White Hollow Horn and Moon-Comes-Up."

Collins suspected she had spent far more time among the Sioux than the soldiers at Fort Shaw had suspected. He sat down and laid his pounding head on the bear-skin. Blood trickled from beneath his bandage. "We will have to go to the cantonment. We need to resupply if we are to pursue Sitting Bull's band."

"You have not had enough of the Lakota?"

"I must complete my commission," he said with his eyes closed against the pain.

"To find a few *wasichu* who fight with *Tatanka Iyotaka*?"

"Yes."

"*Han sni!* You will be killed."

He studied her as she squatted to finish plucking the grouse. "*Is gairid ar gcairt ar an saol seo.* Our lease on life is short. I believe you hold honor and duty as highly as I do."

She lay down the birds and looked back at him. "Perhaps. Honor is not a stranger to the Lakota peoples. But tell me, what is the tongue you used?"

"My native language. It is called Gaelic."

She constructed a rude spit and skewered the grouse over a low fire. "What you said before...how I do not belong in one place or the other. Can this be true also of you?"

No longer surprised by her intuitive and cognitive strengths, he nodded.

She narrowed her eyes at him. "Then you are truly the *sunkmanitutanka wablenica*...the wolf that has no relatives," she told him. "Wolfe with an 'e,'" she added, with her crooked smile.

The pain in his head was steadily reaching a renewed apogee. "I am not alone as long as you are traveling with me," he said, as consciousness slipped its moorings and he descended into gentle oblivion.

# 36

As they rode toward the Tongue River Cantonment the next afternoon, Wakalyapi looked back at Collins frequently.  His head was much improved and he was able to wear his Stetson tipped away from the wound. He had removed the bandage so as not to appear even slightly debilitated in front of Miles.  They forded the Yellowstone easily, given its low waters, and rode into the cantonment from the east.  The camp was full of smoke from many fires in the frigid air.  Soldiers passing on errands and those hunkered by fires glowered at them as they rode by.  They pulled up in front of a building where Miles' tent had previously stood and dismounted.

"Will you stay here with the horses?" Collins asked the woman.

"Yes.  I will stay here.  Do not worry."

He stepped onto the crude porch and knocked.  A voice beckoned and he went in to find Peterson sitting behind a makeshift table piled with papers.  He looked very surprised to see Collins.

"Hello," he said.

"Hello son.  Is the Colonel here?"

"He is here.  Did you wish to see him?"

"That was the general idea."

"A moment, please."  Peterson got up and stepped into the back of the building, partitioned with canvas. C.W. smiled at the boy's interminable courtesy and wondered whether Miles appreciated his young adjutant.

There was muted discussion behind the canvas, then Peterson appeared to beckon him in. Collins entered the cramped space and Peterson slipped by him to return to his paperwork.

"Good afternoon, Colonel," Collins said affably.

"What are you doing back here?" Miles asked without ceremony from behind an ornate oak desk. Even in these hinterlands, Collins thought, the man found the *modus vivendi* for appearing consequential.

"As before," was all Collins told him.

"What have you been doing all this time, Mr. Collins?" the colonel asked rudely. "Looting graves?"

Collins held his gaze for a long moment; long enough for Miles' discomfort to begin to exhibit itself, then said, "I require supplies and some information."

"You can have supplies," Miles said, his previous aggression somewhat mitigated. "What information?"

Collins noticed he had yet to be offered a chair. His head ached mildly. "I understand that you have recently parlayed with Sitting Bull."

"Where did you hear that?"

In truth, White Bull had told Wakalyapi in their brief intercourse during the fracas along the Yellowstone. "I have my sources," C.W. told him.

Miles studied him a moment, then said, "He was exceedingly stubborn and opinionated. He appeared much depressed and suffering from a loss of power. His nephew surrendered just yesterday."

"Is he here?"

"Who?"

"White Bull. The nephew."

Miles seemed taken aback by Collin's informed question. "No. I have accepted five hostages to hold him to his word. They will be sent to Cheyenne River Agency and the others will follow in short order."

"May I speak with them?"

"They do not speak English," Miles said, obviously certain the matter was closed.

"I have an interpreter."

Miles raised his eyebrows. "Do you now?

C.W. held his tongue and waited.

"Who is this interpreter? If it is Culbertson, he has shown himself to be... unreliable. He is a drunkard."

"It is not Culbertson."

"I will need to meet this interpreter before I allow him access to my prisoners."

"Prisoners?"

Miles made a show of impatience. "Well, hostages, then. I still need to assess this man's acceptability."

This was what Collins had anticipated with great discomfort. He feared Miles' reaction to Wakalyapi, either due to her sex or tribal affiliations. He walked out of the building and found her sitting quietly and unobtrusively on the edge of the porch between her roan and gray.

"He must meet you before we may speak with the hostages," he told her. "I need to speak with them. Are you willing?"

She nodded and climbed onto the porch. She touched his elbow lightly. "Do not worry, Charles," she said.

He led her inside and into the back where Miles sat behind his majestic escritoire. The man looked up and raised his eyebrows again, nonplussed by Wakalyapi's appearance.

"This, sir, is your interpreter?" he asked incredulously.

"It is."

"Where did you find her?"

"She speaks, Colonel," Collins said. "Ask whatever questions you require, then leave us to proceed with our commission."

Miles eyes snapped at him and he seemed about to lose composure, but some hidden agenda caused him to restrain himself. "Very well," he said, then turned to observe the woman. "Where are you from?"

"Fort Shaw."

"What were you doing there?"

"Hunt for soldier boys."

Collins noticed she had retreated into her parody of illiterate speech and thought this to be quite prudent given the circumstances. He relaxed a bit.

"Are you Sioux?"

"Oglala. Stole by Absaroka. Now hunt for soldier boys."

Miles looked over at Collins. "She does not appear to be very clever. I had heard there was a half-breed female drunkard hunting for Fort Shaw, but I did not credit the rumors."

Collins glanced briefly at Wakalyapi to see how she was subscribing to this abuse. Her demeanor was apparently unruffled, but her scar was twitching almost imperceptibly and he suspected she was infuriated.

"May we speak to the hostages?" Collins asked.

"I suppose. Although I cannot see how this will further any commission laid upon you by Grant."

"And the supplies?"

Miles called Peterson who appeared with alacrity at the canvas doorway.

"Write out a chit for supplies in the name of Collins." Miles told him.

"Yes sir."

"And inform Sergeant Hammonds that these two are to have ready access to our hostages."

Peterson looked surprised. "Yes sir."

"That is all," he said, apparently to all of them, as he began shuffling through papers on his desk in a dismissive manner.

Outside, Collins pocketed the requisition slip for supplies. "Let us reconnoiter a camp before we proceed further," he told Wakalyapi. "How is it with you?" he asked, using her words.

She cut her eyes at him.  "It is of no consequence," she said, and mounted her horse.  She rode westward toward the Tongue and Collins followed on foot, leading his animals through filthy snow, stained with mud, horse droppings, and urine.  *Is beag an dealg a dheanas sileadh,* he thought, watching the woman's back.  Even a small thorn causes festering.

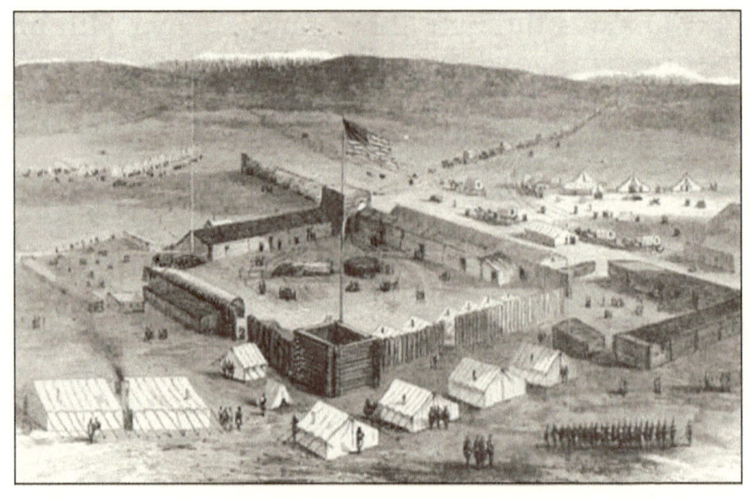

CANTONMENT

# 37

Down along the Tongue River, Wakalyapi chose a sheltered camp and they situated themselves as comfortably as was possible in crusty snow and glacial temperatures.  They spent some time gathering wood, covering it with a hide against the occasional snow squalls that blew through.  The woman pulled bark from cottonwoods and piled it in front of the horses while Collins fed them grain.  The animals needed rest and he hoped they would be able to take a respite for a couple of days.  His head still plagued him as well.

Wakalyapi was singularly quiet, reminding him of their first days together.  The day was swiftly departing as they left their snug camp and walked back toward the nascent fort.

"Let us speak with the hostages forthwith," Collins said.  "I believe that Miles will send them to Cheyenne River as quickly as possible without regard to our need to communicate with them."

She did not respond and they made their way into the cantonment, lit by campfires and lanterns.  Collins nodded at the occasional trooper, huddled by the fires for warmth.  There seemed to be much tension and small joviality among the soldiers, probably due to physical discomfort, given the primitive conditions.  Collins also suspected that the men were ever uncertain as to Miles' next maneuver and the level of danger into which they might be cast.

As they neared the guarded camp of the hostages, a stocky fellow stepped into their path.

"By god, man," the soldier said with a strong Irish brogue. "You are the fella what took my Molly."

"Corporal Murphy," Collins said, shaking the man's hand vigorously. "What a godsend your mule has shown herself to be."

"Have you brought her back to me, then?"

"Not even a possibility. I have a grand story to tell you, but we must hurry now. Shall I find you at the stables?"

"Yes...the stables." The corporal had turned his consideration to Wakalyapi. "What manner of person is this?" he asked.

"This is my guide and interpreter and you must treat her with all courtesy," Collins told him sternly.

The corporal gave him an inquisitive look, then held out his hand to the woman. "I am Corporal Patrick Murphy, at your service."

"Arbuckles," she said and took his hand in her habitually diffident fashion.

"Well, you must both find me later, when you have completed your business, and I will give you a warm meal and a hot cup of coffee. And perhaps a drop of something else to warm you. *Is tuisce deoch na sceal.*"

Collins clapped him on the back. "'Tis true a drink precedes a story, but even in abstention, I will tell you a tale that will astound and amaze."

"I shall await your visit impatiently."

They left him and proceeded to the hostages. One of the guards barred their way.

"I have permission from Colonel Miles to question the hostages," Collins told him. "Sergeant Hammonds was to have been informed."

"Wait here. I will check on this."

The man walked over to another soldier and they spoke briefly. The guard returned. "If you are Mr. Collins then you have permission to approach the prisoners."

C.W. noticed the use of the term 'prisoners' once more. It betrayed the prevailing attitude toward these men who had bravely placed themselves as ransom for their people. "I am Collins," he told the soldier.

Wakalyapi and he walked over to the fire around which hunkered the five Sioux warriors. Collins wondered whether these men had been given adequate blankets or food. The two of them squatted before the Indians. They observed the unlikely couple without speaking. One of them nodded recognition to the woman.

"Tell them I have come to speak to them respectfully. That I am neither with the army nor any agency," he said to Wakalyapi.

She stood and spoke at length in her native tongue. He studied the men and noted the intelligence, patience and fortitude within them. He also remarked the aura of profound melancholy that seemed to permeate the small group.

After she had finished speaking, one of them made a sign to her.

"I have introduced myself. I have told them your words," Wakalyapi informed him. "They are willing to hear you."

Collins glanced around to be certain that the guards were out of earshot. Still, he spoke quietly. "Tell them I seek the white men who are loyal to Sitting Bull. Tell them I mean no one harm."

She spoke again, with eloquent hand gestures. Collins found he admired the sound of the language. One of the men finally spoke. He looked at Collins as if addressing him.

"White Hollow Horn says that these men remain with

*Tatanka Iyotaka.* They have kept themselves away from the blue coats so that they would not be seen."

"Understandable. Ask them if they know where these men came from. Ask them how long they have been with Sitting Bull."

Wakalyapi passed on his questions. The men spoke amongst themselves, then the one called White Hollow Horn responded, once again speaking directly to Collins.

"They say that these *wasichu* have been with *Tatanka Iyotaka* for many many moons. They say that these men are Hunkpapa warriors. They have danced the *Wiwang Wacipi* with honor and have fought with bravery. They do not know where they came from...perhaps from over the sea."

"Ask them how many of them there are."

She asked. White Hollow Horn responded briefly.

"They say not many any more," she told Collins. "They say that some of them wandered away, some of them died of the speckled disease that has taken so many Lakota people, some of them died on the Greasy Grass."

Collins realized this was probably the full extent of information to which he would have access until he found the men themselves. "Thank them very sincerely. Tell them I believe they have done something very brave and that I honor them."

Wakalyapi translated his words. Collins got to his feet and stood beside her, looking each of the warriors in the eye briefly in turn. Each man nodded to him. They spoke to each other then spoke to the woman.

"They are glad to have met you. Moon-Comes-Up tells you to be cautious. That he believes 'Bear Coat' to be of dishonorable character."

"'Bear Coat?'"

"This is the name they have given Miles. He has a coat with bear fur."

"Tell Moon-Comes-Up that I believe the same and for

him to be cautious as well."

The middle-aged warrior smiled at Collins. He smiled back and he wished he could know these remarkable men better. If the enigmatic white men he sought were indeed Irish, he could easily apprehend how they would do well in the company of such people.

One of the other men spoke to Wakalyapi.

"This is Bear-Stop. He says they will leave soon on a steamboat. He wants you to know they will be at the agency downriver and that you may visit them there."

"Thank Bear-Stop. Tell him I hope to live to do so,"

She told them his words and they laughed softly. The guards moved closer, as if they were made uncomfortable by this show of relaxed humor. Bear-Stop spoke again.

"He says we should leave. He does not want us to be in trouble for showing respect and courtesy to them."

"Tell him I am proud to show such men respect and courtesy, but we will leave if he desires it."

She passed this on and Bear-Stop looked at him and made a gesture with his head, clearly signifying they should depart.

Collins nodded, then paused to salute the hostages before walking away from the fire. He was sad to leave their company and felt certain these men would not fare well within the tender mercies of Colonel Miles and the United States Government. Such was the true measure of American justice.

# 38

Corporal Murphy had a cozy hut near the stables composed partly of canvas, partly of mud and log. It was dry and warm and tidy. Somewhere he had scavenged a small wood stove, a camp table and chairs and a narrow wrought iron bedstead with mattress. Collins and Wakalyapi were invited in with great enthusiasm and made to sit. He placed cups before them and poured coffee.

"Are you certain I cannot be sweetening it up a wee bit with a drop of the pure?" he asked.

"No thank you, Corporal. It is best we keep our wits about us," Collins told him. He glanced at his companion and she shook her head. He was forced to admit to himself that he was relieved, as he remained unsure as to whether she had a taste for liquor or no.

"I have some antelope stew here with beans and some biscuits I baked not but a day ago."

"That we will accept and gladly." Collins sipped his coffee and felt it chase some of the chill from his marrow.

Murphy bustled nimbly about his cabin, placing bowls and eating utensils upon the table. He hummed a vaguely familiar tune of Irish origin, filling their bowls to the rim and sitting down with them at the table.

"Now eat," he said. "Afterward, I will be wanting to hear the story about me darling Molly."

Collins found the stew to be delicious. They ate in companionable silence and he sensed that Wakalyapi's angst was melting away in the embrace of Murphy's judicious hospitality.

"Would you take some more?" the corporal asked them after they had emptied their bowls.

"Thank you, but I am replete," C.W. answered.

"No thank you," the woman told him. "It was very good."

Collins noticed she had favored the man with unabbreviated English.

"Well, then I am happy. And now," he said, getting up to clear the table and fill their cups, "I am prepared for a tale."

Collins embarked upon his story of Molly and the grizzly, embellishing the account in true Celtic spirit. Wakalyapi listened attentively, as if she had never heard him tell it before, but rested her chin in her hand, her mouth hidden behind her fingers. Tears rolled down Murphy's cheeks at the telling.

"So you see, man," Collins said to him. "I owe you my life."

Murphy wiped his eyes and nose on a sleeve and sniffed. "I must go to see her in the morning. Aye, I must tell her what a blessed creature she is and bring her something toothsome to eat."

"We are camped due west just outside the cantonment. And now," Collins said, getting to his feet, his head beginning to ache fiercely, "We must take our leave."

They shook hands with the corporal and thanked him again for a fine repast. Outside, the wind was coming up and the temperature felt curiously warmer. As they walked through the cantonment toward their camp, the smoke from many fires lay close to the ground and Collins sensed there was another storm approaching.

As if reading his thoughts, Wakalyapi said, "There will be more snow before morning."

"Shall we rest a day or do you think we should depart?"

"We should rest the horses and your head," she said. "You do not look well."

They walked past the last soldier campfire and the air was easier to breathe. "I am sorry about the opprobrium you have received," he told her.

"Opprobrium?"

"Contempt. Insult."

She huffed softly. "I have grown used to such. It has always been so."

"It should not be so," he said.

The snow crunched and squeaked beneath their feet. They were almost to their camp when she spoke quietly. "I am grateful that you say this," she said and moved away into the night.

Collins stirred up their fire and added wood. The wind whipped sparks into the darkness, like so many summer fireflies. If only it were summer, he thought, shivering with cold. He walked over to where the animals were tethered. They had finished their pile of bark and he resolved to request hay of the good corporal for the morrow. He fetched more grain and distributed it upon the snow before them. They were too fatigued for contention and ate calmly. He returned to the fire and began to lay out his bedroll. He heard someone approaching and looked up, expecting Wakalyapi. Instead, Peterson appeared before him in the firelight.

"Jesus, mary and joseph!" Collins exclaimed. "Do you never rest?"

"I apologize for disturbing you, Mr. Collins, but Colonel Miles wishes to see you. I have been scouring the fort seeking you."

Wakalyapi emerged from the darkness behind Peterson. "How is it, Charles?" she asked.

Peterson gave a start and turned to look at her. "The Colonel requires both of you," he said.

"Can this not wait until morning?" Collins asked.

"We are weary."

"I was not to return without you."

"Well that is not a novelty," C.W. said sarcastically. He thought a moment, then said, "I will accompany you alone.  My guide will stay to guard the camp."

"But that is not what..."

"That is what I have decided," Collins said, interrupting Peterson's protestation.  He looked at Wakalyapi and she nodded, sitting beside the fire.

Collins began walking in the direction of Miles' headquarters with Peterson trailing behind.  He was angry at the proprietary manner of this summons, but equally curious regarding its inception.  He proceeded silently as Peterson caught up with jogging steps.  The boy seemed ever aware of decorum.

The building was brightly lit by lamps and smoke poured from the stovepipe.  They entered and Collins was enveloped in welcome heat.  Peterson stepped in front of him to announce his presence through the canvas partition, pulled back now and tied open.  There was a gruff reply and the young adjutant motioned Collins in.  Miles was seated in a chair by the glowing stove. Collins was surprised that the man had surrendered his consequential desk.

"Collins, come in."  The Colonel gestured toward another chair and glanced around.  "Where is your interpreter?  I summoned her as well."

Collins remained standing.  "In camp.  Why did you wish to see me?"

Momentary irritation passed over the man's features. "Collins, I find that I am without an interpreter at present.  I need to requisition yours."

"That is not possible."

"Dammit, man!  This is not a debate.  The U.S. Army is currently at war with the Sioux.  I will have whatever I require to round them up and put them into submission."

"Last I was aware, your requirements do not take precedence over the President's," Collins said coolly.

"Damn the President, the tired old fool," Miles said, ill advisedly.

"That, sir, is sedition."

Miles stood and took a seat behind his desk, obviously in a maneuver to relinquish his former attempt at informality. "You overstep yourself, Collins. In this cantonment, I wield absolute jurisdiction."

Collins sighed loudly and silently considered the dilemma before him. Miles did, indeed, have the power to forcibly take custody of his companion and guide. His mission would then be fundamentally undone. If, however, he acquiesced, there was a possibility they would be able to slip away in the near future.

"Very well," he said. "But I will accompany her at all times."

"I can always use another man, if you will learn to obey orders," Miles told him disdainfully.

Collins restrained his indignation and nodded curtly.

"We will depart northward toward the Missouri in two days. I will be scouring the country for Sitting Bull and he will not slip through my fingers this time. Colonel Hazen is bringing supplies and more soldiers to Fort Peck from Fort Buford by steamboat. I will have custody of the remainder of the recalcitrant Sioux before spring. Custer and the Seventh will have been avenged."

Knowing this campaign was more about ambition and rivalry with General Crook than retribution, Collins said nothing.

Miles regarded him a moment. "You may go, Collins. Get what supplies you require and be ready day after tomorrow."

C.W. turned and departed without a word. He was angry and frustrated and feared his tongue would betray him. Outside, he strode toward his camp, unaware of the cold wind and the snow that had begun to fall. Wakalyapi was still sitting by the fire when he arrived and she looked at him quizzically.

He threw himself onto his bedroll.  "We have been requisitioned," he told her.

She packed her pipe and lit it.  "You are angry," she said, after a bit.

He dug out his own pipe and tobacco, forcing himself to abandon his ire.  He told her about Miles and his plans.

"I will not go against my people," she said.  "I will not."

"Nor will I.  We will find a way to leave.  There will be an opportunity and we will sneak away."

"Even now, we are being watched," she said.

Having suspected that he had been followed from Miles' headquarters, Collins did not doubt her word. "There will be an opportunity," he said again.

She shook her head.  "I am worried.  We are like the *mastinca*, the rabbit, caught in a snare. I am not safe here among the soldiers and you are not safe among the Lakota."

"I have been in worse predicaments.  Far worse. We will, no doubt, prevail." He spoke with more confidence than he felt.

"It is of no consequence," she said shrugging and knocking out her pipe into her hand.  She dug a hole in the snow and buried the spent tobacco.  "What will take place, will take place. I am in good company."

"'Cowards die many times before their deaths.  The valiant never taste of death but once,'" Collins said.

"Shakespeare?" she asked.

Collins nodded, laying his pipe aside and taking off his boots. "*Julius Caesar*."

"Tell me," she said, and they prepared for sleep as he regaled her with tales of ancient heroes and poetic strife.

⟿✦⟾

# 39

As the coffee brewed and the animals stamped and blew clouds of vapor into the frosty morning air, Wakalyapi and Collins saw to their weapons, cleaning their guns and sharpening their knives. She looked again at the old Green River knife he had found on the Little Big Horn.

"Will you tell me now how you came by that knife?" she asked.

"I will tell you. I found it on the...how do you call it?... the Greasy Grass."

"I know this knife. It belonged to my youngest brother. He had it from an old French trapper who stayed with the Oglala one long winter before I was taken by the *Kagi Wicasa.*"

"That is not possible." Collins said incredulously.

She smiled faintly. "All things are possible."

"Then he fought Custer at the Little Big Horn."

"*That* is not possible. He is dead."

"Will you accept the knife?" C.W. said, leaning to hand it to her.

She shook her head, polishing the barrel of her Hawken with soft leather. "No. It came to you and you must keep it."

Collins placed the blade in a primitive scabbard he had fashioned from old hide. "What happened to your brother?" he asked.

"He died from wounds," she said and did not elaborate.

A hearty voice hailed them from above their camp.

Corporal Murphy arrived with freshly baked biscuits. Collins invited him to their fire and poured coffee.

"I have heard talk this fine morning," Murphy told them, cradling the steaming cup in his hands.

"And what is it?" C.W. asked, his mouth full of biscuit.

"You are to accompany the troops north to Fort Peck."

Collins sighed. "Yes. Miles has not given me a choice."

"Be warned," the corporal said, sipping his coffee loudly. "A couple of the soldiers recognized your guide. They have told around that she is Sioux and is, therefore, not trustworthy. There was also a story about a soldier what had an ear chopped off."

Wakalyapi regarded him phlegmatically.

"Will there be mischief?" Collins asked.

"I am not sure, but I would keep a watchful eye at all times."

"And will you be coming along?"

"I am to stay here with the surplus livestock." He shrugged. "I have no taste for chasing women and children as hounds to a fox."

"Nor I."

Murphy finished his coffee and stood. "I see my darling Molly just yonder. I have some sugar in me pockets and adoration in me heart." He went over to the mule.

"Damn," Collins said. "Would that we could escape this predicament."

Wakalyapi ate the last biscuit. "Our journey lies northward," she said. "There is no escape."

Murphy returned to the fire. "What a gorgeous creature," he said, sitting down. "You must not let her come to harm."

"That mule is providential. If she is lost then all will be lost."

The corporal looked at Wakalyapi. "May I be permitted to ask you a question?" he asked her.

She nodded, lighting her pipe.

"Is it true that you cut off that fella's ear?"

She nodded again from behind a puff of tobacco smoke.

"Was it warranted?"

Another nod.

Murphy reached out a hand. "Then may we shake?"

Wakalyapi accepted his gesture and gave a small smile.

"We need fodder for our horses," Collins told him.

"Then I will send some to you. And grain?"

"Some oats would be welcome."

"It is done," the man said, getting to his feet and stretching. "I must return to my duties. A steamboat is to be coming in today, bringing fresh supplies and taking the hostages away to the agency. If you have a mind to, come by again this evening."

Collins thanked him and watched as he walked away. He poured another cup of coffee and fetched his pipe. "We will go to the supply tent today and obtain more provisions. I do not want to break into those we had from Reed."

"If the Hunkpapa are very hungry it will be best for your survival to offer food."

"Speaking of survival, you must remain vigilant while we are forced to remain with the troops. Stay hard by at all times. And...I think it would be best if you did not wear your army overcoat. Assumptions could be made."

Wakalyapi observed him gravely. "I accept your protection and advice in these circumstances," she said. "Our predicament will be reversed soon enough."

"In which eventuality, I shall be at your mercy."

When they had seen to all their weapons, they took a thorough inventory of their victuals and outfit. As they were sorting their gear, a private arrived with a small cart loaded with native grass hay and grain for the animals. His reticent manner bespoke of the general reception they were to receive from the soldiers. They unloaded the provender and he departed. The horses were fed, then hobbled to roam about the river bottom. Collins chopped a hole in the ice along the bank so that they had access to open water. When all was prepared and secure, they made their way into the cantonment to seek the supply depot with Miles' voucher in hand.

Some of the infantry soldiers were drilling on the outskirts of the camp. Others were sorting equipment, cleaning weapons, and fashioning blankets and buffalo robes into winter clothing. There was a general air of preparation. The two of them attempted to stay clear of the troopers, although they were not immune to unfriendly glances and mumbled comments as they passed. The supply tent was a nucleus of activity with troopers and civilian personnel bustling in and out of the large canvas structure.

They waited quietly for their turn with the quartermaster, standing to the side among piles of government issue wool blankets. Collins presented his note. The taciturn man looked it over.

"What do you need?" he asked brusquely. He was apparently far too busy to be concerned about the presence of Wakalyapi.

Collins listed the items they required and the quartermaster either piled his wares before them or pointed to a location in the tent where they could be found. They packed the goods in wool blankets and tied them into bundles. Wakalyapi was silent and unobtrusive throughout. As they were exiting the tent, a short and bowlegged private blocked the woman's path.

"I know you," he said in a malignant tone.

Wakalyapi stood impassively, holding her woolen parcel in both arms.

"Let us pass," C.W. said, laying down his pack and

stepping over to stand in front of her.

"This yours?" the soldier asked, nodding toward the woman and sneering.

"This is my guide and she has been commissioned by Colonel Miles.  I suggest you leave whatever grievance you are entertaining and let us pass," Collins said in a low and calm manner.

"Who are you?" the private asked.

Collins leaned closer.  "Just the man you should avoid provoking," he almost whispered, placing pressure on the man's belly with the tip of the Green River knife.

"Fuck," the soldier exclaimed and jumped back.

"We finished here?" Collins asked, sheathing the blade.

"Maybe," the private said boldly from behind the mound of buffalo robes to which he had retreated.

"I believe it would be best for your prolonged well being," C.W. told him, retrieving his provisions.

As they walked away, Wakalyapi glanced back.  "I do not know him," she said.

"It does not matter.  We need to abscond as soon as it is remotely possible.  I fear there will be more such confrontations."

"There is a saying I have heard... 'from the pot to the fire?'"

Collins gave her a look of chagrin and they walked back to their camp, both carrying a load of supplies and a sense of foreboding.

WINTER MARCH

# 40

Three battalions of the Fifth Infantry marched northward out of the Tongue River Cantonment, fording the
Yellowstone and proceeding into arctic cold and some
of the wildest country in Montana Territory.  Many of
the troopers were mounted on captured Indian ponies.
Winter clothing had been shipped in by steamboat and
the soldiers wore an array of standard issue and improvised apparel against the falling temperatures, wind and
snow.  Collins and Wakalyapi both wore layers of gear,
although the woman's cavalry overcoat was conscientiously replaced by a buffalo robe.

Snow squalls blew periodically through the ranks
and the concomitant howling winds, perforce, thwarted
all idle conversation.  Assigned to ride alongside Colonel
Miles with Captain Snyder's battalion, they were unable
to confer with each other regarding plans for escape.
Hunkered in the saddle, Collins' mind revolved around a
variety of schemes for fading out of the military column.
It had become patently clear that Miles was having them
watched.  He assumed that Wakalyapi was hatching de-
signs of her own and that, between the two of them, they
would be able to confound Miles' plans for their disposition.

Three days of bitter weather and abject discomfort
brought them the opportunity Collins had awaited.  In
selecting a campsite, Wakalyapi cleverly chose a location
hidden in a willow thicket along the banks of Little Dry

Creek. Eschewing all sleep during the night, they slipped away into a blizzard before dawn. Heading northeast, away from Miles and his destination of Fort Peck, they rode without respite until they reached the headwaters of the Redwater River. Nearly frozen, they made camp along the river, just as the brutal wind and snow began to abate.

Collins thought he had never been so tired as he unloaded the packs next to the fire. Their animals stood with heads hanging, desultorily picking at the cottonwood bark and oats piled before them. Using a canvas bucket, Collins hauled water for them. As he was seeing to the livestock, Wakalyapi gathered wood and made coffee. Sitting at last to warm himself by the crackling flames with a hot cup of coffee in hand, he looked at his companion and gave a theatrical sigh.

"We are now deserters from the U.S. Army," she said, her scarred mouth lifted in a weary half smile.

"*Nil aon dli ar an riachtanas.* Necessity knows no law."

"Still, I am convinced you are full of *witkopi* for pursuing these white men," the woman said, pouring more coffee.

"Then how foolish is it of you to remain here with me when you could leave me to my fate?" he asked, blowing on the steaming liquid and sipping it gingerly.

"Did you not say that I hold honor and duty as highly as you do?"

Collins smiled. "Then we are both compelled to continue on this path of self-destruction." He lifted his coffee. "*Slainte,*" he toasted.

She raised her cup. "*Wozanni.*"

They dined on roasted potatoes, tins of "soldier" beef and more biscuits courtesy of Corporal Murphy. After smoking and tethering the horses for the night, they rolled into their bedding. Collins read a bit of Shakespeare aloud at the woman's request. As she banked the fire and they prepared for sleep, a heavy snow began to fall.

"We will follow the Redwater downriver to the Missouri. If the Hunkpapa need supplies and ammunition, their only hope is to trade with the *Slotas* that hang around Fort Peck and the Medicine Line." Wakalyapi said the next morning as she ground coffee beans.

"What is the Medicine Line?"

"The border with the Grandmother Country."

After coffee and a cold breakfast of biscuits, they saddled and packed their animals. When they were almost finished, Wakalyapi left to scout their back trail. Warming Ulysses' bit in his hands before bridling him, Collins watched her climb an old cottonwood with the agility of a young man. She sat upon a large limb and used his field glasses to scan the western horizon from which they had come.

"No sign?" he asked when she had returned and handed the glasses to him.

"No sign. Do you plan to ride all over this land until you find your *wasichu?*"

"Let us ride to the Missouri. Perhaps we will find a trail. If not, we will go to Fort Peck," Collins said, mounting his horse and gathering up Molly's lead.

The woman tightened her cinch and swung onto her gray. It had begun to snow again. "What do you think Bear Coat will do if he finds you?" she asked, moving northward out of their camp.

"You will not let him find me. I am not worried," he told her, as he moved Ulysses into his customary position behind her roan packhorse.

"I am worried," she said. "I am worried about many things."

"'Oh god! That one might read the book of fate,'" Collins quoted and pulled his hat down against the growing breeze.

# 41

As the rifle barrel thumped him again in the small of the back, Collins had to fight the urge to turn and attack his abuser.  The tall warrior had pulled him out of his saddle, sending Ulysses bolting.  He could not help being concerned about the welfare of both his animals, now that he was the prisoner of this small band of Sioux.  He had no idea where Wakalyapi had gone.  As he was shoved through deep snow toward the smoke of a village, C.W. wondered if she had left him to his fate.  Somehow she had escaped the ambush, leaving her packhorse and riding at full speed into the prairie beyond the river.  He held himself straight, with head high, as women, children and other warriors began approaching the little group from the gathering of lodges ahead.  Dogs barked and yipped in excitement. There was much talk and the people poked and touched him, wanting to examine his Stetson, now worn by one of his captors, and the packs on Molly and the roan, both led by a thin young man with a limp.

Enveloped by the curious crowd, Collins was moved toward a tipi of grand proportions.  A man of apparent status stood before the lodge, surrounded by warriors.  Collins thought him to be around fifty years old.  He had a broad forehead and strong features, with eyes that showed obvious intelligence and reasoning.  He wore a long buckskin shirt decorated with tassels of some type of hair and his braids were wrapped in fur.  The warrior with the rifle pulled him to a halt by grabbing his shoulder and holding him. Another Indian took a handful of his hair, grown longer on the trail, and waved a large knife before his face while speaking animatedly. C.W. looked into the eyes of the leader before him and held a steady gaze, in spite of the trepidation that rose within him.

"*Hanta!*" the man said softly, but with force. The commotion around them died down and the warrior let go of his topknot. Then the sound of galloping hooves could be heard and a gray horse came bounding around a nearby tipi to come to a sliding stop near the crowd. Wakalyapi leapt down and pushed through the people, brandishing her Hawken, coming to stand beside Collins. She spoke fervently, gesturing at him. When she had finished speaking, the head man seemed to consider her words carefully, then threw open the door flap of his lodge and motioned for them to enter. Wakalyapi took Collins by the arm and attempted to pull him away from the tall warrior. When he protested, she spit angry words at him so that he let go of Collins. She led him to the entrance of the tipi and they waited to follow their host into the dark and musky interior.

Pulled down to a sitting position, Collins saw the shapes of more people entering the dwelling as his eyes adjusted to the dim light.

"You have found Sitting Bull," Wakalyapi told him in a low voice, leaning close.

"He has found me," he muttered.

The infamous chief sat across the fire from them, leaning against a willow backrest. He was examining the two of them. After a while, he spoke. Wakalyapi got to her feet and answered him at length. Once again, she gestured in Collins' direction. Then she squatted down and there was silence in the lodge. Sitting Bull spoke to a woman and she fetched a bundle. She took out a small soap stone pipe, filled it with tobacco and handed it to the chief, who lit it with a stick from the fire. He smoked quietly, apparently thinking. One of the younger warriors spoke impatiently and the older man raised his hand. When the warrior was quiet, Sitting Bull spoke again.

"You are safe," Wakalyapi whispered to Collins. "He is curious about you."

Collins looked at the chief, who nodded to him and said something to the woman who had given him the pipe. She took it from him and brought it to Collins.

"Smoke," Wakalyapi told him.

Collins puffed on the stone pipe, liking the taste of the tobacco mixture. *Tatanka Iyotaka* watched him, then gestured that he should pass the pipe to the man on his left. Collins handed it over and glanced at Wakalyapi.

"I will not be asked to smoke at this time," she told him. "It is tradition."

"Does he know you?"

"Yes. He knows me," she said quietly. "That is why you are still alive."

"I thank you," Collins said, moved by the friendship of this strange woman beside him.

"It is of no consequence," she said.

An older woman came out of the back of the group around the fire and knelt down in front of Collins. She studied his face, touched his hair, and ran a finger across the fresh scar from the coup stick. She leaned in and looked into his eyes, then she smiled a sweet smile and stood. She spoke to Sitting Bull and made her way back to her place in the lodge.

"That is Her-Holy-Door, *Tatanka Iyotaka's* mother," Wakalyapi told him. "She has much influence. She said she likes the color of your eyes. She says they are *th'olah-kaka*. Very blue."

"I am glad she likes them," he said.

Sitting Bull spoke and Wakalyapi stood to answer him.  She left the lodge and returned carrying the grizzly hide from Molly's packs.  She walked around the back of the tipi, winding her way through the group of people that now that filled the dwelling.  She respectfully knelt beside Tatanka Iyotaka and handed him the bundle. He unrolled it and ran his hand appraisingly across the thick fur. Wakalyapi returned to her place beside Collins.

"It is your gift to him," she said.

"Yes." He gave a nod to the chief.

The pelt was passed around and there was much talk among the Indians.  Now that Collins was not in imminent danger of losing his life or scalp, he was able to observe his surroundings more closely.  Without wanting to appear too inquisitive, he casually glanced around the lodge, seeing for the first time that many of the ornaments suspended from the lodge poles consisted of strings of scalps and various weapons.  Flamboyant beading and painting on the handles of war clubs, arrow quivers, shields, coup sticks and rifle scabbards exhibited the Indian penchant for decoration.  Bunches of dried plants and nondescript packets were also tied to the poles.  A distinctive necklace hanging high in the tipi appeared to be manufactured of human fingers.

"You must speak now," Wakalyapi told him, nudging him gently in the side.

Collins looked across the fire and saw that the chief was once again watching him attentively and all conversation had died down.

"What should I say?" he asked.

"Tell him you have brought gifts of food.  Tell him why you have come seeking him.  Be honest.  Tatanka Iyotaka will know if you are not speaking the truth."

"Should I stand?"

"Yes."

Collins got to his feet with Wakalyapi beside him.  "My

name is Charles Wolfe Collins. Thank you for inviting me into your home," he said directly to Sitting Bull.

Wakalyapi translated his words. The man nodded to Collins.

"I have come to find answers to a riddle. I mean no harm or disrespect and do not come at the behest of the army or other agency."

Sitting Bull listened as the woman interpreted. He gestured for them to sit down, then spoke.

"He wants to know what riddle," she said, after they had resumed a seated position. "He wants to know if it is worth the price of your own life." Wakalyapi told him.

Collins smiled and shrugged. The chief saw this and smiled back.

"Tell him I do not know if it is worth the price of my life, but a duty that is accepted is a task that must be honorably completed."

The chief nodded.

"Tell him I have come to find the identity of the white men who are loyal to him. Tell him that they have nothing to fear from me."

Sitting Bull considered this new information carefully before speaking. Some of the other men became agitated and the chief raised his hand to pacify them. He spoke to his warriors, then to Wakalyapi.

"He says he must study this. Now he wants to see what gifts you have brought to him and his people. He says that food is always welcome and shows good manners."

Tatanka Iyotaka stood and everyone within the lodge came to their feet. Filing out from left to right in a clockwise motion, the crowd exited the tipi into a breezy day of intermittent sun and patchy clouds. Collins and Wakalyapi came out in their turn and he was surprised to see Ulysses, Molly, and the woman's roan and gray standing together under the care of the crippled young man Collins had noticed earlier. The packs were intact and apparently untouched. The Winchester remained in its place on his saddle.

"I thought they would have pillaged our outfit by now," he told Wakalyapi.

She looked at him askance. "My people have great courtesy. It would not be proper etiquette to disturb another's belongings before being invited."

"I apologize for my ignorance," he said, ashamed of his assumption, and went over to Molly.

Undoing the buffalo robe and canvas tarp covering the load, he began unpacking goods they had procured from Reed's trading post. Laying the items upon the tarp, he displayed the tins of beef, tins of beans, the flour, the dried apples, sides of salt pork, Hudson Bay blankets, coffee, sugar, tobacco and other articles. Sitting Bull stood back and evinced approval. The women and children showed subdued excitement. The warrior who had taken C.W.'s Stetson handed it back to him.

The chief turned to Wakalyapi and spoke at length.

"He says we should find a place to camp near the village. He is sorry there is no room in any of the lodges as he is sheltering a great many people who have come to him for protection from Bear Coat and the other soldiers who have come to Fort Peck on the *wata p'oyela,* the steaming boat. He tells us that he needs to consider this other problem and will need to speak to his white brothers about it."

"Other soldiers?" Collins asked.

"We will find out about this," she told him. "But now we must make camp."

Collins nodded to the chief, who came over to them.

"Thank you, Collins," the man said in heavily accented English, holding out his hand. His voice was deep and resonant.

C.W. took Tatanka Iyotaka's hand in the retiring

fashion he had learned was proper in Indian custom. "Thank you, sir," he said respectfully.

Wakalyapi spoke briefly in Lakota, then gathered her horses and led them away from the crowd.  Collins followed suit, leading Ulysses and Molly and followed by a group of dogs and a couple of children.

SURVIVAL

# 42

They made camp a little south of the village in the river bottom.  All but one scrawny dog lost interest after a while.  The children departed at a stern word from Wakalyapi.  Collins constructed a primitive shelter of branches, canvas and hides in anticipation of more snow.  The yellow dog lay nearby and observed him.  He dug in his pocket and tossed a piece of jerked meat in its direction.

"You have a dog," Wakalyapi said, watching the animal devour the morsel.

"I do not."

"You have fed it.  Now it is yours."

Collins grunted and finished piling branches around the perimeter of their humble lodge.  "What is your opinion?" he asked, admiring his own efforts.

"We will share this?" the woman asked, striking flint and steel to light the fire.

"Is it not proper?" Collins asked, vaguely disconcerted.

"It is not improper.  We will be protected from the weather."  A small glow flickered and she blew into the kindling until a flame grew.

The dog watched as they completed the final touches to their campsite, stripped bark from surrounding trees for the horses and gathered more wood for the fire.

"Now I will hunt," Wakalyapi announced, when all necessary chores had been completed.  She picked up her bow and quiver of arrows.  "I will hunt silently, so

Miles and his 'walk-a-heaps' will not hear."

"'Walk-a-heaps?'"

"This is the name these people have given to Miles' soldiers. They are loaded down with clothing and equipment."

Collins smiled. "Very descriptive."

"Now I will go."

"It is coming night fall," Collins said with concern.

"It is of no consequence. We need fresh meat. These people need meat," she said, tilting her head in the direction of the village. "I am a hunter," she added, picking up her McClellan saddle, decorated with beading and brass tacks.

"Shall I accompany you?" he asked, as she saddled her horse. He was not completely comfortable at the notion of staying in close proximity to the Hunkpapa village without his interpreter.

"No. You are safe and I will return." She placed a lead rope on her packhorse and swung into the saddle. With the roan in tow, she rode to the east, crossing the Redwater River without another word.

Collins sat on a log by the fire and put a few more sticks of wood on the flames. The dog bellied nearer, obviously expecting to be rebuffed. He coaxed it closer with soft words and hand gestures. The animal crawled to him in fits and starts, until he could reach out a tentative hand to touch its head. The dog growled and retreated to the base of a nearby cottonwood tree, where it lay down to watch him.

Shrugging, Collins fetched the coffeepot, filled it from the hole he had chopped earlier along the stream bank and placed it on a rock in the fire. He ground coffee and threw a generous handful of grounds into the pot. Then he regained his seat on the log and took out his pipe to smoke, resigning himself to peaceful solitude until his guide's return. He thought about Sitting Bull's willow backrest and thought he might attempt to replicate it. After he had finished his smoke, he took his knife and went in search of willow brush. The dog skulked along behind, keeping its distance. Collins cut a pile of stalks and carried them back to the fire. He strove to weave them into a basket type of framework, using some sinew lacing to secure the structure. He failed miserably.

About to abandon his endeavors and turn his efforts to supper, the dog barked suddenly and C.W. looked up to see the handicapped warrior coming into camp. He limped to the fire and sat. With the bottom of his leggings pulled up, Collins could see there was something terribly wrong with the young man's right ankle.

"*Kcanptepte*," the Indian said, patting his chest.

"Collins," he said, pointing at himself.

The Indian studied the pile of willow stems. He gestured his chin toward it inquisitively. C.W. shrugged and held up the part of his experiment that had held together. Kcanptepte grinned and waved his hand in a way that let Collins know he wanted the pile brought to him. He gathered it up and laid it at the boy's side. Then he went to the packs and procured a hunk of salt pork and some dried apples. He took out two cups and pointed to the coffeepot.

"Coffee?" he asked his guest, using his hands to signify his meaning, then remembered he knew the Lakota word. "*Wakalyapi?*"

Kcanptepte looked up from his efforts with the willow frame and nodded. Collins settled the grounds and poured him a cup. He accepted it then made a stirring motion with his finger. Guessing he wanted sugar, Collins took out the sack and handed it over to him. The young man put a good amount into his coffee and handed it back with a smile of thanks. He drank with enthusiasm. C.W. cut the salt pork into chunks and placed them in a frying pan on the fire, then tossed the dried apples in with the meat. After pouring himself a cup of coffee, he refilled Kcanptepte's cup and gave him the sugar sack. The boy promptly stopped his work, added the sugar and sipped the hot liquid until it was gone.

"*Omawaste*," he said.

Collins figured this meant he liked the coffee. He smiled and nodded to his guest. Squatting to stir the pork and apples, he noticed that the day was swiftly waning. He stood to walk to the edge of the river, with the dog shadowing him, and scanned the eastern horizon for Wakalyapi. There was no sign of her and it was becoming increasingly difficult to see in the fading light. After checking on the animals, he returned to the fire. A tightly woven backrest awaited him where Kcanptepte had been seated. The young man had disappeared.

Trying out the rest, he found it to be quite sturdy and serviceable. The unexpected kindness was meaningful in his isolation and uncertainty. Filling a plate with the fried pork and apples and refilling his cup, he sat comfortably by the fire and ate, occasionally tossing a tidbit to the dog. The night grew colder and he added wood to the fire, shaved off several days' growth of beard, smoked his pipe and waited anxiously for Wakalyapi's return.

It was late and he had read an entire act of *As You Like It* before C.W. gave up on Wakalyapi's reappearance that night. Leaving the fire's warmth, he beat a hasty retreat to his bedroll in the brush shelter. The dog followed him and lay down near the doorway, his head silhouetted against the dying light of the fire. He fervently hoped that the woman had found sufficient protection against the freezing temperatures, given that he not only had become quite fond of her, but also because his chances for survival would be severely diminished without her.

Worry kept him wakeful. In the early hours of the morning, he climbed out of his refuge to relieve himself. The dog jumped up and scurried out of his path. The velvet black sky was clear and the stars seemed more plentiful than he had ever previously observed. The aurora borealis filled the northern horizon with eerie pulsing streams and arches of colored lights. He walked over to the horses, rubbing and scratching Ulysses and Molly until the cold drove him back to bed. Snug in his heavy bedroll beneath a buffalo robe, he finally drifted off to sleep with fitful dreams of his childhood in Ireland.

# 43

The sound of Ulysses whickering in the dawn brought him into the early light with rifle in hand. Wakalyapi was approaching from the southeast and her roan was loaded with two deer carcasses and several rabbits. The dog barked and raised its hackles. She rode into camp and dismounted stiffly. Collins laid aside his gun and stirred up the fire, adding kindling. He went over and helped her unload the meat, unsaddle her horses and rub them down. Shedding the buffalo robe she wore, the woman went to the fire and hunkered down, adding more wood and warming her hands. C.W. grained their horses, filled the coffeepot and put it to boil.

"How was it?" he asked.

"It was far. Game is scarce."

"Did you sleep?"

"I could not. It was very cold."

"Are you hungry?"

"I am tired," she said and got up to disappear into the shelter, carrying her buffalo robe.

Collins made coffee and fried some bacon. The sun appeared on the horizon, sending thin light across the hoary landscape. After a while the woman returned, yawning and stretching. She accepted a cup of coffee and a plate of bacon and beans. Collins had strung the deer carcasses from a tree branch and the dog lay beneath, licking blood from the snow.

"Where are the *mastinca?*" she asked.

He gestured to a fork in a nearby tree where the rabbits were cached.

"I must take this meat to Tatanka Iyotaka," she said, finishing her breakfast and putting her plate aside. "Have you been left alone?"

"I had a visitor. Kcanptepte. I gave him coffee. He made me this." Collins nodded at the backrest.

"It is good. Kcanptepte is nephew to Little Knife, a head man here in camp."

They resaddled the roan and loaded the horse with the deer and rabbits, keeping two for themselves. Leading the animal, they walked toward the village. Collins looked for the dog and saw that it remained near their fire. Children and dogs came to meet them, creating a din that brought the rest of the people out of their lodges and shelter tents. Tatanka Iyotaka appeared outside his lodge and they led the packhorse to him. Wakalyapi spoke and waved a hand at the game. The chief nodded and said something to a nearby woman. She took charge of the roan and led it away.

Sitting Bull beckoned them into his lodge and they went in. This time Wakalyapi was allowed to smoke with the few men who had joined them. After standing and making a prolonged speech, she sat back down and smiled at Collins.

"I found a small herd of buffalo. I think we will go hunt them," she said.

"What of the soldiers?"

The herd is far to the southeast near the *Hehaka Wakpa.* No soldiers there."

Collins became aware of a man sitting away from the fire in the dimness of the tipi. The Indian seemed to be closely observing him and he felt slightly disconcerted. Despite Collins' attempts to scrutinize the figure, the man's distance from the firelight made it impossible to ascertain much about him. Sitting Bull spoke.

"He says we should go hunt buffalo," Wakalyapi told C.W. "A runner has come from *Tasunka Witko* asking that they meet him on the Powder River with ammunition. Tatanka Iyotaka says they will hunt and wait for Miles to leave Fort Peck at which time they will go there for trading. Then they may travel south to reunite with their allies."

"Who is Tasunka Witko?"

"You have, perhaps, heard of him as 'Crazy Horse.'"

"Yes."

"What about the other soldiers at Fort Peck?"

"Some of the soldiers are waiting for Bear Coat to arrive. Tatanka Iyotaka has learned that the others left on the boat and did not wait."

Sitting Bull began speaking, looking directly at Collins.

Wakalyapi interpreted. "He says you are free to go your own way. He says his white brothers do not wish to meet with you."

"Tell him I would like to stay with his people for a while. Perhaps his white brothers will change their minds. Tell him I shoot well and wish to hunt."

Sitting Bull thought about this when the woman had translated Collins' words. After a while he spoke and Wakalyapi answered at length. The chief responded.

"Tatanka Iyotaka asked whether we could not go to the fort for ammunition. I told him that Bear Coat is angry with us and it would not be safe. He says you may stay with us as long as you keep to yourself and are not too...*wawiyunge s´a*...inquisitive. He says they can always use another hunter."

"I give my word that I will be honorable and not too inquisitive," Collins said, looking at Sitting Bull.

"He will keep a close watch on you, Charles," she told him. "You must be very careful."

"I will be. How do you say thank you?"

"*Phila´mayaye*" It is the men's way.

Collins attempted to repeat this, looking at the chief. There was a derogatory laugh from the strange man in the shadows. Sitting Bull spoke sharply to the man, then turned to smile and nod at Collins.

"Let us depart," Wakalyapi said and they rose to leave. She spoke to Sitting Bull and he nodded and waved them out.

The day was bright and Collins' eyes smarted and watered from the wood smoke in the tipi. He wiped them clear. He saw that the crowd had dispersed and that the people were busy with various chores throughout the village. The woman brought the roan back to Wakalyapi and they returned to their camp. The yellow dog lay before the fire and slunk away as they approached.

"Your *sunka*...your dog is guarding the camp."

"It is not my dog."

"Let us have some coffee," she said, adding wood to the fire.

# 44

Standing on the sandstone butte, they looked down upon the carnage in disbelief.  The snow was splattered crimson with spilled blood and naked frozen carcasses were scattered like grisly insect larvae, pale and unmoving.  The wooly heads each vomited forth gouts of scarlet where the tongues had been removed. When they climbed down to see if anything could be salvaged of the buffalo meat, they discovered it had been riddled with strychnine.

"Those who are *sica*, evil," Wakalyapi said and Collins noted tears of rage in her eyes.

"I do not understand," he said.  "They poison the meat in order to kill wolves?"

"And any other living thing that might eat of the dead," she answered.

"This is heinous...atrocious," he said, shaking his head and finding no word sufficient for the enormity of the crime before him.

"There have been other wanton acts committed by these men that far outweigh what you see here."

"These men?  Who are they?"

"Buffalo hunters.  Wolfers. Old fur traders.  They make their living in butchery... 'Having acquired by habit a kind of pleasure in the discharge of their horrid office,'" she said, distractedly quoting Sir Walter Scott.

Tatanka Iyotaka and his warriors knelt in the snow and some of them sang and some of them wept.  Collins sensed their grief had to do with more than the loss of meat after traveling so far. They were grieving for relatives, slaughtered and abandoned. Heartsick and bereft, they eventually moved off to find their ponies and return to the camp where hungry children would remain hungry this night.

Positioned slightly apart from the others, Wakalyapi and Collins sat dejectedly beside their fire, the yellow dog hovering nearby. The wind was coming up and before long a storm raged in, forcing them to take refuge beneath buffalo robes. Miserable, they chewed on moldy bits of jerky and smoked their pipes, waiting for the weather to break and their mood to lighten.

The next morning, the sun came up brilliant on the glacial horizon and tenuous smoke from the village fires sent tendrils into the still, thin air. Collins made coffee while Wakalyapi went to find out what the Hunkpapa chief had decided.

"We will now journey north to the Missouri. If it is frozen and we can cross, he will seek to trade with the *Slotas* for ammunition so that he may bring relief to Tasunka Witko and his people...if we do not starve to death first," she told C.W. upon her return.

"Are there no other herds of buffalo to be found in this region?"

"I do not know. I doubt it." She drank some coffee. "I saw one of your *wasichu*," she said.

"Did you speak to him?"

"No. He saw me and moved away. They are not ready."

"Will they ever be?" he asked, dejectedly.

"Well Charles," Wakalyapi said with a slight smile, "You can either remain with us and solve your mystery or make your way back to Bear Coat at Fort Peck. I am certain he will give you a heartfelt reception."

"Oh lord," Collins said, smiling wryly.

They roasted some shriveled potatoes for breakfast and broke camp when they observed the lodges nearby being struck for travel. They were packed and saddled when it came time to move out with the others. Riding behind the procession of Indian people, the yellow dog following as had become its custom, Collins scanned the group for any sign of white warriors. He thought he glimpsed red hair beneath a bison headdress in the distance, but could not be sure. Wakalyapi held in her gray and waited for him to catch up with her.

"I will leave my packhorse with you. I must try to hunt," she told him.

"Now?"

"Yes."

She dismounted and tied the lead of her roan to Molly's breeching.

"When will you return?" he asked as she swung back into her saddle.

"I do not know. Share the rest of our food with the people and you will be as one of them. Kcanptepte has said he will be company for you."

"Should I not go with you?"

She shook her head and turned her horse eastward. "We cannot use rifles to hunt. We must be cautious," she said over her shoulder. "And you do not use a bow."

Collins watched her move away, slowly becoming a speck on the far horizon and disappearing into the frozen expanse of featureless landscape. He was not sure if or when she would return. Resigning himself to an uncertain fate, he nudged Ulysses into a fast walk, following the trail of broken snow.

SLAUGHTERING FOR THE HIDE

# 45

Many days passed of below-freezing temperatures and frequent blizzards. Kcanptepte and the dog were his only close companions, although Her-Holy-Door would randomly appear at his fire with small gifts of food. On one occasion she offered a buffalo wool hat, which he accepted with much gratitude, stowing the Stetson in his packs. Kcanptepte had named the dog *'ziyela'* according to its color, or so Collins surmised. The young man camped with him and attempted to teach him words of Lakota with much patience. There was very little food to eat, as he had shared the bulk of it with the starving Hunkpapa, saving back only some jerked meat and a bit of salt pork and cured bacon. Ziyela had become more gaunt than Collins could bear and Molly, Ulysses and the roan horse were showing the privation of long miles with diminishing rations of grain.

Wakalyapi's prolonged absence caused him great anxiety. He had almost despaired of her return as they finally came to the southern banks of the Missouri River. The river was frozen, so they camped in the bottoms and prepared to cross in the morning. Sometime in the night there was a commotion of horses and dogs barking. Collins and Kcanptepte crawled out of their shelter tent to find Wakalyapi riding into camp. Behind her she was dragging a buffalo hide folded and tied around a pile of frozen meat and three antelope carcasses. Her gray looked all in and Collins unsaddled him and rubbed him down, graining him and fetching some cottonwood bark for the tired animal.

Wakalyapi went over to the fire as Kcanptepte blew on the coals and added kindling. Collins ground coffee and put the pot on to boil. The woman sat very still and was breathing deeply.

"*Wicotoketu?*" he asked. "How is it?"

She looked at him in surprise. "*Blomakit´e,*" she answered, taking out her pipe and filling it from her dwindling supply.

Kcanptepte spoke to her and they talked until the coffee was ready. Collins dug in the packs and pulled out the bacon he had been saving. After he fried it up, they all had some with their coffee, giving the largest share to Wakalyapi. The dog was allowed to lick the grease after it had cooled. The eastern skyline was beginning to lighten as she dragged her bedroll over to the fire.

"Take the meat to Tatanka Iyotaka," she said before falling fast asleep.

Pausing to slice off a small portion of frozen organ meat for Ziyela, Collins and Kcanptepte rigged a primitive rope harness for Molly and used her to drag the meat-laden hide into the Hunkpapa camp. Finding Sitting Bull's lodge, they scratched on the door covering as the few remaining dogs in the village began gathering to the smell of blood. The chief threw open the flap and came out, wrapped in a buffalo robe. Kcanptepte gestured grandly at the pile of meat and antelope as if he were responsible. Collins smiled at his pretension.

The Indian policemen, the *akicita*, as taught to Collins by Kcanptepte, were called upon to distribute the meat to approximately two hundred families under Sitting Bull's protection. It was a vastly insufficient amount to share with so many, but all made a show of exceeding gratitude. The chief sent a choice bit back with Collins so that the hunter might eat well for one night. He also sent her a tobacco pouch of fine buffalo calfskin, beautifully worked with dyed porcupine quills and stuffed with a fragrant mixture.

Wakalyapi was awake and drinking more coffee when they returned to their camp. Collins gave her the meat and the pouch.

"You will stay with me now?" he asked simply.

"Yes. I must earn my wages. Although it seems that you have been learning the Lakota language and will soon have no need of me," she said, smiling.

Opening the pouch, she shared tobacco with Collins and Kcanptepte, whose pipe was old with a broken stem. They smoked companionably until activity in the Indian camp told them it was time to move. When they were packed and saddled, Wakalyapi again left the roan with Collins, saying she needed to ride ahead and convey some news to Sitting Bull.

The crossing of the frozen Missouri River was uneventful. Ulysses moved across the ice with excessive caution while Molly and the roan followed patiently behind. Kcanptepte walked with them, as he had no horse of his own and few belongings. Collins had stowed the boy's modest bundle on Molly's packs so he could travel without any more burden than his physical disability.

A short distance beyond the river, Wakalyapi returned to them. "*Has!*" she exclaimed.

"What is it?" Collins asked.

"There is a *wahtesni t´a* among us. A man who sneaks and cannot be trusted." She rode over and untied the roan from Molly.

"Who is it?"

"A *Slota*, a mixed blood called 'Big Leggings.' I have heard he made a deal with Bear Coat at Fort Peck."

"How did you hear that?" Collins asked incredulously.

"My search for game took me very far. I circled close to Fort Peck and sought news from those who beg there.

I learned that Bear Coat is looking for these people far to the west."

"Did you warn Sitting Bull of this man?"

"I made the attempt, but he is very fond of him and listened with only one ear. I fear no good will come of this." She said something to Kcanptepte and momentarily stopped her horses. The young man came over to her and she gestured at the roan. He climbed onto its back, making a seat on the packs.

"What else of Miles?" C.W. asked her.

"Not much. He has split his soldiers into three columns and they are traveling up and down between the *Hehaka Wakpa*, the Yellowstone, and the Missouri. It is a good plan to stay north of this river."

Shadowing the tide of Sitting Bull's followers, they traveled west along the Missouri, camping each night in the cover of the river bottoms. Intermittent blizzards and terrible cold added to the misery of the hungry people. On the third day, a warrior came to them bringing a message from Sitting Bull.

"There is a small herd of buffalo to the north of us," Wakalyapi told Collins after the messenger had departed. "We will go to hunt them. You are invited."

"There is something else," he said. "Tell me."

"That sneaking man, Big Leggings, has disappeared. Tatanka Iyotaka now believes he was scouting for Bear Coat, as I told him. He is worried."

They made camp in a sheltered place and left Kcanptepte and the dog to tend it. Loaded with only spare ammunition and a minimum of gear, they rode to join the others.

# 46

Struggling through waist deep snow, Collins approached the laboring brute cautiously. The animal foundered desperately in its frozen snare of soft powder. He aimed his rifle and shot the cow behind a left rib, as Wakalyapi had instructed. The animal bellowed and blew steam and foamy blood from its nostrils. He shot again and the buffalo shivered and twitched as it died.

Looking around, he saw several warriors moving nimbly across the surface of the snow on snowshoes, a mode of conveyance he had heard of, but had never witnessed for himself. Several of them dispatched the buffalo with lances, as ammunition was short. Women were already hard at work, gutting and butchering the carcasses. The strategy of pushing the herd into a coulee of drifted snow had made their hunt successful and relatively safe. There were a couple more gunshots, then all the animals lay still. Wakalyapi came over to where he stood, exhausted from wading in the snow.

"You killed three," she said. "Have you ever hunted buffalo?"

"No. This was my first time."

"In the old days, there would be celebration and dancing. You would be honored as one of the hunters. But now..."

"I am glad the people have meat."

She nodded. "And robes to trade for ammunition."

Kcanptepte appeared, riding the roan and leading

Molly.  "You must begin cleaning your animals.  Do not throw anything away.  It is all useful."

Collins went over to the last cow he had killed and knelt beside it.  He pulled out the Green River knife and opened the animal.  Kcanptepte came over to help.  He told him the Lakota words for each organ as they pulled the entrails from the abdomen.  He offered Collins a piece of warm liver, which he ate from courtesy, eschewing the condiment of a proffered amount of bile. They worked through the night, butchering and loading their bloody bounty.  Back in the main camp of the Hunkpapa, the meat and robes were piled for distribution.

When there were so many in need, Wakalyapi explained, all was shared and no carcasses were the sole property of the hunter.  The *akicita* again performed the duty of fair distribution.  There was joyous singing and laughing throughout the village, lightening the hearts of all the people. Collins and his two companions returned to their camp to sleep and to await their portion of meat. He tossed a small tidbit of liver to Ziyela, hidden in his pocket for the starving dog.

The sound of the *akicita* announcing their arrival woke them.  These powerful men of status presented a largesse of two robes, a tongue, two front shoulders, some ribs and a variety of organ meats.

"*Phila´mayaye,*" Collins said to them.

The three warriors grinned widely and slapped him on the back.  One of them spoke.

"*Mnicasniyanyanla* says you are a good hunter and they are glad you are with us," Wakalyapi translated.

Kcanptepte immediately stirred the coals and built a large fire.  Wakalyapi cached the meat high in a nearby tree, having first carved three generous steaks from a shoulder. Draped over sticks above the flames, the meat sizzled and spat, emitting an almost unbearably delicious aroma.  With full bellies for the first time in days, the three of them tended the horses, banked the fire and rolled into their robes for a good long nap, while the dog worked over a hunk of meaty gristle.

The next day the village moved to a place near the Milk River chosen by Tatanka Iyotaka. It was situated near a Métis settlement where they could engage in trading. Wakalyapi and Collins chose to avoid the Métis so that their presence with the Hunkpapa could not be reported back to Miles. Kcanptepte engaged in some trading as their proxy. He also helped C.W. construct a pair of snowshoes. Collins and the young man spent hours moving about the snowy prairie, building snares for rabbits and ptarmigan and exploring the banks of the river. Wakalyapi cleaned and cured the two buffalo robes and visited in the village, always keeping an eye for the elusive white warriors. In their present location, several other Sioux families sought refuge with the great chief, making food more scarce and their situation more desperate.

Collins realized he had lost all track of time and that, in all probability, the presidential election had taken place and Grant would soon be leaving the White House, swiftly depriving his mission of significance. It was becoming patently evident that he was ensnared in a difficult predicament from which there was no ready escape. In the dead of a terrible winter, he could not travel alone to Fort Buford and, until Miles withdrew from the region, he could not reasonably consider Fort Peck as a port of refuge. Collins was also obliged by honor to complete his sworn duty, no matter how absurd it was becoming. Whatever white allies remained with the Sioux, they had been rendered harmless and soon, if Miles was successful in his enthusiastic campaign, all the Indians would be dead or forced onto agencies.

For better or worse he would see it through. He would find a way to make a report to Grant prior to the new president's inauguration, whether it be Tilden or Hayes. The weather was bound to break eventually. Meanwhile, it was not unpleasant spending time in the company of his friends and the Lakota people. He was definitely learning that many of the prejudices and shopworn assumptions regarding Indians were vastly fallacious. As a man ever eager to acquire new knowledge, he was actually enjoying himself in spite of the extreme physical privations.

Trading had been favorable for Sitting Bull. He had procured some fifty boxes of ammunition and mules to carry them. Soon, according to Kcanptepte, they would move south to rendezvous with Tasunka Witko and again fight the white soldiers to a standstill. It had become apparent to Collins that his young companion maintained an all encompassing hero-worship of Crazy Horse. He wondered if he would actually have the opportunity to meet the legendary warrior or would, in fact, survive such an encounter, given the Indian's notorious hatred for whites.

After a few days in camp, he had gotten into the habit of laboring each day to clear snow from buried grasses and there picketing the horses to graze. Using a shovel he had improvised from a tin plate, a forked tree limb and some sinew lacing, he was able to expose modest sections of forage for the hungry animals. As he was thus employed one morning, Wakalyapi came up to him.

"We must begin packing before nightfall. I have gotten word that we are to begin our journey south to the Powder River early tomorrow."

"I have made no progress on my search. I am at an impasse."

"You are gaining status. You are being noticed."

Collins took off his buffalo hat and scratched his head. "Will this serve my objective in the end?"

"Perhaps. Perhaps not."

"I do not doubt these men fear exposure as traitors, but I am one man and not sufficient to pose a threat."

"If you reveal their whereabouts, you are very much a threat."

Collins conceded the point with a wave of his hand. "Then what must I do to prove myself further?"

"Be patient. I have spread word among the people that you are no friend of Bear Coat and his walk-a-heaps. I have caught sight of your men several times. They are still here among us."

"I will try to be patient, but I cannot stay with these people forever, nor do I wish to witness their destruction at the hands of the U.S. Army."

She shrugged. "Who knows what you will witness before you part with them," she said and turned to walk away.

SCOUTING

# 47

Collins was woken by a hand over his mouth. Wakalyapi bent over him and whispered to be quiet. He sat up in their shelter and heard wild winds blowing about them, but under this he could make out the crunching of many feet in the snow and the occasional clinking of equipment. Pulling on his boots and grabbing his rifle, he followed the woman out into stinging snow. Kcanptepte appeared and spoke hurriedly.

"Soldiers," Wakalyapi said softly. "We must go now."

Fumbling in the dark and a crippling storm, they saddled and loaded the horses. Joining the others, they moved almost silently across the ice of the Missouri River. On the south bank, they faded into the breaks, ensuring the safety of the families. Wakalyapi left Kcanptepte with the horses and asked Collins to accompany her. They worked their way back to where warriors had gathered overlooking the river. As daybreak came, a company of soldiers attempted a crossing, but they were met with a volley of gunfire. They retreated hastily and took up a defensive position. Some of the warriors spread out to harass the troopers and give the people time to escape. Collins and Wakalyapi returned to their outfit and took time to readjust the packs and grain the animals.

With Kcanptepte in his place on the roan and Ziyela following, they rode southeast with the Indian families as the snow relented. Wakalyapi rode ahead to speak with some of the men.

"The soldiers are pinned down. The warriors will keep them so until we have traveled some distance," she told him upon her return.

"Who gave the alarm?"

"You have met Jumping Bull?" she asked.

He nodded. "Sitting Bull's brother."

"Yes. Jumping Bull was out seeking the attentions of another man's woman when he heard them moving nearby. He even rode his horse up to the soldier boys, but they did not fire at him. I suppose they thought him to be one of their own scouts. He came to his brother and warned the camp."

"That was lucky," Collins said.

"Very lucky, but Jumping Bull has always been fortunate."

They rode without resting throughout the short northern day, eating *wasna*, powdered meat that was rich with lard and marrow, and chatting idly to pass the time. The daylight began to fade and a temporary camp was made beneath a small butte. As they were preparing a fire, another storm struck, blowing hard from the north and bringing driving snow. Abandoning the fire, they sheltered their horses in some brush and retreated into their bedding, covering themselves with buffalo robes and smoking their pipes to chase away the cold.

The next morning dawned brightly. They received word that the warriors had pursued the troopers upriver back to Fort Peck. Two *wamalalakapi*, hangers-on from the fort, had shown up during the night to inform Tatanka Iyotaka that Bear Coat had gone south to the Tongue. They also imparted that Big Leggings was the one who told the soldiers where to find them.

Wakalyapi was angry at this news. "The man was almost killed by the people when he came to camp, but Sitting Bull gave him his protection. He is a thief of trust."

Collins set the packsaddle onto Molly's back. It pained

him to see that her ribs were showing. "*Na' tabhair tao-bh le fear fala.* Trust not a spiteful man," he told her. "Surely he will come to no good."

"Perhaps. Perhaps I will see to it."

The Lakota village continued its migration south and east. Wakalyapi often rode out to hunt and Collins sometimes accompanied her, although she would not allow him to use his rifle. After the attack on the Milk River, no one felt certain they were clear of Miles' walk-a-heaps, despite the brutal weather. On occasion, Collins and Wakalyapi would scout the back trail as a favor to Sitting Bull, although the *akicita* were constantly vigilant.

One day, as they were riding to the east of the Lakota procession, they stumbled onto a hollow covered in weathered pole scaffolds. Tattered hides, hair, bones and other debris dangled eerily from the frames.

"Is this Lakota?" Collins asked as they pulled in their horses to survey the peculiar scene.

"Probably Crow. They must have strayed too far into Lakota territory."

"Do the Lakota dispose of their dead in such a manner?"

"Yes, but see the beading on some of the bodies? It is Crow. Sometimes the Lakota have other ways of keeping the dead. It is not for the ears of strangers."

Ulysses blew and pawed the snow impatiently. "Do you believe these white men I seek have become privy to all of the Lakota's secrets?" Collins asked, feeling a trifle disaffected.

"Maybe. Maybe not. It is not good to share too much with outsiders." She scanned the horizon. "We must go. The *wanagipi*, the spirits of these men may be restless here so far from their home."

As they turned their horses west to rejoin the others, Collins was oddly disappointed that he would never be fully embraced by the people he had come to respect and for whom he felt genuine warmth.  Not even Wakalyapi, despite all the perils they had shared, would ever consider him to be more than an outsider, notwithstanding her own peripheral status.  When he considered the impossibility of Wakalyapi being accepted into the coastal Irish village of his birth, he realized the absurdity of this sentiment.  Oh well, he thought... *nil aon tintean mar do thintean fein.*  There is no fireside like your own fireside.

# 48

Ziyela allowed Collins to stroke his head, ever prepared to make good his escape. Wakalyapi was sitting by the fire, smoking her pipe and watching.

"What will you do with this dog?"

"What do you mean?" He rubbed an ear. The animal remained alert to sudden moves.

"When you leave us." Her look was inscrutable.

"I will leave him in your good care."

"How do you know I will not eat him?"

Collins smiled at her. "I will ask you to give your word that you will *not* eat him."

Kcanptepte walked into camp with a snowshoe hare. He spoke to Wakalyapi.

"He says you have caught this in one of your snares," she told C.W.

"Glad to be of service."

Camped back on the headwaters of the Redwater River, they were sheltered in a valley beneath a rim of bluffs. The weather had turned very cold and the ground was covered in deep snow. Sitting Bull had told them they would rest in this place for a few days before heading south to the Powder River and their rendezvous with Tasunka Witko. Much fatigued, the three of them were pleased to sit by the fire, smoke, nap and eat. Occasionally, some of the people from the village would come to visit and drink coffee, as this was a most popular beverage. The sugar had long since run out due to

Kcanptepte's sweet tooth.

"Why not stay with us?" Wakalyapi asked Collins, who was skinning the rabbit. Kcanptepte had fallen asleep on his robe with Ziyela tentatively curled up next to him.

Really quite flattered, he formulated his answer carefully. "Unfortunately, I have other obligations. Also... do you truly believe these people have a future off the agencies? You, no doubt, have a clear understanding of the military and its vagaries. Bear Coat and the others will never leave the Indians to their own devices."

"Tatanka Iyotaka wants to go to the Grandmother Country."

Collins was astonished. He had not thought of such an exigency. "Are you in earnest?"

She nodded. "He has said so."

The man called Mnicasniyanyanla came running into their camp, talking in great excitement. Wakalyapi jumped to her feet, hurriedly speaking to Kcanptepte, who had been awoken by the commotion. The boy ran to where the animals were picketed.

"Soldiers are coming down the valley. Will you shoot at your own?" Wakalyapi asked, fetching her Hawken, powder horn and pouch.

"They are not mine," he answered, running for his rifle and spare ammunition.

The boy brought them their horses and they led them following Mnicasniyanyanla up a small rise into the bustling village. Women were pulling down the lodges and warriors were swarming down the valley toward where the troopers could be seen, spread out in formation. Mounting their ponies, the men charged at the soldiers, firing their rifles. There was a volley from the troopers, mostly ineffectual due to the evasive maneuvers of the Indians. Collins held in his excited gelding and fired round after round from his Winchester. Wakalyapi had dismounted and was resting the barrel of her Hawken on a boulder, firing and reloading with great speed and precision.

All seemed to be in their favor until a loud blast suddenly issued from the ranks of the soldiers. A cannonball whizzed by Collins' head, making a sound most recognizable from the war. It took him a moment to control poor Ulysses, who was beside himself with terror. Wakalyapi had remounted and was now shooting arrows into the line of troops. Nearby a warrior rode at full gallop to scoop up a wounded comrade and carry him back to the women. Another explosion created greater chaos among the warriors and their ponies.

"They have a Howitzer," Collins yelled to Wakalyapi.

"They are not hitting anything," she answered and sent another arrow into the soldiers, now losing formation.

Collins levered another cartridge. A warrior rode by, yelling to Wakalyapi.

"He says we are pulling back. We must cover the retreat of the people."

Another shot sounded from the Howitzer and it seemed to provoke the warriors into a concerted movement to the rear, heading in the direction of their families and firing behind them as they rode. Despite the dire circumstances, Collins could not help but note the remarkable horsemanship of his fellows and he felt certain he had witnessed several white faces among them. They rode pell-mell through the previous location of the village and he saw that many lodges, blankets and buffalo robes, as well as a substantial herd of horses and mules, had been left behind in the impetus of departure.

When they caught up with the retreating camp, they reorganized and made certain that all children either rode pack animals or were placed on lodge pole drags. Kcanptepte had carefully packed all their belongings and made an enthusiastic show of his joy at their safe return.

Ziyela hovered behind the shelter of Molly's rear hocks. Collins reached out a hand to squeeze the boy's shoulder affectionately, nodding his gratitude. Kcanptepte grinned happily from his place on the roan's packs.

Forced once more to travel in the worst of winter conditions, the Hunkpapa band pushed southeast. Word reached Wakalyapi that much meat had been lost, but Sitting Bull had managed to retain the full supply of ammunition and pack mules for Crazy Horse. As snow squall after snow squall obliterated their trail, the procession of weary and disheartened people moved toward the camp of another legendary leader. Perhaps, thought Collins, the two great warriors together would inspire a final and foolhardy stand against the U.S. government and its inexorable policies. He fervently hoped he would not be there for the final chapter.

# 49

Having returned from an invitation to eat with Sitting Bull in his lodge and having left Wakalyapi behind to smoke with some of the men, Collins found that Kcanptepte and Ziyela were gone from their campsite and there was a stranger sitting by the fire. In the glow of twilight, Collins could plainly see that the man had his back to him and was pouring himself some coffee from their pot. A bear skin hat was beside him on a stump and his red hair hung between his shoulders in a thick braid.

"Come to me have you?" Collins asked, rounding the fire cautiously and standing before him.

"I have. This is good coffee. Will you not have some?" The man's brogue was patently Irish.

"Maybe," Collins answered. "Where's the boy?"

"He is off visiting. He knows me well and I requested to wait for you alone."

C.W. sat on a log and reached for a cup. The man picked up the coffeepot and poured.

"How many of you are there?" Collins asked, blowing on his steaming coffee.

"Not many. Your name?"

"Charles Wolfe Collins"

The man sipped from his cup. "My name is Aidan Mulhaire from Roscommon."

Collins studied his face. It was weathered and scarred, seated with deep green eyes. He had an agreeable manner.  "Sligo," he said.

"Ah, Sligo.  From fishing folk then?"

"Aye."

"Well, Mr. Charles Wolfe Collins...why do you seek us?  Word is that you are not here as an official emissary of the U.S. government seeking its own revenge.  The sight of you firing at blue-coated troopers was not unconvincing."

"No doubt." He poured more coffee for the both of them.  "There was an official report made of white men among the Indian forces at the Little Big Horn.  I was sent to find out if this report was accurate and, if so, to find the identity of these men."

Aidan Mulhaire's green eyes narrowed.  "Sent?"

"By President Grant...really rather unofficially," Collins told him with a wry smile.

"To what end?"

"The President expressed concern that you might be "Galvanized Yankees," renegade gun runners, even Mormons."

Mulhaire gave a sharp laugh.  "Mormons. No fear."

Wakalyapi walked out of the darkness.  "How is it, Charles?" she asked, cradling her ubiquitous Hawken.

"There is coffee," he told her.  "This is Aidan Mulhaire," he said, waving a hand toward their guest.

Mulhaire spoke to her in her native tongue.  She sat down between the two men and set her rifle aside.  "He speaks well," she told Collins.

"How long have you been among these people?" Collins asked Mulhaire, filling a cup for Wakalyapi and handing it to her.

"Many, many years."

"And the others?"

"We came together.  But we have been leaving separately.  *Nil a fhios ag aon duine ca´ bhfuil fod a bhais.*"

"Nobody knows where his sod of death is," Collins

translated.  "I met one of your confederates in Helena."

Mulhaire studied him.  "How is that possible?"

"His name was Thomas Cronin.  He was in jail."

"Thomas…how came he there?" Mulhaire asked, frowning.

"The drink.  He caused a row and was incarcerated.  The scalp of a white man was found in his possession."

"Jesus, mary and joseph! The fool!"  The man stared at the fire a moment.  "Did they hang him?"

Collins shrugged.  "I cannot say."

"Come man.  They could not let him live."

"I suppose not.  He suspected as much when I met with him."

Wakalyapi took out her tobacco pouch and offered it to the men.  They all filled their pipes.

"Cronin asked that I send you a message, if I indeed caught up with you," Collins told Mulhaire.

"Aye?"  Mulhaire lit an old briar with a hand carved stem wrapped in beaded leather.

"*'Is milis da ol e ach is searbh da ioc e.'*"

"The fool," Mulhaire said again.  His air of sorrow spoke more eloquently than his words.  "He disappeared in the Big Horn Mountains.  We thought perhaps he had met with an accident.  Poor Thomas was ever prey to the wiles of the drink and after he looted a flask from the battlefield, I feared he would crave for more."

They smoked silently for a while.  Ziyela crept back into camp carrying the frozen carcass of some small animal, lying down at the edge of the firelight and devouring it with zeal.

Mulhaire knocked out his pipe and stood.  "I must retire."

"Will you return?" Collins asked.

The man sighed heavily.  "Will you depart without knowing the full extent of our identity?"

"I will not."

"I feared as much," Mulhaire said and disappeared into the darkness.

❦❧

PRISONER

# 50

"What did you think of your white man?" Wakalyapi asked as they rode through unremitting inclement weather the following day.

"I do not know what to think," Collins answered honestly. He rubbed ice from his mustache. "What did *you* think?"

"I have heard he is honorable. He belongs to a warrior society."

She turned to speak to the boy on the packhorse behind her. He answered her at length, with Collins attempting to pick up any recognizable Lakota words.

"Kcanptepte's uncle, Little Knife, admires this man. He killed several blue coats on the Greasy Grass."

"Does he have a Lakota name?"

"*Hehak iktomi.*"

"And what does it mean?"

Wakalyapi grimaced. "It means moose."

"Oh." Collins said, smiling.

They rode in silence for some distance. Then Wakalyapi spoke again. "Maybe you would care to know what name you have been given."

He looked at her dubiously. "Maybe not."

She shrugged and turned to say something to Kcanptepte, who looked at Collins and grinned.

"*Wicasa leha'nkata.*"

A blast of wind pummeled them for several minutes, bringing gravelly sleet and making conversation an impossibility. When the brief gale had passed, he said, "I suppose you had better tell me the meaning."

"It means a man that has fallen in with us. A foreigner," Wakalyapi told him.

"That is not bad. I thought perhaps it might be insulting."

"It is a little insulting," she said, hiding a smile with her hand.

Kcanptepte spoke.

"He says they also call you something else...something not insulting." she translated.

"Yes?"

"*Wazi S´e.* It means very tall. Tall as a pine tree."

Collins was naturally more pleased with the second name. In truth, he was taller than many of his Hunkpapa companions. He still had no notion as to what Wakalyapi's real name might be. He knew better than to ask as she would, no doubt, dissimulate. Also, he had learned that it was not considered to be good manners to ask direct personal questions.

They rode across open prairie, now having crossed the Yellowstone. Sitting Bull and the others thought it best to cross the river east of Bear Coat's new fort then swing back around to the west in search of Crazy Horse's band in Powder River country. The plan, according to Wakalyapi, was to camp on the *Ptan´unpi Wakpala*, Pumpkin Creek, for a brief respite. No word had come as to the exact whereabouts of Tasunka Witko, but they obviously expected news. Meanwhile, they had heard that the Cheyenne village of Little Wolf and Dull Knife had been destroyed in a canyon on the Powder River. The Cheyenne had managed to kill and wound many soldiers, but had lost maybe thirty people and most of their possessions, including food, clothing, horses and lodges. Children died from exposure. Eventually, it was said, they found refuge with Crazy Horse.

Collins was always mystified how information came to the Hunkpapa leaders. It seemed that the eddies of people in and out of the forts and around those who scouted for the military carried tidings of conflicts and tragedies. According to these questionable sources, 'Three Stars' Crook had sent one of his men, Mackenzie, and around a thousand troops to attack the village. It appeared to Collins that Crook and Miles were locked in a deadly competition that would result in calamity for the Lakota and Cheyenne peoples. They had heard that military equipment bearing Seventh Cavalry markings had been found in Dull Knife's village. If this were true, retribution would be swift and painstaking.

The three companions reached Pumpkin Creek that evening and worked to build a comfortable camp fit for a few days' repose. High winds over the past days had cleared significant patches of fodder for the horses and they were hobbled to graze freely. Together, they contrived a sturdy hut of branches and hides, reminding Collins of some of the Yaqui shelters he had seen. As darkness fell, Kcanptepte roasted a hunk of remaining buffalo meat over the fire while Collins and Wakalyapi gathered more wood. The sky cleared and the aurora borealis shot parabolas of pulsing light across the blackness.

"*Hohetamahpiya*," Kcanptepte said, seeing Collins watching the lights.

Collins attempted to repeat the word. His tongue had great difficulty with the complex language. More proof, he thought, that these people were not the simple savages they were presumed to be. His companions refrained from mockery and helped him improve his pronunciation of the word. The meat was soon cooked and they ate hungrily. Having replenished their stores of coffee and tobacco through Kcanptepte's trading with the Métis, they made a full pot, packed their pipes and indulged their vices.

Someone coughed politely at the edge of their firelight and Ziyela barked from his hiding place nearby.

"*Hoakicipapi*," Wakalyapi greeted the person.

A short, slight figure came to their fire. In the flickering light, Collins observed that their visitor was another white man, very swarthy, with a black growth of beard. He had pale gray or very light blue eyes creased with deep wrinkles.

"Sit down," Collins invited.

The man took a seat on a rock. "Ta," he said.

Wakalyapi dug a spare cup out of their gear, filled it with coffee and handed it to him. He nodded his thanks, cradling the hot coffee carefully in his hands.

They sat quietly, waiting for their guest to speak.

"This is excellent... *Omawaste*." he said, after a few sips from his cup. "I decided to come to see you," he told Collins. "I believe there is some history you should know. Some truths should not die with us so that we will not be judged as harshly as may be. We did not know anyone was aware of our existence prior to your coming."

"Will you give me your name? I am Charles Collins."

"Yes. Charles *Wolfe* Collins, named for the honorable Theobald Wolfe Tone?"

"That is correct. And you?"

"Me *Da* named me for 'The Liberator.'"

"Daniel O'Connell is your name?"

"Aye. Daniel O'Connell Kinealy."

"Pleased to meet you, Daniel. I have come a long way to do so."

"Aye and you are persistent."

Collins smiled and repacked his pipe, handing the pouch over to Kinealy. The man shrugged. "I lost me pipe in the fracas with the troopers."

"I will share with you," Collins said, lighting his briar

with a stick from the fire and handing it over.

"Ta," Kinealy said and puffed with vigor. "One may live without one's friends, but not without one's pipe."

"True enough. Now, Mr. Kinealy, will you not tell me some of your story. I will report it as you tell it, upon my word."

"I understand you have the ear of the President himself," he said, handing the pipe over.

"I do indeed. Do you wish to return to white society?" Collins asked.

He laughed loudly, exhibiting a mouthful of intermittent teeth. "None of us either crave it nor believe it possible."

Kinealy turned pensive. He helped himself to more coffee and took another turn with Collins' pipe. After a while, he asked, "Do you have any notion of what has been happening to these people, Mr. Collins?"

"Some. I am fully aware that the U.S. government has been culpable in their dealings with them...in spite of Grant's 'Peace Policy.'"

"Once we might have returned to life among the *wasicu*. Even after the circumstances that perpetuated our... apostasy. Then we witnessed too much. We became sensible to atrocities sanctioned, nay, even authorized by the federals."

Wakalyapi was listening with interest. "He does not know much. He has not seen enough," she told the Irishman.

"I wish to know," Collins said, simply.

"Women and children...especially children, are targets. The worst of it began before the war had even ended. We were already living with the people and heard of Chivington's massacre of the Cheyenne."

"Beckwourth went to the Cheyenne," Wakalyapi said, eloquently spitting into the fire. "He tried to get them to surrender."

"There was an investigation, was there not?" Collins asked.

"The Cheyenne and Arapahoe were pushed off their ancestral lands," Kinealy said. "Of what use was an investigation? When has the government ever punished its own?"

"There was gold. Just as there is now in the Black Hills," Collins said. "I suppose justice must always be subjugated by greed."

"Just so. Just so," Kinealy said, nodding. He laid Collins' spent pipe on a rock nearby. "Do you know of the most coveted souvenirs to a lowly blue-coat on the northern plains?"

"No." Collins had a presentiment that he really did not wish to know.

"Well, let me tell you. One is a tobacco pouch fashioned from the...sack of a warrior."

Collins was not certain he understood correctly. "The sack? You surely do not mean..."

"The scrotum, Mr. Collins. The scrotum," Kinealy said.

Collins glanced at Wakalyapi, who nodded in agreement. "There are also hat bands," she said.

"Hat bands?" Collins asked, with growing dismay.

"Aye sir," the man said. "Hat bands manufactured from the lips of the private parts of women."

"That is not possible," C.W. said. "It cannot be possible."

"Soldiers will gut pregnant women while life remains in them. They show them their own unborn children as they lay dying. Chivington made a spectacular exhibition of scalps in Denver to great acclaim...some of which were the scalps of ...women's parts."

Collins shook his head in repulsion. He was speechless. Kcanptepte, sensing his consternation, placed a hand on his arm.

"After we became aware of these and other heinous acts committed by emissaries of the government, my comrades and I perpetually shunned the trappings of civilization."

Collins sighed, smiling briefly at Kcanptepte and retrieving his pipe to refill it. "Never will I cease to be amazed by the infinite supply of human cruelty. 'I am stifled with this smell of sin.'" he said, quoting the Earl of Salisbury and lighting his pipe.

"It is late," Wakalyapi said. "Will you tell us your story?" she asked Kinealy.

"I will so," the man said. "But perhaps the story will be better served by more than myself, alone."

"Are you deserters?" Collins asked abruptly. "Is that why you dissemble so?"

"We are deserters, sir." Kinealy answered. " 'Tis not an easy confession."

"No doubt."

"Are *we* not deserters?" Wakalyapi asked wryly, her scar pulled up in a lopsided smile.

"I think not," Collins said. "We chose discretion."

"As did we, my son. As did we," Kinealy said, reaching for the coffeepot to refill his cup.

MOURNING

# 51

The next day word came to the village that Miles and Crazy Horse had engaged each other in a conflict near Hanging Woman Creek. Miles had used artillery to good purpose and an attempt at ambush had failed on the part of Crazy Horse, due largely to the premature actions of a handful of young warriors. Even so, according to the reports, a storm had ended the skirmish without untoward bloodshed on either side. Tasunka Witko had taken his people down the Tongue River to the Big Horn Mountains in an attempt to hunt buffalo. On the following morning, the village would be struck and they would follow.

After a day of sorting through gear, cleaning their guns and seeking feed for their animals, the three of them sat by the fire dining on stew made from ptarmigan and tubers and tree fungus gathered by Kcanptepte. Collins thought it tasted similar to some unpleasant Chinese cuisine he had sampled in San Francisco, but they were hungry and it was soon dispatched.

Kinealy had promised to return with a few of his confederates and give Collins the full history of their desertion and alliance with the Sioux, but he failed to appear. Again frustrated by the circumspection of his quarry, he determined to track these men down and coerce them into narrating their stories; at gunpoint if necessary. Wakalyapi did not believe this to be a very advisable scheme and talked him out of it.

"What are your plans after we find Tasunka Witko?" she asked.

"I will admit to a great amount of trepidation in regard to this fellow. Does he not find enmity with every white man?"

"Perhaps. But I believe you now have the protection of Sitting Bull, No Neck and several of the other warriors. My worry is that you are becoming more ensnared in the fight between Bear Coat and the Lakota. Will you not have difficulty explaining this to your Washington?"

Collins smiled. He was stroking the head of the yellow dog, who was beginning to seek affection on the rare occasion. "'My Washington' will appreciate the vicissitudes of my current predicament if I can get back to him having completed my assignment. These white Lakota are more elusive than...Ziyela here."

The skittish dog had heard a noise, growled and run for cover. Kcanptepte spoke.

"He says there are wolves about. He said he saw much sign," the woman translated.

They smoked in silence. Collins could feel the wind growing in strength and feared another blizzard. He could not remember being as cold as he had been on this expedition. He resolved to seek his subsequent assignments in warmer climes. If he survived this one, he thought grimly.

Early the next morning, they rolled out of their buffalo robes into another few inches of fresh snow and temperatures that seemed a trifle warmer. Collins went out to where the horses were picketed and found Wakalyapi's old roan lifeless in a snowdrift. He called to her and she stood looking at the animal. He thought a moment she would weep, but she said nothing and turned to walk back to camp. He felt a remarkable sense of loss, having spent much time with the creature and having appreciated its stamina and endurance.

Kcanptepte and he began packing up their outfit, as Wakalyapi was nowhere to be found. While Collins was saddling Molly and Ulysses, the boy borrowed his knife and disappeared in the direction of the roan. He returned with several hunks of meat. Collins shook his head vigorously.

"We need the meat," Wakalyapi said behind him. He turned to see her holding the lead of a stocky bay horse, thin from lack of rations, but appearing to be strong and able.

"What did you trade?" he asked.

"A fine blanket I had been saving. It was of no consequence."

"I am sorry," he said, placing a hand on her shoulder.

She met his eyes a moment. He always sensed a depth of sadness within her and now it seemed to have become more profound. "It was only an old horse," she said and turned away. "We must hurry."

Kcanptepte handed Collins his knife, wiped clean of blood. As they mounted their horses, the boy climbing onto the new bay's packs, Ziyela appeared with his muzzle red from feasting. They took their accustomed position following the body of migrating Lakota village, crossing the frozen creek and traveling southwest toward the Tongue River.

Around midday, Kinealy found them. He was riding a bony buckskin mare, with a roman nose and missing the tips of her ears. His saddle was an ornately beaded Indian affair and he rode carrying a Springfield carbine in his left hand. The man's thin black hair hung loosely around his shoulders beneath a worn beaver hat.

"Charles Wolfe Collins," he said. "I am mortally ashamed." His breath made clouds in the chilly air.

"Of what?" Collins asked.

"I did not keep my word to you, the truth being I could not convince my brothers to meet with you."

"I am completely at your whim," Collins said. "I truly mean you no harm, but as deserters I can well understand your reluctance to reveal yourselves."

Kinealy smiled. "We have been well pleased with our defection overall, but there is an abiding sense of shame at having abandoned our comrades. Did you fight in the war?"

"I did, although not always in the capacity of a soldier."

Molly had taken a dislike to the new bay gelding and laid her ears back to bite him. Wakalyapi made a scolding noise and pulled the packhorse out of her reach.

"It seems very long ago now," Kinealy said quietly, gazing ahead into the distance.

"Were you and your mates with the Irish Brigade?"

The man looked over at him. "We were. Most of us were with the Fighting 69th and had all been members of the Fenian Brotherhood under O'Mahoney."

"And, no doubt, you hoped that one day you would use your military experience to strike a blow for the liberty of Ireland?" Collins asked, without derision.

"I suppose so...did you happen to have your pipe handy?"

Collins reached into his pocket and handed the man his pipe and tobacco pouch. "How many of you were there?" he asked. "How many of you at the first?"

"In Company K?" Kinealy asked, laying the reins across his mare's withers and balancing his rifle on his lap. He packed the pipe. "Did you have a match? I have not had any for many a long day."

Collins reached in another pocket and handed him his battered nickel match safe.

"There must have been around sixty or so of us what joined up together. It was Thomas Meagher, you see. A hero of the Battle of Balingarry." Kinealy lit the pipe and handed the tobacco and matches back to Collins. "Ta," he said.

"You are welcome," said Collins.

"We had no idea of the disintegration of the man," the Irishman said, obviously enjoying his smoke. "How could we? After the first Bull Run and Fair Oaks, we had begun to notice inconsistencies...erratic behavior and such. Despite our growing reputation and his, the drinking was reaching Homeric proportions. And we were losing terrible numbers of men. McClellan was already questioning the high rate of casualties *before* Antietam. We did great work at Gaines' Mill, but lost too many of our fellows."

"I had heard the rumors of his drinking," Collins said. "There are always rumors, especially when a man is climbing in the ranks."

"Aye, but the gossip was not amiss. By Antietam his judgment was gravely impaired. We were slaughtered at 'Bloody Lane,' losing hundreds of our mates in each volley. He fell off his horse, for chrissake! Later, McClellan made a report that his horse had been shot. It was a grand humbug."

Collins did not respond. He let the man assemble his memories at will and felt a bit as if he were waiting for a wild animal to approach. He feared any responding remarks on his part might frighten off the long sought information Kinealy possessed. Wakalyapi had been listening with interest and rode nearby, keeping the bay a little distance from Molly.

Kinealy tamped the pipe with a finger and cupped his palm over the bowl to suck more smoke from the tobacco. "Then came Fredericksburg," he said. "That ungodly hell of bloody death. Do you know of the battle?" he asked.

"I know the Irish Brigade broke its back on Marye's Heights," Collins told him quietly.

"We were utterly destroyed. Meagher ordered us to

charge uphill straight into the mouths of Confederate artillery. French and Zook had already been flattened. We charged, by god... up that hill all slick with mud and blood...tripping over those what had fallen before us. Some of the wounded pulled at our pant legs, begging us to stop, the poor souls. But on we went, as Meagher withdrew to the safety of the town. I will tell you, Collins...the heart went out of many of us that day. Some of us made it close to the Confederate position, but as the day waned, such a force of fire came down upon us that we were razed as corn to the scythe." Kinealy raised a hand to wipe his eyes. "Most of us withdrew in the night and worked to find what was left of our original mob. Whilst Meagher and his followers made a drunken celebration over new flags for the brigade, we gathered our wounded and faded out of that bedeviled arena, sure that only annihilation lay in our future if we stayed."

Kinealy knocked the spent pipe out on his knee and handed it to Collins. He sighed deeply and retreated into silence.

"By December of 1862, over a hundred thousand soldiers had gone missing," Collins said after a while.

Kinealy looked at him in surprise. "That many? We ran into some of them as we made our way west. Some were bound for Canada. We figured we would vanish into the frontier wilderness. We doctored our wounds as best we could and did a wee bit of robbery to buy wagons and supplies. We would get some distance behind us, then maybe find gold or do a bit of farming...I cannot rightly remember all the schemes we gnawed upon."

"I found a diary at Little Big Horn," Collins ventured. "It hinted at retribution."

Kinealy gave him a guarded look. "Do you have it still?" he asked.

"Yes. Is it yours?"

"Not mine. It was Cronin's. Aidan told us you met

him in Helena."

"I did not think to mention it to him. I showed him a claddagh he seemed to recognize."

"Must have belonged to his younger brother, Daniel. We lost him on the Greasy Grass. Could not find his body and Thomas went back to craving the drink."

"And the reprisal? Was it one of you that drowned Meagher at Fort Benton?"

Kinealy smiled without humor. "Some of us stumbled upon him by accident. Dolan, always a hand on water, was piloting a riverboat on the Missouri. Many of our number had already fallen in with our Hunkpapa brothers, but Thomas and Daniel Cronin, James Dolan and a few others preferred to sojourn among the settlements. After Meagher had been...dispatched, they came to us and became Lakota as we remain."

"And how many are you now?" Wakalyapi asked.

Kinealy looked at her a moment. "Eight of us now. We lost many to disease, battle and mishap. Some left for Canada before winter set in. The ones with families feared the ire of the army after the Little Big Horn." He turned his light eyes to Collins. "Will you now turn us over to Bear Coat?"

"Of course not, Kinealy. I gave you my word. I report to Grant and that is all."

"Charles is no friend to Bear Coat," Wakalyapi told Kinealy. "Perhaps Miles would like to hang him," she added, smiling behind her hand.

"Perhaps," Collins said, smiling back. "I have a watch, the diary and the ring I will return to you," he said to the Irishman. "I am seeking a valuable pistol that belonged to a friend of mine. It is an over and under pistol made by J. Manton & Company. It had the name of Keogh upon it."

"I know naught of such a weapon, but I will ask around. How did your friend come to lose it?"

"He was killed at the Little Big Horn."

Kinealy rode in silence as the sun briefly emerged from a blanket of clouds and shone pale light upon the frozen land. At last, he said, "I am sorry you lost your friend. I hope to christ I was not the one to kill him."

"He was a soldier. He died a soldier's death."

"And I? What manner of death shall I die?" Kinealy asked, pensively.

"'Conscience doth make cowards of us all,'" Collins said, quoting Hamlet. "I believe you are a soldier still, for are you not yet defending hearth and home?"

"A shrewd reply," Kinealy said, "for it seems to me you have come into our fold."

"And will be leaving it forthwith," Collins told him, sincerely hoping he was not wrong.

# 52

Collins need not have been concerned about his reception from Tasunka Witko.  His presence was barely remarked in the excitement over the arrival of boxes of ammunition, extra robes and blankets, old friends and relatives and, of course, the great chief, Sitting Bull. From Wakalyapi, he learned that he was in the midst of some of the most illustrious warriors of the Lakota and Cheyenne people.  The Sans Arc, Oglala, Miniconjou and Hunkpapa were all represented, as well as those Cheyenne of Dull Knife's band that had fled the soldiers on the Powder River.  Collins found several opportunities in which to study Crazy Horse and was much taken by the man's light brown hair, hazel eyes, innate capacity for leadership and otherworldly mien.

As had become their wont, they made their camp a little apart, sheltered at the base of the Big Horn Mountains.  There had been a successful hunt in the mountains and meat was distributed to the newcomers, including Wakalyapi, Kcanptepte and Collins, but the quantity would not be sufficient to long sustain all the people in such a large village.  Kcanptepte had smoked the horse-meat and it was held in reserve for leaner times.

The leaders were seriously divided as to whether the people should surrender to Miles or continue to fight, the Sans Arc and Miniconjou generally being the ones who wished to give up.  The *akicita* made certain the families that attempted to sneak out of camp were brought back.

Many of the people were sick and wounded, crowded into lodges and suffering terribly. Vehement disputes were not uncommon. Collins avoided the village as he desired to remain as unobtrusive as possible, given the heightened passions and anger toward the whites. As a result, he did not see Kinealy, Mulhaire or any of the others for several days.

There was not much to occupy their days, except hunting, setting snares and exploring their surroundings. Collins spent much of his time finding forage for the animals. One day, Wakalyapi took Collins to the site of Fort Phil Kearny, a mound of burnt rubble beneath the snow.

"We were certain we had won our land forever," she said, looking east across the open plains.

"It was quite a victory. To force the U.S. Army to relinquish its forts."

"*Han.* But to what end?"

"Were you here, then?"

She studied him a moment. "I was here. I am like the bat...a winged creature or a land creature as it serves. Sometimes with the bluecoats, sometimes with the people. I do not regret the *wasichu* I have wiped out."

"And now? When you are rid of me will you return to Fort Shaw?"

A raven croaked in a nearby tree, sounding to Collins like a rusty hinge. Wakalyapi kicked at a blackened timber and reached down to pick up a broken china cup. It was delicately painted with roses and bluebirds, oddly incongruous to their surroundings.

"I will see you safely away. Then, I think, I will never return to the company of white people."

Collins looked at her, standing in the ruins of the fort wearing the beaded cavalry overcoat of unknown origins, her strong and damaged face silhouetted against the blank sky. To him, she was an anomaly of tragic history.

"Do you mind an impolite question?" he asked.

"No," she said, tossing the broken china aside.

"Did you have children?"

The woman did not respond for a long while. "No," she finally said. "Beckwourth."

"He hurt you?"

"It is of no consequence," she told him, walking back to her horse. "We will hunt now."

That evening, as they were licking their fingers after a fine haunch of roasted venison, several figures approached their fire in the darkness. Ziyela barked fiercely until silenced by a stick thrown by Kcanptepte. Wakalyapi reached nonchalantly to pull her Hawken across her lap.

"*Tuweska?*" she asked.

" 'Tis Kinealy. I have brought guests."

The Irishman walked into camp with seven other men, one of them Mulhaire and all apparently white. Collins could not see well in the flickering firelight, but it seemed that many of them had light hair and eyes. Their clothing was a diverse amalgam of civilian, military and Indian origins.

"Collins," Mulhaire said in greeting.

"Mulhaire," Collins said, with a tilt of his head.

"*Hokahe,*" Kcanptepte said, waving his hand.

The men arranged themselves on the ground around the fire ring. Wakalyapi laid her rifle aside and took out her pipe and tobacco.

"Smoke?" she asked.

Some of the men pulled pipes out of their pockets. They accepted her pouch and filled their pipes in turn, lighting them and sharing with each other. Collins fixed his own pipe and shared it with Kinealy, next to him.

They smoked in silence, then one at a time the men introduced themselves by their Christian names. There was Lorcan Connor, James Flanagan, Sean O'Hara,

Duffy Ryan, Colm Kelly, Rory O'Higgins and Mulhaire and Kinealy. Connor and Ryan were brawny men while the others were of average build.

"It is a pleasure to finally meet you," Collins said.

Ryan eyed him suspiciously. "It is passing strange that you would take this much trouble just to meet us," he said.

"Not so strange," Collins told him. "President Grant was made aware of your presence at the Little Big Horn. He commissioned me to find you."

"To what end?" the man named Flanagan asked gruffly.

"Politics. It does not bode well for Indian policy that white men would be sided with the Indian. Grant's Quakers and Unitarians have been unpopular enough. The President needed to know who you were. I feel certain he will not pursue this further."

"And what is in this for you?" Ryan asked. "You are on a very dangerous mission."

"I am a private agent for hire. I have been at Grant's disposal since the war."

"Are you proud of this?" Kelly asked, laughing derisively. Collins recognized his laugh as the one that had girded him days before in Sitting Bull's lodge.

"It is a living. My god, man...I am Irish. Do you not remember how it is?"

"We do so," Mulhaire said, frowning at Kelly. "We are not the ones to judge," he added.

Wakalyapi handed the coffeepot to Kcanptepte and spoke to him. The boy got up and limped to the nearby stream to fill it from the hole in the ice they kept open for their use. When he returned, he ground coffee beans and added them to the pot on the fire. Collins went to their packs and handed out the few cups they possessed.

"I understand now *why* you are here," Collins said after a while. "I would like to hear the story of your attachment to these people."

The men talked amongst themselves in their adopted language. Wakalyapi did not translate and Collins surmised it would have been considered rude to intrude upon the private confabulation.

"I suppose there is no harm in it," the man called Connor finally said in English. "Daniel here is the bard." He gestured at Kinealy. "We will let him tell it."

Kcanptepte settled the coffee grounds with cold water, as Collins had taught him, and began to pour coffee. Pipes were laid aside for cups and all was shared. Kinealy waited until everyone settled back with coffee, then began.

"It was summer of '63. We had avoided settlements and were fast running out of food. Some of us had finally succumbed to wounds sustained at Fredericksburg, the rest of us were badly malnourished and two had died from cholera. We found ourselves on a vast, desolate prairie and we had only two wagons left. Our oxen and horses were dying from lack of water and all the grass was dried out from drought and held little nutrition for them." O'Hara handed a cup to Kinealy, who drank and handed it back.

"We stumbled onto a colossal herd of buffalo. Those of us capable of hunting took our rifles and went to pick off stragglers while the others made camp. We had seen the effect of a buffalo stampede on some wagons before and did not wish to excite them. In the twinkling of an eye, we were surrounded by fierce men on horseback... warriors of the Oglala and Hunkpapa come to hunt the *tatanka* and not kindly disposed to our ragtag bunch about to spoil the game."

Some of the men nodded in remembrance.

"They herded us back to the others at the wagons without stripping us of our weapons and we stood bravely together, prepared for the end and glad to meet it in each other's company. We had been through so much and dying in battle was still honorable in our thinking. We held our rifles, axes, knives, whatever came to hand… some forty of us of the Fighting 69th. The warriors talked much, gesturing at us. There must have been around eighty of them all around us, their horses dancing restlessly, their feathers fluttering in the breeze. We could smell the wood smoke and bear grease on them and it smelled like death."

Collins thought to himself that Kinealy was, indeed, a storyteller. He noticed that Kcanptepte was listening in rapt attention as if he could understand every word.

"Of a sudden, many of them dismounted and came at us with coup sticks, quirts, war clubs and fists. The assault came so precipitously, we did not have the chance to fire a single round. They beat us ferociously, took our weapons, most of our clothing, our boots and hats. They used *wikan*, leather cord, to bind us in a line, while many of them raided our goods in the wagons, butchered our oxen and secured our horses. A group of them returned to the herd to hunt buffalo. The rest of them found matches and piled whatever they did not want next to the wagons and burned the lot. Finally there seemed to be an argument and we found out later that many of them wanted to just kill us and be rid of us, while others thought we could be traded at Fort Laramie for rifles and ammunition. If we had known then, we could have assured them that nobody would have traded aught for us as we mattered to no one except to hang as deserters."

The wind came up and blew a shower of sparks from the fire into the night. Collins passed his lit pipe to Kinealy, who thanked him and smoked for a moment before continuing.

"The faction what thought we might be valuable as trade goods won out, so a few of the men were left to haul us back to their camp while the rest of them joined the hunt. Several of us suffered from head wounds from their beating and all of us were weak from hunger, so their impatience grew as they dragged us behind their horses. We helped each other keep walking and after an eternity of cactus spines and rock bruises in our feet, we entered the village, mostly empty, as the women had already departed to begin butchering buffalo carcasses. We were thrown down in a heap near the edge of camp, a pile of desolate pilgrims bereft of hope and desperate for water.

"They all became caught up in the hunt and the feasting and we were mostly forgotten, until late in the night some raw scrap meat was finally tossed in our direction along with a bladder of water. We shared the bounty and, with our bodies somewhat restored, we began to hope for escape or, at least, survival."

Kinealy reached for an empty cup and filled it from the coffeepot. He handed Collins' pipe back and sighed.

"We survived," he said. "But it was hell for many days."

Many of the Irishmen nodded and smiled in assent. "They used us as pack animals," O'Hara said.

"Aye," said Kinealy. "They saved their horses and used us instead. When the butchering and feasting was done and the village was struck, they loaded us poor souls with hides and meat and all variety of goods. We were given enough food and water to keep us alive, and finally some cast off footwear, so we could continue to travel. In stubborn Celtic fashion, we would not submit nor show how gravely we suffered. At last, this earned respect and the abuse diminished. Mulhaire, a real scholar when it comes to languages, learned the language swiftly and used it to good purpose. By winter, we had been adopted into the fold. Some of us found our darling wives soon after and began our families."

Kinealy paused in sadness. "We mourn for them," he said after a moment, gazing desolately into the flames.

"*Hunhunhé*," Wakalyapi said, in commiseration.

Finishing his coffee and visibly shaking off his grief, Kinealy continued. "The Lakota tribal lifestyle is not unsimilar to that of the ancient Irish. It came naturally to us and as we learned their ways and religion, we saw many aspects what seemed similar to the old tales and beliefs we had been taught in our youth. Some of the men gravitated back to white settlements, yearning for money and whiskey, but most of us found fulfillment in the aboriginal life. And here you find us. In truth, I believe it is books we have missed the most."

Several of the men nodded.

"So those of you left here have no families?" Collins asked.

"No longer," Flanagan said quietly.

"Aye," O'Higgins said bitterly. "The anger that fueled Little Big Horn was much inspired by vengeance. They were coming again at our families. It was cowardly and unmanly."

"You have fought many battles against the U.S. Army?" Collins asked.

"Why would you want to know?" Kelly asked suspiciously.

"I was merely being curious. After all, I fought them myself."

"So you did," said Mulhaire, who seemed to function as a leader to the Irishmen. "The answer is that we have engaged in every battle with the Hunkpapa and sometimes the combined forces of other bands. Instead of fighting for the liberation of Eire, we now fight for the liberation of our adopted people. We are only ashamed of our desertion of the 69th...but at the time there seemed to be no other options."

"I understand," Collins said truthfully. "'By being once false for ever to be true,'" he said, quoting from *Love's Labour's Lost*.

"Well said, even for an Englishman," Mulhaire said.

"Shakespeare had the soul of an Irishman," Collins told him.

"That may be more of a curse than a blessing," Mulhaire said philosophically. "For I believe we were placed upon this earth to suffer passions that far exceed those of other men."

"Perhaps," said C.W. "But…a vessel holds only its fill."

FREDERICKSBURG

# 53

Over the following days, the Irishmen visited frequently, sometimes en masse, sometimes individually. Collins returned the claddagh and the diary to Mulhaire to dispose of as he saw fit. The watch, he discovered, had belonged to James Flanagan's best friend, Patrick Connell, killed on the Little Big Horn. The woman depicted in the daguerreotype was, indeed, the man's mother. Flanagan became quite sentimental at receiving the memento and vowed to carry it with him to the end of his days.

Collins joined the men in reminiscing about their boyhoods in Ireland and singing old ballads and the supply of coffee beans was greatly depleted as they sat by the fire while day followed day. He was unable to discover news of Keogh's pistol until Wakalyapi found a warrior who had looted and traded it to a Métis near the Missouri. The band to which the trader belonged had long departed for Grandmother Country. Collins was forced to relinquish his maudlin aspiration to obtain the weapon.

He found himself becoming restive and eager to return. Grant would soon, no doubt, be replaced by the pending inauguration of the new president. As inconsequential as his mission had become, he yet intended to make his report and exact final remuneration. Violent arguments regarding surrender continued to break out in the village and Collins feared that the relentless Miles might find and attack their position any day. Wakalyapi refused to consider leaving the security of the village to risk capture by soldiers. Her fear was not unfounded and Collins was certainly hesitant to hazard another encounter with Miles.

As the unrelenting winter weather brought more snow and intense cold, the large population of the village pressured surrounding resources and their situation became more desperate. Wakalyapi returned from visiting one morning and brought word that Sitting Bull had reached a decision.

"We are moving north," she told Collins. "He has pleaded with Tasunka Witko, Red Bear and many of the others to join him, but most believe the agencies are the only possibility for survival. Black Moon and his band have already traveled across the Medicine Line and Tatanka Iyotaka will follow." She sat by the fire.

"And us?" C.W. asked, braiding hide into a new lead for Molly.

"We will travel with them until we reach striking distance to Fort Buford. When we are close, I will leave you."

"If you do not accompany me to the fort, I cannot pay you what I owe you."

"It is of no consequence, Charles. Pay me what you can." She sat down near the fire and took out her pipe. "Perhaps you own something I covet."

"And what might that be?" he asked, flexing his fingers, stiff from the cold.

"Your Winchester repeater."

He grinned at her. "You covet my rifle?"

"Yes," she said, stone faced.

"Well...I am not certain it is advisable to provide weapons to hostiles. It is an act that could be easily censured."

"Perhaps," she said, inscrutably. "Perhaps I can take it by force and you would be held blameless."

Collins laughed loudly and Ziyela jumped from his

place nearby. Kcanptepte came into camp excited by the news of imminent departure. He signed to Collins that he desired some of his tobacco. Collins handed over his nearly empty pouch and the boy took out his dilapidated pipe and packed the bowl.

"What will happen to him?" Collins asked Wakalyapi.

"He and the dog will stay with me and I will promise not to eat either of them."

"And you will go to Canada?"

"I will go to Canada. There is nothing left for me anywhere." She reached over with a burning stick and lit Kcanptepte's pipe for him. "Where will you go after Washington?"

"Back to my home north of San Francisco. I have a small house on the coast that reminds me of Ireland."

"You might visit Canada sometime?" she asked, avoiding his eyes.

"I might. It might be nice to go there, but not in the winter. Never in the winter."

"You might have friends there who would want to see you," Wakalyapi said shyly, getting up and walking away.

They left the next morning, packing their animals with their diminishing supplies, making fortuitously light loads for the weakening livestock. The Lakota bands parted ways unceremoniously. There was resentment and suspicion as some of the Cheyenne, Miniconjou and Sans Arc had decided to join the Hunkpapa rather than give up their ponies and guns to the agencies. Wakalyapi told Collins that Crazy Horse intended to hold the Powder River Country, but would have few warriors left to fight with him.

As two flocks of birds, the people separated and journeyed north and east respectively. Women called to each other as the distance grew between the bands. The Irishmen stayed with their Hunkpapa brothers and some of them joined Collins and Wakalyapi as they rode behind the assemblage. Kinealy frequently sought their company and Collins wondered whether or not the man had grown attached to his guide and interpreter. They seemed to be of a similar age and both were suspended between two cultures. He fervently hoped that simple contentment could find Wakalyapi in her waning years and thought, perhaps, this belabored Gael might lend solace.

"So it is back to kith and kin with you, Mr. Collins?" Kinealy asked as they put the wind to their backs.

"No kith nor kin, Mr. Kinealy. And you? To Canada then?"

"Aye. With so many Irishmen already there, what notice will a few more take?"

Flanagan and Connor were riding alongside Wakalyapi and Kcanptepte, conversing in *Lakol*, the Lakota language.

"You will not stay with the Indians?" Collins asked.

"I will so. As long as I may evade reprisals. I am well up in my years and do not favor the notion of a military prison."

Collins shifted in his saddle to ease his back. He had found himself thinking lately of hot baths. "I do not believe there would be a viable danger in Canada," he said. "Besides, I am aware of a few dubious veterans who now receive a pension. The government has engaged itself in new concerns, such as the obliteration of these people here."

"Maybe so," Kinealy said, slumped on his wizened mare. "But there is always the Little Big Horn."

"Yes," Collins was forced to admit. "There is the Little Big Horn."

# 54

Again, they crossed the frozen Yellowstone well east of the confluence with the Tongue River.  Word reached them that Bear Coat was hunkered down at the cantonment and they sought to avoid him at all cost.  Game was scarce and, at last, Collins was forced to eat horse-meat or abide debilitating hunger.  The fell weather tested their endurance.  Compelled to keep moving for fear of the soldiers, the children, elders and livestock suffered greatly and heartrending wails heard in the Lakota village testified to the loss of loved ones.

Kinealy had taken to camping with their little group, sharing the work and whatever he had to offer.  He had somehow acquired a pipe made of deer bone, but tobacco was running short and smoking was reserved for after the evening meal, such as it was. The coffee had long been used up. They spent a great amount of time foraging for the animals and themselves.  Kcanptepte was depended upon to seek out the remnants of edible plants and tubers to add to their stores.  Ziyela disappeared for long periods and Collins did not wish to know what he survived upon.

They reached the Redwater River very near to the location of their skirmish with the blue coats.  Following the stream northeast, Collins knew they were nearing the point of divergence.  Already desolate due to hunger and the audible mourning in the Hunkpapa village, his spirits sank lower at the thought of leaving his friends and the others to an unknown fate.  By the campfire one evening, Wakalyapi quietly told him they would be taking their leave on the following day.

"I will guide you to the Missouri a day's ride west from Fort Buford," she said.  "We will go into the village so that you may speak to Tatanka Iyotaka."

The next morning, while Kcanptepte and Kinealy packed up camp, Wakalyapi took Collins into the village, bustling with preparations for the day's journey.  They found Sitting Bull sitting by a fire speaking to his mother, Her-Holy-Door.  She smiled at Collins and he greeted her.

Wakalyapi spoke to the chief and motioned toward Collins.  Sitting Bull studied him, looking up from his seated position. Collins noticed he was wrapped in the grizzly bear pelt, fully tanned and beaded along the edges.  He spoke to Wakalyapi.

"He wants your word you will not betray his location to the soldiers," she told Collins.

He held the chief's dark eyes and said, "Tell him I give my word.  Tell him I have grown very fond of the people and would do no harm to them."

She translated and the chief, still looking at Collins, spoke again.

"Tatanka Iyotaka thanks you for your friendship.  He sends his best wishes for your health."

"*Phila´mayaye*," Collins answered.

Sitting Bull said, "Goodbye, *Wazi S´e*."  He gave a small hand gesture and a kind smile.

"Goodbye, *Tatanka Iyotaka*."

They walked away from the chief's fire and back to their camp without speaking.  Collins felt remarkably saddened by the leave-taking and was not relishing the idea of parting ways with his closest companions.  The animals were all saddled and packed upon their return and Kinealy and Kcanptepte were standing by their mounts waiting for them.

"We have decided to accompany you," Kinealy said. "At least until you are in sight of the fort."

"I am glad," Collins said, grinning at the two of them. "I am very glad."

As they prepared to separate from the body of the village, the other Irishmen came to say their farewells. Mulhaire gave him a bit of smoked meat, Flanagan and O'Hara presented him with a small supply of tobacco, and the rest of them wished him luck in Irish and Lakota blessings. As they parted way, it occurred to Collins, that had fate slightly altered his course, he might well have been one of these men, sharing the uncertain destiny of a people on the brink of disaster. Not so different, he thought, than the Irish in the Great Famine. Perhaps his mother had not been amiss. Perhaps the Irish were indeed targeted by the heavens. But then, it would seem, so were the Lakota peoples.

Wakalyapi was much preoccupied during the journey to the Missouri. She hunted far a field and, to everyone's gratitude, returned the third day with a mule deer doe. That evening, they feasted until they could hold no more and Ziyela was satiated on scraps and gristle. Their spirits lifted, they smoked and talked until late. Camped in the sheltered lee of a bluff, their firelight danced upon the sandstone cheerily above and Collins knew he would always fondly remember the night.

On the following morning, they came to the Missouri River, stretching wide within its snowy banks. They sat upon their horses, looking down from the brink and eastward seeing the far distant low-lying smoke of Fort Buford on the confluence with the Yellowstone.

"We will go now, Charles," Wakalyapi said simply.

"Yes."

"Let us smoke one more time together."

They dismounted and found an overhang in the sandstone rim along the river. They took out their pipes and shared Wakalyapi's pouch. Collins produced his match safe and offered a light to everyone. The four of them smoked quietly, sitting on the sandy dry floor of their refuge and looking at their feet. When they were finished, Collins went to Molly's packs and took out his remaining supply of coin, as he had learned that paper money had little value on the frontier. He placed the silver and three golden double eagles into his tobacco pouch and held it out to Wakalyapi.

"I will also give you my Winchester," he told her as she accepted the pouch. He walked to his saddle and retrieved the rifle. "May it keep you safe in all eventualities," he said, handing it to the woman. His vision blurred momentarily and he turned toward Ulysses until he had regained composure. When he turned back he saw that Kcanptepte was weeping openly. Slipping the Green River knife from his belt, he gave it to the boy and placed a hand upon his shoulder.

He looked at Kinealy, standing aside politely. "I would like to present you with my volume of Shakespeare."

The Irishman's eyebrows rose in disbelief. "Oh now you cannot mean it. That would be lovely."

"With the provisional agreement that you share it with Wakalyapi," he said, pulling the book from his saddlebags and handing it to him.

"Wakalyapi?"

"That is the name I gave him to use for me," she told Kinealy, smiling behind her hand.

"Will you tell me your other name? Your personal name?" Collins asked. "I have been very patient."

"You have been patient. It is *Winyan Psunpsunwahela*. Something akin to 'Woman with many things fallen off,' or 'Broken Woman.'"

"I prefer Wakalyapi."

"Then you may always call me Wakalyapi. It is your

name for me."

They had to end it then, for the moment had become too painful and awkward. The four of them mounted their horses, Kcanptepte on the bay packhorse. Collins paused to pat Ziyela, but the dog dodged behind Kinealy's mare and cowered. He shrugged, swung onto Ulysses and reached a hand to Wakalyapi. They gripped each other's forearms and held each other's eyes with complete understanding. Then Collins released his grip and turned Ulysses and Molly to head down the eastern riverbank. He allowed his gelding to pick its own way, for he was blinded by tears.

WESTERN FORT

# 55

At Fort Buford he was welcomed and resupplied. Washington had arranged to forward much needed funds for his return journey. As a result of several communiqués from Bradley and the White House, Collins' arrival had been anticipated with widespread curiosity. His first priority was to see to his animals. During his brief stay, he spent many hours with them, brushing and talking with them, filled with guilt at their debilitated condition. The rest of his time was mostly spent in sleeping and sitting close to the wood stove in his quarters, conscientiously evading probing questions from some of the officers.

Colonel William Hazen was present at the fort, but General Terry had returned east. Collins was relieved to not have to field his questions, although he remained curious as to Terry's reasoning in passing on Reno's report of the white men to begin with and his failure to mention Bradley's white captive. Despite the suspicions exhibited by some, Hazen was singularly uninquisitive, which suited Collins perfectly. The Missouri was frozen, thereby thwarting travel by river and no messages could be sent.

Due to the impending inauguration of Rutherford B. Hayes on March 4, Collins resolved to allow his horses to recuperate for a few days, then make a forced ride to Bismarck. Hazen would be sending dispatches with a company of soldiers to this nearest railroad terminus and he would accompany them downriver. He requisitioned paper and ink to compose a succinct and not altogether comprehensive report of his findings. In the writing, he revisited many memories of his remarkable friend and guide, precipitating a forlorn and nostalgic humor. It seemed impossible that they might never see each other again.

Ulysses and Molly recovered swiftly and Collins was pleased by their renewed energy as they embarked upon the journey to Bismarck. The days passed quickly and uneventfully, although Collins found himself stupefied by the unintelligent and biased conversation engaged in by the soldiers, mostly new recruits. Their officer, a Captain Thorpe, was young and inexperienced and full of regret at the thought that the Indian Wars were coming to a close without having yet presented him with the opportunity to "kill a hostile savage." Strong feelings ran among the men regarding the martyrdom of Custer. Collins held himself apart and endeavored to maintain a cold detachment.

Most pleased to arrive in Bismarck and free himself of his undesirable companions, he sought out Jenkins' livery stable. He found it under the ownership of a burly young blacksmith named Toby Howell. He told Collins that Jenkins had died of pneumonia a scant month before and he had purchased the business in a town auction. Howell was an affable young man and Collins made arrangements to board Ulysses and Molly there until his return from the East. The temperatures remained quite frigid, so C.W. opted to find passable lodging that provided a bed and a wood stove. As the number of transient miners and prospectors was somewhat diminished by the daunting winter weather, he was not forced to 'double up.'

He purchased a train ticket and sent a telegram informing the White House of an approximate time of arrival and apprising the President of the successful completion of his mission in their prearranged code. On inquiring after Major Reno, he was informed the man had been transferred to Fort Ambercrombie in December. Collins sought a tonsorial parlor and indulged in a long, hot bath, a shave and a haircut. A steak in the hotel restaurant completed his first day back in civilization, such as Bismarck could claim, and he took to his bed relaxed and satiated.

Two days later, somnolent from boredom despite his serendipitous discovery and subsequent purchase of a tattered volume of Shakespeare, he boarded the train. His parting with Molly and Ulysses had been far more difficult than he had anticipated. He sincerely hoped that Howell would care for them in keeping with the exorbitant fee Collins had pressed upon him. As the train crossed frozen wastelands of endless prairie, he could not help but revisit the past few months. It had been an extraordinary journey and one, he was well aware, that had profoundly affected him. He was weary and despondent to the core.

# 56

Signs of packing and impending departure filled the White House.  President Grant's office was in disarray and he appeared to be in ill health and much depleted in stature.  Collins removed his Stetson and sat across the desk from the President.  Grant studied him for a moment.

"You look as if you were rode hard and put up wet," he told Collins.

"Something like that."

"You were incommunicado for quite some time.  I thought perhaps you had gone native."

Collins did not respond as this was uncomfortably close to the truth.

"Well...I am glad you have returned intact, Charles. You do appear as if it must have been a difficult assignment."

"Unequivocally."

"Your telegram imparted that you had been successful."

"I was."  Collins placed his narrative upon the desk. "This is my official report."

Grant glanced at it.  "Thank you.  I would oblige you to give me an oral synopsis."

"Yes sir.  The men we sought were deserters from the war."

"Were there many of them?" Grant asked, offering Collins a cigar and lighting one for himself.

"Originally.  There are not many now.  Only a handful." Collins puffed on the fine cigar with pleasure.

"No threat?"

"None whatsoever. Just beaten men suffering privation and an uncertain future."

"What regiment did they desert from? When?" the President asked.

"They were all Irishmen from the 69th. Meagher's brigade."

Grant leaned back in his chair. "The Irish Brigade. *'Clear the way!'*" he said, sardonically. "After Fredericksburg?"

"Yes."

"Any chance their existence could become public knowledge?"

"No sir. They do not want their existence known. They fear reprisals, not just for desertion but also for their participation on the Little Big Horn."

"I see." Grant squinted through a thick cloud of cigar smoke. "And you visited the battlefield?"

"Yes."

"How was it?"

"Ghastly."

"Terry reported they had efficiently buried the dead. Was this correct?"

"Most definitely not...but you have to remember the bodies had been exposed to extremes of temperature for some days before he arrived."

"Yes. You can only ask your men to do so much under such circumstances."

Collins nodded.

"And Custer?"

Collins shrugged.

Grant retreated into his thoughts. C.W. glanced out the window. The maple tree was naked and grim.

"I will be leaving the White House in a few days." Grant said. "Julia and I are soon embarking on a tour of Europe.  I am weary of political wrangling and life on the public stage.  I do not believe I will bear up well in posterity."

"You will always have my respect and admiration," Collins said truthfully, stubbing out his cigar.

"Thank you, Charles.  I am not certain a military man is suited for politics."

"I do not believe an *honest* man is suited for politics."

Grant smiled.  "Well said...well said."

Collins waited a moment, then asked, "What is Hayes' attitude toward the Indians?"

"I have the distinct impression he intends to support Sheridan and Sherman in any policy that removes the Indian and promotes peaceful settlement of the West.  I fear he will not advocate for their humane treatment as I have done. He seems to be preoccupied with finances and the situation in the southern states and not overly concerned with the ultimate fate of the red man."

"As you well know from your acquaintance with Commissioner Parker and your visits with Red Cloud, Ouray, Spotted Tail and others, these people are not blood thirsty savages.  They deserve respect and dignity."

Grant relit his cigar and regarded Collins.  "It is far too late for me to be able to aid their cause in any way." He reached over to pick up Collins' report. He laid it before him, absentmindedly smoothing it with his hand. "Did you meet hostiles?" he asked.

"I did."

"Sitting Bull?"

"Yes.  He is an inspired leader."

"He has certainly grown in fame since the Custer debacle.  Newspapers would hazard that he is a mighty strategist with supernatural powers of prophecy."

"He is a holy man and dedicated to the welfare of his people."

"You admire him." Grant said flatly.

"I do.  So would you."

The President turned his chair to stare out the window.  "These Irishmen...what is your opinion?  Should they be punished?"

"They are already being punished.  Many of them have lost their families in conflicts with the army.  I do not believe the incendiary emotions brought about by the Little Big Horn would be well served by the revelation there were white men fighting on the side of the Indians.  These men will fade into oblivion with the nation being none the wiser."  Collins was not about to reveal Sitting Bull's plan to escape into Canada.  Such knowledge would surely compel the President to action.

"Very well," Grant said, turning back and laying aside the stub of his cigar.  He stood and walked around his desk.  Collins came to his feet and they shook hands.

"Thank you for your commendable discretion during your years of service to me.  I have valued our acquaintance," the President said and cuffed him on the shoulder.

"As I have valued yours, sir," Collins said.  "Good luck in your future endeavors."

"The same to you," Grant said, returning to his seat.  "If there is ever a service I may perform for you, please do not hesitate to inquire."

"Thank you.  And likewise," Collins responded, retrieving his hat.

"My secretary has instructions as to your final compensation. Farewell."

"Farewell," Collins said and left the office with an abiding sense of finality.

*The End*

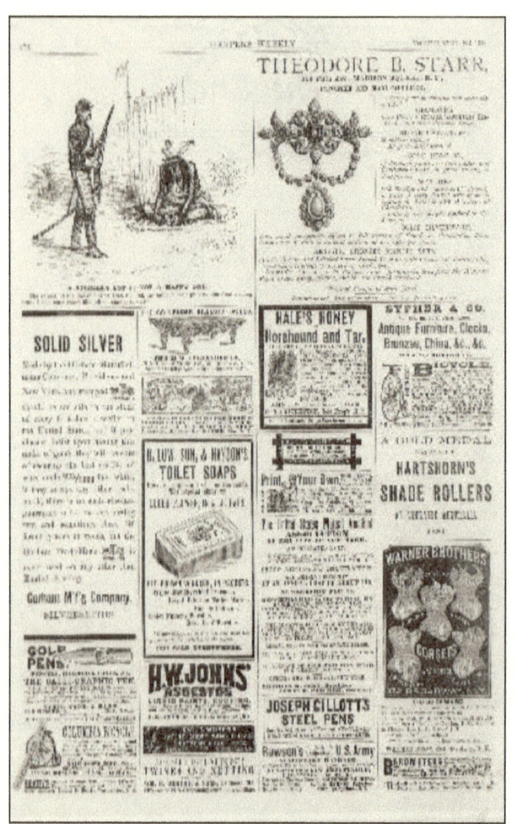

SIGN OF THE TIMES

# Epilogue

Obviously, many of the individuals involved in this work of fiction were historical figures. No disrespect is meant them, with the possible exceptions of George Armstrong and Elizabeth Custer and Nelson Appleton Miles. The ultimate fates of some of these figures embody the tragedy that was the expansion of the American West.

Lieutenant James H. Bradley was given the command of a mounted detachment of the 7th Infantry in the 1877 campaign against the Nez Perce´ (*Niimiipuu*) peoples under General John Gibbon. At dawn on the 9th of August, he led a handful of soldiers and civilians into the lower end of a Nez Perce´ village encamped in the Big Hole Valley of Montana Territory. Bradley was cut down by a bullet at close range in the dense willows surrounding Chief Joseph's camp, ending a burgeoning military career and a remarkable life. His journal was later published in *Contributions to the Historical Society of Montana*, Helena State Publishing Company, 1896. In 1902, Granville Stuart found a copy of the first volume of Montana history, published in 1876 by the nascent historical society. The volume was in a second hand store in Butte and had been inscribed to Lieutenant Bradley from Colonel Wilbur Fisk Sanders, Territorial Governor, on April 19, 1877. The book bore a bullet hole in its upper left hand corner.

Having endured relentless calumny resulting from the efforts of Elizabeth "Libby" Custer's confederates, Reno faced an official Court of Inquiry, convened on January 13, 1879 for the express purpose of reviewing Reno's conduct during the Battle of the Little Big Horn. The Court of Inquiry found nothing with which to censure the man. By March of 1880, ongoing defamation and his own increasing consumption of alcohol and concomitant lack of judgment prompted his dismissal from military service. Marcus Reno spent the remainder of his life seeking reinstatement in the U.S.Army. On March 30, 1889, he died of pneumonia following an operation for cancer of the tongue. He was buried in an unmarked grave in Washington D.C. As the result of a hearing held in 1967, Reno received an honorable discharge retroactive to 1880. Major Marcus Reno was exhumed and reburied at the Custer Battlefield National Cemetery with full military honors. During the hearing of 1967, the opinion was expressed that Elizabeth Custer had been obsessed with placing the blame on someone other than her husband and her chosen scapegoat had been Major Marcus Reno.

Myles Keogh's bloody gauntlet and the guidon of his Company I of the 7th Cavalry were supposedly recovered in Dull Knife's village on the Powder River after Colonel Mackenzie's attack in November of 1876. His papal medals were returned to the possession of his family. Keogh's remains were reinterred in Fort Hill Cemetery, Auburn, New York on October 26, 1877. The Cantonment on the Tongue River was renamed Fort Keogh in 1878. In 1877, a trader in Canada claimed to see Keogh's English pistol in the hands of a Sioux warrior. He supposedly recognized it from the name engraved on the pistol's grip.

Sitting Bull and his people entered Canada in May of 1877. They resided there for four years, in spite of General Terry's efforts to repatriate them to the agencies. Tatanka Iyotaka supposedly told the Commissioner of the Mounted Police that he could not trust One Star Terry or any Americans because they were liars. Finally, as a result of the Canadian Government refusing aid and an official reserve to the starving Lakota people, Sitting Bull and his followers surrendered at Fort Buford on July 19, 1881. The great chief became a prisoner of war and was held at Fort Randall. In May 1883, he was transferred to the Standing Rock Agency near Fort Yates. He spent the summer of 1885 as a star of Buffalo Bill's Wild West Show. Four years later, specifically blamed for the spiritual movement of Ghost Dancing, which he merely tolerated, Sitting Bull's arrest was ordered by Bear Coat Miles. On December 15, 1890 Tatanka Iyotaka was murdered by Sioux policemen at the behest of Indian Agent McLaughlin. Much of Sitting Bull's personal belongings came to be in the possession of McLaughlin, who profited nicely from displaying the souvenirs. The U.S. Army perpetrated a final massacre of the Lakota people on Wounded Knee Creek, December 29, 1890.

After the end of his second term of office, President Ulysses S. Grant spent more than two years touring Europe with his wife Julia. By 1884, having been swindled by an investment banker and having been diagnosed with throat cancer, Grant found himself destitute. Mark Twain offered a contract to Grant for his personal memoirs and a desperate and dying Grant finished the book a few days before his death. As a result, the Grant family earned over $450,000. Ulysses S. Grant died on July 23, 1885 at the age of 63. His body lies in Grant's Tomb in New York City's Riverside Park.

Charles Wolfe Collins spent several months in New York City, visiting old friends and particular Irish families and exhausting his funds on expensive hotels, meals and entertainment.  By the end of the summer of 1877, he was somewhere in Montana Territory.

# Author's Note

Special thanks to Tiokasin Ghosthorse for kindly editing the Lakol used in this book and offering his insight and encouragement.

Native American readers will hopefully understand that any denigrating or otherwise objectionable terminology in this text is used to illustrate prejudices and attitudes of the historical period within which this story occurs.

THE NOBLE RED MAN

Although the mysterious identity of the white men who, according to Reno, fought alongside the Native Americans at the Little Big Horn is mere conjecture in this work, it must be stated that as research proceeded, there existed a surprising bit of evidence that they could have actually been Irishmen. Certainly, a steamboat pilot named Dolan did entice Meagher aboard the *G.A. Thompson*, from which he fell to his death. There were, indeed, many, many deserters from the Irish Brigade after Fredericksburg and it is also a fact that many of them ventured west. Other coincidences, too numerous to mention, have convinced the author that Irishmen could well have found allegiance with the Lakota people, enough so to have earned their trust and fought with them as fellow warriors.

Some place names, such as Little Big Horn and Redwater River may be spelled alternatively. Variations in spelling are common throughout the American West.

Note: Blackfoot peoples traditionally live north of the Medicine Line and Blackfeet peoples live south of the Medicine Line.

# Suggested Reading

For further reading, the author suggests the following:

*U. S. Grant: American Hero, American Myth*, by Joan Waugh, 2009, University of North Carolina Press

*Sitting Bull: Champion of the Sioux*, by Stanley Vestal, 1989, University of Oklahoma Press

*The Lance and the Shield: The Life and Times of Sitting Bull*, by Robert Marshall Utley, 1993, Henry Holt and Company

*Frontier Regulars: The United States Army and the Indian, 1866-91*, by Robert Marshall Utley, 1984, Bison Books

*Crazy Horse: The Strange Man of the Oglalas*, by Mari Sandoz, 2004, Bison Books

*The Battle of Little Big Horn*, by Mari Sandoz, 1966, Amereon Limited

*Bury My Heart at Wounded Knee: An Indian History of the American West*, by Dee Brown, 2001, Henry Holt and Company

*March of the Montana Column: A Prelude to the Custer Disaster*, by Lieutenant James H. Bradley, 1991, University of Oklahoma Press

*Killing Custer: The Battle of Little Big Horn and the Fate of the Plains Indians*, by James Welch, Paul Stekler, 1995, Penguin Books

Juliana "Hoolihan" Clayton

# About the Author

Juliana "Hoolihan" Clayton is an indigenous woman of Turtle Island (First Nations Nehiyawak) who was adopted by a white family and raised on a cattle ranch in Wyoming. She has lived and worked with Native Americans and cowboys throughout the West during her years as a ranch hand and wild land firefighter. She has engaged in extensive research on various topics and has been published in western historical magazines, such as "True West" and "Wild West." Through her research, she has stumbled upon enigmas of the past and has accumulated abundant topics for a succession of detective stories pertaining to the 19th century American West. She has a degree in history and education from the University of Montana and it has long been her goal to create a series of novels that are entertaining, but at the same time rife with impeccable research and unique cultural perspectives on American history. *Commendable Discretion* is the first book of this series.

"Throwing the hoolihan" is a technique that old time cowboys used for roping horses. It has been Juliana's nickname for many years

# About the Artist

Robert Szucs attended the Cleveland Institute of Art for five years, majoring in illustration and painting. After moving to Montana in 1977, he gained a reputation for drawings of local cowboys and paintings of western landscapes. His artwork has shown in the Hole in the Wall Gallery in Montana, the Ed Morgan Gallery in New Mexico and has been purchased by collectors around the world. He currently lives in northern New Mexico.

# List of Illustrations

All illustrations are used with explicit permission from *Harpers Weekly,* and are available through the Library of Congress Prints & Photographs Online Catalogue.

www.ingramcontent.com/pod-product-compliance
Lightning Source LLC
Chambersburg PA
CBHW020906060726
47591CB00004B/1102